ESCAPADES

Visit us at www.boldstrokesbooks.com

By the Author

Shots Fired

Forbidden Passion

Initiation by Desire

Speakeasy

Escapades

ESCAPADES

by

MJ Williamz

2014

ESCAPADES

ISBN 13: 978-1-62639-182-6

This Trade Paperback Original Is Published By
Bold Strokes Books, Inc.
P.O. Box 249
Valley Falls, NY 12185

First Edition: July 2014

Credits
Editor: Cindy Cresap
Production Design: Susan Ramundo
Cover Design By Sheri (graphicartist2020@hotmail.com)

Acknowledgments

First of all, a huge shout out to Dini for always being there for me, every step of the way, in all my endeavors. Also, major thanks to my son for always believing in me and giving me my time and space to write.

I also need to thank ABR and Speed for beta reading this book for me. I appreciate all their input and support.

Of course, I offer my gratitude to Cindy and Stacia for all their hard work in getting this work ready to be published.

And last, but not least, to Rad for giving my works their home.

Dedication

For Dini—Forever

CHAPTER ONE

Joey Scarpetti's tongue lapped at the blonde's pussy while her fingers worked frantically inside the redhead. She glanced up and saw the women kissing, mouths open and tongues entwined. She sucked on the swollen lips in her face and continued to watch as the others fondled each other's breasts. She watched as nipples were tugged and twisted, even as she plunged her fingers deeper in one and her tongue farther in the other.

The taste and scents that surrounded her left her dizzy with need. She wanted to fuck them harder, faster, and better than they'd ever been fucked before. The sounds of one cunt sucking her fingers while the other one closed around her tongue had her fighting to maintain control.

Breathing got heavier as Joey continued to tend to their needs. She was aware of them panting harder and heard soft mewling sounds as they teetered near the brink. She felt them twitching and moved her mouth to suck on one's clit while her thumb rubbed the other's.

The women's bodies tensed as they rode Joey, and they both screamed as the orgasms rocked their bodies. Exhausted but pleased with herself, Joey continued to tease the women until they pulled away, too sensitive for more.

Through the curtains, Joey saw the sky growing light, indicating that her adventure was over and it was time to get back to the community of women where she lived. She slipped out of the women, then out of bed and quietly dressed while watching the two dozing together. She washed up briefly before letting herself out into the morning.

The sun was just making its presence known as Joey climbed into her old Ford F-150 and headed out of the college town of Somerset toward Maybon Tir, the sixteen-thousand-acre community ten miles west of town, bordering on the Pacific Ocean. It was a community of women for women that had been founded in the sixties. And it was where Joey felt most comfortable.

She turned off Highway 101 onto the gravel road that led to the community of women Joey called home. She drove down Main Street with most buildings still dark but the restaurants and coffee shops just opening for business. She parked in front of Nature's Bounty and went in for a much-needed cup of coffee.

"Joey, you're looking like crap this morning," Nancy, the matronly owner, called to her from the kitchen. "Were you out breaking hearts last night?"

Joey grinned, her reputation well deserved. "I might have stayed up a little late."

"Anybody I know?"

"No, ma'am. I spent the night in Somerset."

"Smart woman, keeping your escapades away from the locals. One of these days, you're going to bring someone back here with you and we're all going to faint."

"Don't count on it." Joey was a confirmed bachelor, and all members of their little haven knew it.

"You're not getting any younger." Nancy handed her the largest cup of black coffee they served. "You'll be turning thirty this summer, won't you?"

"I've got a lot of years ahead of me. I see no reason to slow down yet." She threw a couple of wadded ones on the counter and waved as she hurried back to her truck.

Joey pulled up to the worksite on the south side of town as the rest of the crew was beginning to work. She was buckling her tool belt when her best friend, Mel, walked over to her.

"Damn, woman! You smell like a fuckin' whorehouse."

"You wish you knew what a whorehouse smelled like."

"Whatever. Sorry I had to bail so early last night."

"You're fuckin' whipped. I get it."

Mel blushed but let the comment slide. "So which one did you end up going home with?"

"Both," Joey tossed over her shoulder as she walked toward the rest of the crew.

"Both?" Mel yelled.

❖

The crew got the concrete poured and took a break in the morning heat as it settled. Joey sat on her tailgate, her short, sweaty hair plastered to her head.

"Now you smell like a distillery," Mel said.

"You seem to have a lot of opinions on how I smell."

"You look like shit, too. How much sleep did you get last night?"

"Sleep is overrated."

"You've got to be hurting."

"The worse I feel, the more I remember the good time I had. It's worth it."

Mel shook her head, her shaggy blond hair falling in her eyes.

"Break's over!" the forewoman called. "I want to get some walls up today. Let's go."

Joey slid off the truck and joined the others in framing the walls. After a quick lunch, she and Mel were holding one wall up while Kelsey, a coworker, made sure it was plumb. A silver Dodge Charger pulled up, and when its door opened, a shapely leg slid out, followed by a tall, tanned woman with silky blond hair that cascaded down her back. She wore a pink sundress that showed off her ample breasts and long legs. She sauntered over to Brenda, the forewoman.

"Holy mother of Gaia," Joey breathed. "Who is that?"

"No clue," Mel said.

"She wants me."

"She's out of your league."

"No such thing, sister."

"You two mind holding the wall steady?" Kelsey yelled.

"Sorry!" Joey called back, never taking her eyes off the newcomer. She watched as the beauty and Brenda conversed briefly, then allowed her gaze to follow her back to her car. By the time the crew was left in the car's dust, Joey was a wet mess.

"I've got to have her," she told Mel, who rolled her eyes in response.

"Keep your pants on. You don't even know who she is."

"No, but I will soon enough."

The crew worked until early afternoon, when the sun was beating down on them and the temperature hovered in the high nineties.

"How are you feeling now, stud?" Mel asked.

"Like I need to catch some waves."

"I'll meet you at The Shack?"

"Head over to my place. I'll catch up with you there." Joey sauntered over to Brenda.

"How do you do it?" Brenda asked.

"Do what?"

"Work as hard as you do as hung over as you've got to be."

"Who said I was hung over?"

"Mel was right. You smelled like a distillery."

"Yeah, whatever. So, anyway, who was the blonde?"

"Oh, no, you don't." Brenda's eyes got wide as she shook her head. "Don't even think about it. She's off limits."

"No such thing. Now who is she?"

"There is such a thing, Scarpetti. And she's it. She's going to run this day-care center when we get it built."

"Oh, man!" Joey was disgusted. "She's into snot gobblers?"

"Into what? They're called children."

"Is she financing this job?"

"When did you become a gold digger?"

"I'm not. Just curious."

"You take your overactive libido somewhere else."

"You know the more you tell me I can't have her, the more I want her."

"Joey, please. She's not like the women you're used to. She's got class."

"Aren't you funny? Well, I'm gonna have her. It's just a matter of when."

Brenda grew serious. "Look, she just lost her partner and is moving here for a little solace and recovery. Give her some space?"

Joey nodded. "I hear what you're saying."

"And?"

"And I won't do her right away." She laughed as she walked off.

"Joey!" Brenda called. "I'm serious."

Joey didn't turn around as she raised her arm and waved to her boss. She climbed into her beat-up truck and drove home. She walked in through the open door to find Mel already in her board shorts sitting on her couch drinking a beer.

Joey grabbed a cold one from the refrigerator and stood staring at her friend, seated comfortably among the mess that was Joey's great room. The floor was gray linoleum with a braided navy blue surface rug in the center that was barely visible under empty pizza cartons and beer bottles.

Mel sat on one dilapidated couch with her feet on the coffee table. The other couch was covered in laundry that Joey never bothered to put away. She grabbed a pair of shorts and a muscle shirt from the pile and walked down the hall to her room.

"You ever going to clean this place?" Mel called after her.

"Just 'cause you have to keep things clean nowadays doesn't mean I do."

She quickly stripped out of the clothes she'd worn for the past thirty hours and jumped into the shower. She washed quickly, then got out and pulled some shorts over her hips. The shirt hung loosely over her small breasts and showed off her muscular arms.

She drained the last of her beer as she walked back out to the front room. She grabbed a six-pack from the fridge. "Let's get out of here. I'll drive."

They put their boards and cooler in the back of her truck and drove the short distance to the beach. They parked at a local burger joint called The Shack. They crossed the parking lot and hopped their way over sand that burned their feet through their sandals.

Joey set the cooler down and stepped into the water. "Oh, yeah. Much better."

"Take your shoes off and let's catch some waves." Mel walked past her, board under her arm.

Joey grabbed her board and paddled out to where the waves would soon be breaking. She sat up and straddled the surfboard.

"So she's gonna run the day-care center."

"Who?"

"The hottie. Remember? From the job site?"

"Oh, shit, Joey, let it go."

"No can do. I feel I owe it to her to give her the best night of her life."

"You're so gallant."

"No kidding."

"So does this woman have a name?"

"I forgot to ask. Not that it matters. As long as she knows my name."

"Why's that important?"

"Because she'll be screaming it out all night."

The swells were getting bigger, and Mel paddled away, shaking her head. Joey laughed, enjoying the cool ocean on the hot day. By the time Mel had put some distance between them, the waves were coming in at decent sizes. There were no massive waves along the coast at Maybon Tir, but they were fun to ride nonetheless.

She watched one form and lay on her stomach, her strong arms cutting easily through the water. When the pull of the water was just right, she stood on her board and caught a seven-foot wave.

She felt the power of the ocean through the board and rode the wave until the force was gone, then lay back down and paddled out to catch the next. Mel caught her attention in the distance, and they exchanged thumbs-ups as they readied themselves for the next ride.

After a couple of hours of nonstop surfing, Mel paddled over to her. "I'm ready for some brews."

"I'm right behind you."

They maneuvered to the shallow water, then carried their boards to the sand where they stood them on end, then sat on their towels.

"Nice waves today," Joey said.

"No kidding." Mel downed half a beer. "I'm about starving now, though."

"We'll dry off, then go grab some burgers. Unless you need to get home to the little woman."

"Very funny. We've been dating a couple of months. Don't go marrying me off."

"Still. I've never seen you like this."

"You know, being in a relationship isn't the end of the world."

"You just keep telling yourself that."

Mel popped the top off another bottle and stared out at the water. "Remember, I was with you in college. I remember Randi. I know she burned you, but don't you ever wonder if maybe there's someone else out there? Don't you ever think how cool it would be to have someone to be with?"

"Believe me, I remember those days. And now that you have a new girlfriend, you tell me. Why bother?"

"I can't really explain it. It's kinda cool knowing someone cares about you."

"When women start caring, I start leaving. I don't like clingy. I guess it works for you though."

"Bess isn't clingy. She lets me do my own thing."

"Yeah, like last night when you couldn't stay out and play."

"It was getting late. So I felt like spending a little quality time with my woman before I went to sleep. Some of us still sleep, by the way."

"I'll sleep when I'm dead. And I spent some quality time with a couple of women. So I still don't see the pros of a ball and chain."

Mel brushed her bangs out of her eyes, only to have them fall right back down. She finished her beer. "I wonder if there's a woman alive who could tame you."

"Doubtful."

"Hey, do you ever wonder what happened to all our big plans?"

"What do you mean?"

"Remember when we met as freshmen? You were going to be a business bigwig and I was going to be a marketing genius? We were going to find ourselves some nice women and live in big houses with white picket fences next door to each other?"

"Living among many women took precedence. Maybon Tir called to us. I, for one, am happy living here working construction."

"So am I. I just think about that sometimes."

"And getting burned was enough to keep me from wanting that white picket fence anymore."

"Still…it was fun having dreams."

"It's not fun getting all nostalgic. I'm famished. Let's get some food."

They gathered their things and started back to The Shack.

"Holy shit! What's going on here?" The parking lot was full, and there was loud music and laughter coming from within.

"What time is it?" Mel asked.

"It's not even five o'clock yet. I wonder what gives."

"Good thing we're up for a party." Mel laughed.

"Always."

As they entered the place, they walked past the origin of the noise. There was a large group that occupied five big tables around the jukebox. The tables were full, and people were milling around, talking and laughing and singing with the music.

Joey and Mel found an empty booth close to the kitchen.

"What can I get you gals?" the waitress asked.

"Two monster burgers with fries and a couple of Coronas." Joey motioned to the gathering. "What's going on over there?"

"Tiffany Swanson's eighteenth birthday party."

"No way," Mel said. "That runt is eighteen now?"

"Makes you feel old, don't it?" The waitress walked off.

Joey glanced over at the crowd, almost feeling sorry for the men who clearly felt out of place. She scanned the group, and her gaze fell on a lovely young woman whose purple tube top barely covered her shapely breasts. Her belly piercing shined against her flat tan stomach, and the legs of her jeans shorts came just to the tops of her thighs.

"Damn, that Tiffany's grown up."

"Eighteen really isn't grown up."

"You're not looking at her."

Mel craned her neck around the booth to see what Joey was talking about. "Damn. That's scary. She's just a kid."

"Not the way I see it."

"Joey, don't."

"I'm just saying she doesn't look much like a kid."

"That's not what you're saying, and we both know it. Be cool. Her grandmother founded this place. She'd roll over in her grave if she could read your mind. Joey Scarpetti after any of her womenfolk would have terrified her."

Joey nodded absently. "Mildred was a special woman. I miss her."

"We all do. Her death last month was a blow to the whole community."

Their burgers arrived, and they devoured them, washing them down with more beer.

"I suppose we should go say happy birthday," Joey said.

"Sure, why not? Just remember we used to babysit the birthday girl."

"Would you relax?"

They had barely crossed the restaurant when Tiffany walked up to them.

"Hey, squirt," Mel said. "Happy birthday."

"Thanks." Tiffany looked at Joey. "I'm eighteen now."

"So I hear."

Tiffany closed the distance between them and leaned against Joey. "That means I'm legal."

"Oh, shit!" Mel said.

"Don't mind her." Joey smiled. "Are you enjoying your party?"

"I am now."

"We were just leaving," Mel said. "But we wanted to say hi first. So enjoy your party."

Tiffany pouted, her full pink lips teasing Joey. "But you just got here."

"Right," Joey said. "It would be rude to just take off like that."

Tiffany smiled and tucked some chestnut hair behind her ear. "So you'll stay?"

"No, really. We can't." Mel looked pointedly at Joey.

Joey fished her keys from her pocket and handed them to Mel. "If you need to go, take my truck. I'm sure Tiff here'll give me a lift later."

Tiffany's face lit up. "I'd love to. Oh, I'm so happy you're staying."

Mel glared at her but took the keys. "Don't stay out too late. Remember, we're working stiffs."

"Have I ever been late to work?"

"You were close this morning."

"Details. I'll see you tomorrow, Mel." She watched Mel walk out of the dive and felt Tiffany's warm hand on hers.

"Let's get out of here," she whispered.

"But this is your party." Joey laughed.

"It's been going on long enough. Go out back and I'll swing around and pick you up."

Joey's crotch was wet from Tiffany's boldness. She couldn't wait to peel those tight shorts off Tiff and taste her wares. The thought made her clit hard. She walked behind the building and leaned against the back wall.

Less than ten minutes later, a new yellow convertible Mustang pulled up with Tiffany behind the wheel. Joey smiled appreciatively at the sight.

"Nice ride." She slid in.

"I like it."

"Where are we going?"

"I'm staying at my grandma's."

"Why?"

"Just to make sure nothing happens to it before it sells."

"You're not seriously worried about vandals in Maybon Tir? And even if we did have them, no one would dare touch Mildred Braun's place."

"I know. She's like a hero here. But my mom worried, so I'm staying there over the summer."

"It's got to be nice for you to have a place of your own for a few months."

Tiffany lifted a slim shoulder. "I enjoy my independence. But it's kind of hard to be tied to Maybon Tir all summer."

Joey shifted in her seat and stared at Tiffany. "I suppose there's not a lot to do here at your age."

"Not a lot meaning nothing."

"Will you be going to college in the fall?"

"Yep. I'll be at Somerset."

"What about after that? Any plans?"

"Honestly?"

"Sure."

"Well, my dad wants me to be a hotshot lawyer in Los Angeles or somewhere, but I think I might make Maybon Tir my home. It may not be fun to live here now, but I can see what a cool place it would be to live when I grow up."

"Really?" Joey was genuinely surprised.

"Sure. I could spend the rest of my life surrounded by nothing but women."

"I like you." Joey laughed.

"I was kind of counting on that." Tiffany pulled up in front of one of the larger houses in the community. Mildred Braun started with a cottage when she was establishing the community, but that was now an outbuilding, and the Georgian-style house she'd had built sat on a curved driveway lined with palm trees.

There were six balustrades in the front section of the wraparound porch, all whitewashed to look brand new. Green shutters accented the white of the house and all looked freshly painted, as well.

"This place was your grandmother's pride and joy."

"You helped build it. I remember."

"You do, huh?"

"I decided the first time I saw you that I had to have you."

"You were just a kid. I remember your long hair in braids and those braces on your teeth."

"Aha, so you did notice me."

"Not the way I notice you now."

CHAPTER TWO

Tiffany smiled and walked around to the back of the house. Joey followed and gazed at the swimming pool she had poured concrete for. She sat on the diving board and let her feet dangle just above the water.

"You're not getting in?" Tiffany asked from the shallow end.

"Are you?"

"I was thinking about it."

Joey sat mesmerized as Tiffany lifted the tube top over her head, her large breasts bouncing free. Her nipples were large and hard and only slightly darker than the mounds on which they sat. The distinct absence of tan lines was not lost on Joey, who grew wetter by the moment.

Tiffany kept her focus on Joey as she unbuttoned, then slowly unzipped, her tight denim shorts. Joey's focus was on the shorts as she strained to see what was underneath. Her mouth was dry, her throat tight as she watched in anticipation.

Tiffany slid her shorts down, and Joey saw a tiny purple patch of cloth covering an area she knew she'd see soon enough. She enjoyed being teased and smiled that Tiffany was obviously no stranger to the role she was playing.

Tiffany stepped onto the top step leading into the pool.

"Careful," Joey called. "Your panties might get wet."

"They already are."

Joey swallowed hard, using every ounce of self-control to stay on the diving board. She watched as Tiffany moved down to the next step, the water halfway up her thighs.

"How's the water?" Joey asked.

"Why don't you get in and find out?"

"Maybe I'm enjoying the view from here."

"You never struck me as someone who'd be satisfied to just enjoy the view."

Joey stood on the board and quickly stripped out of her shorts and shirt. She saw Tiffany's appreciative gaze as she bounced into the air. She sliced into the water, making barely a splash. She crossed the pool underwater, surfaced just in front of the steps and knelt on one, her face level with Tiffany's breasts. She brushed her cheek against them. She opened her mouth and fought the urge to close it on the pert nipple. Instead, she stood and placed her hand on the back of Tiffany's neck.

She moved her mouth closer, feeling Tiffany's ragged breath on her lips. Intent to drag the moment out, she kissed Tiffany's cheek, her jaw, then licked and sucked her earlobe. She stood and looked again at the hardened nubs protruding from Tiffany's breasts. They were puckered and tight, leaving no doubt about Tiffany's arousal.

Blood rushed in her ears, her own need making her dizzy. She brushed her open mouth against Tiffany's once, then again before closing it on her lips, finally tasting Tiffany's perfectly full pink pair.

Her own breath catching, Joey moved her mouth against Tiffany's while she pulled her body against hers. The feel of Tiffany's soft breasts against her made her clit swell. She was all desire as she slid a hand up Tiffany's shapely rib cage and rested it under her breast. She ran her thumb along the soft underside as her tongue finally entered Tiffany's mouth. She traced the breast with her thumb as the kiss intensified. Unable to resist any longer, she moved her thumb over the hard nipple and pinched the tender tip.

She felt Tiffany's moan as her hands were in Joey's hair, holding her in place while she kissed her harder. Joey finally broke the kiss and, breathless, leaned her forehead against Tiffany's. She moved the palm of her hand over one nipple and then the other. She cupped one full mound and bent to suck its offering. She rolled it in her tongue and sucked hard, drawing it deep.

Joey slid her hands down Tiffany's back and cupped her firm ass, gliding her hands over her smooth cheeks. She peeled the thong down Tiffany's legs and helped her step out of it. She tossed the satin undergarment on the side of the pool and moved her hand between Tiffany's legs while she moved to suck the other nipple.

Tiffany pulled away from Joey and stepped up one step.

"Where are you going?"

"Over here." She got out of the pool and walked along the edge, finally sitting down and lowering her legs into the water.

Joey cut through the water and stood before her. She separated Tiffany's thighs and stared at the smooth, creamy pussy briefly before running her fingers along it. She watched as she dipped her fingertips inside, turned her hand over, and pulled them out. She reinserted them and spread them out while withdrawing them again.

Tiffany placed her legs over Joey's shoulders and Joey dipped her tongue inside her. She lapped at the juices that were pouring from her before taking her swollen clit in her mouth. Joey buried her fingers deep inside her once again as she licked and sucked the hard clit.

Tiffany pressed herself into Joey, rubbing against her in a perfect rhythm. Joey licked her clit harder, rubbing perfect circles on it while her fingers moved deeper with each thrust.

Tiffany threw her head back and screamed as Joey felt her crushing her fingers in the force of her orgasm. Joey slowly withdrew her fingers and replaced them with her tongue, savoring the flavor of Tiffany's come. She sucked her lips and pressed her thumbs into her clit, forcing Tiffany to climax again.

Joey backed up and grabbed Tiffany's ankles, abruptly pulling her into the water. Tiffany surfaced and grabbed Joey, kissing her hard and running her hands over her muscled arms.

"Happy birthday to me!" She laughed against Joey's mouth.

"I'm glad you're enjoying it." She kissed down Tiffany's neck, sucking where it met her shoulder.

"You have a way with that mouth," Tiffany said.

Joey moved lower and took Tiffany's nipple in her mouth once more. She kneaded and squeezed the breast while she sucked and moved her free hand between Tiffany's legs again. She easily slipped three fingers inside her while she continued to suck and pull on the nipple. She felt Tiffany's fingernails digging into her upper back while she continued to please her and was rewarded with yet another round of convulsions as Tiffany came around her fingers.

Tiffany lifted Joey's mouth to hers and moved her hand between Joey's hard thighs. She found her clit hard and slick. "What gets you off, huh?"

"Beautiful women usually do the trick."

Tiffany slid her fingers inside Joey while she pressed her palm into her clit. "I'm so glad you came by The Shack today."

"Me too." Joey kissed her hard, all her need apparent in the kiss as she rocked against Tiffany's hand. She felt the pressure against her throbbing clit and moved to take her fingers deeper.

"I want you to come for me," Tiffany whispered.

Joey threw her head back, closing her eyes at the sensations. She felt Tiffany's tongue on her neck and struggled to remain standing as she felt the waves building.

"You're so fucking hot," Tiffany said. "I feel you twitching. Are you close? Oh, God, I can't believe Joey Scarpetti is going to come for me."

Joey lost it then, giving herself over to the orgasm that crashed through her. She grabbed hold of Tiffany so as not to fall over and slip underwater. When she was back in control, she tried to move away, but Tiffany had other plans.

"Not yet." She slid another finger inside Joey.

"Easy, baby. We have all night."

"But I want you again now."

"You're about sexy as hell, aren't you?" Joey felt her body responding again.

"I'm so glad you think so." Tiffany smiled. She moved her fingers in and out and pressed her thumb against Joey's tight rosebud. "You like that? Can I fuck you there?"

Joey was used to being the one doing the exploring, but there was something insanely arousing about this young woman wanting to fuck her every which way. She felt Tiffany's thumb barely penetrate her, and her clit swelled even more. She knew one touch would get her off again. She grabbed Tiffany's free hand and pressed it into her. She rubbed it against her as Tiffany continued to fuck her. The explosion started at her very core and shot through her limbs, leaving her limp when it ended.

❖

Fog rolled in as the sun went down, dropping the temperature an easy twenty degrees. Joey saw goose bumps on Tiffany and knew they weren't from being turned on.

"Maybe we should head inside and warm up," she suggested.

"Or we could just move to the hot tub," Tiffany said.

Shivering, they climbed out of the pool and into the warmth of the hot tub.

"Do you want bubbles?" Tiffany asked.

"No way." Joey moved closer to her and rested a hand on her upper thigh. "I want to be able to see every inch of you."

She watched as Tiffany's legs parted and moved her hand between them. She enjoyed the magnified view as she slid two fingers inside her. Tiffany pulled her hood back, exposing her clit for Joey's view, as well.

"You're beautiful." Joey kissed her and plunged her fingers deeper. She felt Tiffany's fingers brush hers and pulled away to see Tiffany rubbing her protruding clit. Joey got comfortable and watched, sliding another finger in as Tiffany rubbed either side of her clit, pinching it between her fingers and getting Joey hotter by the minute.

Tiffany placed her free hand on Joey's clit and rubbed it hard and fast as she continued to play with hers.

Joey drew a deep breath and gave up thinking. She focused only on the feel of Tiffany's slick cunt and her own clit, straining against Tiffany's fingers. Through the haze, she heard Tiffany breathing heavily and knew neither of them would last much longer. She felt her orgasm sear through her body just as Tiffany cried out yet again.

"You just don't stop, do you?" Joey finally found her voice.

"Why should I?"

"I'm not saying you should." Joey laughed. "You're a lot of fun."

Tiffany slid over and rested her head on Joey's shoulder.

"Don't tell me you're finally satisfied."

"I'm just taking a break."

Joey, finally starting to feel tired after her two nights of play, kissed Tiffany's head and tried to formulate her escape.

"Hey, you, I hate to do this, but I've got to get up early and get to work tomorrow."

"Sucks to be you." Tiffany laughed. "What time do you all start work? And what are you working on now?"

"We start at six. And we're building the day-care center."

"That's so cool that enough of us residents have kids to warrant an actual day-care center."

"I guess. I mean if you're into kids and all."

"I just think it's nice that women who choose to have kids will have a place here instead of having to take them to Somerset."

"True. The more self-sufficient we are, the better."

"Exactly."

There was a long pause in conversation.

"Oh, I get it. You were trying to leave, weren't you?" Tiffany asked.

"Well, as much as I hate to, I really should."

"It's all good." Tiffany smiled. "I had a blast. You fucked me senseless. You made my birthday dreams come true."

Joey wondered if she was just putting on a brave face. She seemed genuinely fine. "And you're okay if I don't stay the night?"

"I don't need you here when I wake up if that's what you're asking. I'd love to fuck some more, but I already wonder if I'll be able to walk tomorrow as it is."

Joey threw her head back and laughed. "You're something else."

"I'd like to fuck again some time."

"Works for me." Joey climbed out of the hot tub and shook in the cold night air. She looked around and realized they had no towels.

"Check the pool house." Tiffany seemed to read her mind.

Joey hurried over and found a towel. She quickly dried and dressed. Tiffany remained in the hot tub, her young body looking inviting as ever. Joey walked over and bent to kiss her.

"I had a really good time," she said.

"Me too." Tiffany said. "Hey, you want a ride home?"

"No, I don't live far." She walked out of the backyard and hurried home.

Chapter Three

The sun beat down on them as they broke for lunch late the next morning.

"Tell me you showed some restraint last night," Mel said.

"Actually, restraints are about all that didn't happen." Joey laughed.

"She's just a kid."

"No, she's an adult. And believe me, she's all adult."

"So it was another night with no sleep?"

"I slept. I got home around midnight."

"You didn't stay the night?"

"Nope. She was fine with it, too." Joey turned her attention to the Charger driving toward the site. "Hey, look who's back."

"Are you going to talk to her today?" She watched the woman step out of her car.

"She's talking to Brenda again. It's like she's all business. I really need to help her learn to relax."

Joey jumped off the tailgate and sauntered toward them. She got there just as the blonde turned toward her. She looked Joey up and down and gave her an appreciative smile before lowering her sunglasses and walking past.

Joey brazenly stared after her, watching hips sway in beige capris. She watched the woman drive off before turning back to Brenda.

"Seriously, who is she?"

"I told you yesterday. She's the director of this center."

"Yeah, yeah, but she's got to have a name."

"Her name is Samantha."

"Samantha," Joey said softly, reverently. "It fits her."

Brenda shook her head.

"Does she have a last name?"

Brenda stared at her, apparently contemplating answering her. "Brewer," she finally said.

"Brewer." Joey nodded, then stopped. "No relation, right?"

"She's his daughter."

Leonard Brewer was the homophobic mayor of Somerset. He encouraged his residents to boycott the women's booths at their farmers market and asked the town's businesses not to provide goods or services to them. If he could have forbidden residents from ever entering Maybon Tir, he would have.

"What the fuck? What's she doing here?"

"I told you."

"Is she a spy? For Leonard so hated Maybon Tir that he sent his only begotten daughter…"

"Paranoid much? She has every right to be here. And he didn't send her."

"Are you sure?"

"Listen to yourself. She's a lesbian, just like the rest of us."

"So she says. I guess I'll have to find out for myself."

"I've told you to leave her alone."

Joey shrugged and smiled. "I owe it to the rest of the community. We need to find out if there's an impostor in our midst."

As she walked off, Brenda called to everyone, "Lunch is over. Back to work."

❖

"What did you find out?" Mel asked as they went back to work.

"She's Leonard Brewer's daughter. Says she's a lesbian. Yeah, right."

"No, wait. She is. I remember reading about him disowning a daughter a few years ago."

"The asshole disowned his own daughter? Where has she been? How come she didn't move to here then?"

"I heard she moved to San Francisco as some bigwig lawyer or something."

"And now she wants to run a day care? I'm even more suspicious."

"Maybe I don't remember right. I remember something about San Francisco anyway."

"Well, we don't need some hotshot big city gal poking her nose around here."

"I thought it was you who was going to do the poking?"

"You know it. I'm going to find out for sure if she plays for our team. It's the least I can do."

"You're too kind."

"Don't I know it."

"Nothing would please you more than sticking it to Brewer's daughter, would it?"

"Not a damned thing."

❖

The workday finally drew to a close. Joey was loading her tools in her truck when Mel walked over.

"I've got a few things to do this afternoon, but I was thinking we might catch some waves a little later."

"That sounds good. I've got no plans for the day. I may head over to the community garden and put in some time there. I haven't put in any hours this month."

"Not cool. We're each supposed to put in twenty a month."

"Don't quote the rules to me. I know I need to do some time. I'm sure there are plenty of weeds that need my attention. Anyway, come by the house, and if I'm there, we'll surf."

"Sounds good to me."

Joey got home and stripped her shirt off as soon as she got inside. She untied her work boots, slipped them off, and left them by the front door. She was down the hall, unbuttoning her shorts when she got to her room and stopped.

There, tied to her bed, pussy open and on display, was Tiffany. Joey couldn't enjoy the view. The cold dread in her stomach was spreading throughout her body. All she could think about was Glenn Close in *Fatal Attraction.*

"Tiffany, we need to talk."

"Oh, shit! Don't get weird on me."

"Me get weird? You're the one tied to my bed."

"I was horny and thought this might be a nice surprise."

Joey scratched her head. "Last night was fun."

"And this afternoon can be, too."

"What if I'd brought someone home with me?"

"We'd have a three-way."

Joey fought to suppress her smile. "I'm serious here."

"You're too serious. You're making more out of this than you need to."

"This is something a girlfriend does." Joey almost choked on the word.

"Seriously? I'm eighteen years old! The last thing I want is a girlfriend. I had hoped you wouldn't be able to resist this." She strained against the handcuffs that had her held to the bed frame.

"You look great. Don't get me wrong. But I can't have sex with you now. You'll think we're in a relationship."

"I won't."

"Really, I know how these things go."

"I want you to fuck me. I figured we'd fuck for a while, then I'd go see my mom for dinner and you'd go surf or whatever and that's all."

"I really wish I could believe you."

"Okay, in retrospect, I totally see where you're coming from. I look like a crazed teeny bopper who thinks she has the right to let herself into your house and make herself comfortable."

"Exactly." Joey nodded.

"I was horny and not thinking clearly. I really just wanted to surprise you."

"Well, that you did."

"So untie my legs and unlock the handcuffs and I'll get going."

"How did you do this anyway?" Joey moved to the side of the bed.

"I tied my ankles to your bedposts, then cuffed one hand and threw the other cuff over your frame for the other hand. It was quite easy actually."

Joey was warming up to the idea of a romp with her. Her fear of further disillusioning Tiffany warred with the warmth that was starting in her crotch. She slipped her hands in her pockets and looked over the young body laid bare for her.

"You've made your point. Now I'm embarrassed and uncomfortable. Please untie me and toss me my clothes."

"You really think we could have more sex and you wouldn't go thinking we're an item?"

"You're not going to believe me if I say yes."

Joey ran a hand over Tiffany's breast, coaxing the nipple to attention.

"You're not helping."

"No?" She pinched the nipple and smiled down at Tiffany. "Not at all?"

"You said no sex. It's no fair teasing me only to send me on my way. Trust me, I've learned my lesson."

"So you're not going to let yourself into my house again?" She dragged her hand down Tiffany's torso, stopping with her fingertips just below her smooth mons.

"No." Tiffany could barely breathe.

Joey pulled back Tiffany's hood and ran her finger over her clit.

"Enough already. Either fuck me or untie me."

Joey laughed. "You sure are demanding. Funny how you're really not in the position to call the shots."

Tiffany strained against her restraints.

"You did a great job there. I don't think you're going anywhere. But please, keep struggling. I like to watch your breasts jiggle."

"Now you're just being an asshole."

Joey laughed again as she left the room and walked down the hall.

"Where are you going?" Tiffany called, but Joey ignored her. She finished undressing and stepped into a hot shower. She quickly washed off the sweat and dirt of the day, then grabbed a towel and dried herself as she walked back to her room.

"How long do you plan to leave me like this?" Tiffany asked, the harshness in her voice softened by the longing in her eyes as she looked over Joey's naked body.

Joey ran her hand over Tiffany's body. She pinched her clit between two fingers and ran her middle finger over it.

"You can't expect it to be all big and hard when you've told her she's not going to get any attention."

Joey didn't answer but moved her fingers lower, running them over Tiffany's opening briefly before slipping a fingertip inside.

Tiffany started to say something, but Joey tossed her towel over her face. She shook her head but couldn't dislodge it. "That wasn't very nice."

Joey stared at Tiffany's body and wondered where to start. She looked at her face and, satisfied Tiffany couldn't see her, she absently stroked between her own legs while she admired Tiffany.

"What are you doing?" Tiffany's muffled voice said. "Are you still here?"

Joey smiled and ran her wet fingers over Tiffany's cunt. She used it as lube as she dipped a finger inside her. She was tight and hot and getting wet. Joey moved her finger around inside, then folded the towel slightly, exposing Tiffany's pouty lips. She ran her finger over the lips, then slipped it between them.

She inhaled hard when she felt Tiffany's talented tongue move along her finger as she sucked on it. Her own clit was bulging, and she reasoned she'd deal with the consequences later. There was no way she could walk away from this smorgasbord.

She moved her hand back between Tiffany's legs, teasing her. She watched as her clit swelled and felt her pussy getting wetter. She ran three fingers inside her and plunged them deeper and deeper.

"Funny. That feels like fucking to me."

Joey thrust them harder, pounding her insides, seeing how much Tiffany could take. Tiffany moved her hips as much as possible, meeting each of Joey's thrusts. Joey moved to the head of the bed again and put her fingers in Tiffany's mouth while she bent to suck a nipple between her teeth.

Tiffany sucked her clean while Joey suckled her. She had Tiffany's nipple hard and taut. She licked it and teased it with her tongue before dipping to suck on it once more. Joey removed her hand from Tiffany's mouth and crossed the room to her dresser. She opened the bottom drawer.

"Now what are you doing? You're making me crazy," Tiffany whined.

Joey just smiled and unwrapped a toy from its cloth confines. It was thick and black and phallic-shaped with a thinner, beaded protrusion, as well. She flipped open the lube and poured generous amounts on it.

She placed the tip of the toy against Tiffany's clit and rubbed.

"Oh, my God, that feels good." Tiffany tried to arch her hips to get more pressure.

Joey moved the toy lower and placed the large tip just inside Tiffany. She slowly pressed onward until it filled her.

"How big is that?" Tiffany asked.

"You tell me."

"It feels huge."

"Do you need more?"

"Not at the moment."

Joey withdrew the toy until just the tip was inside, then pushed it to its base again. She was dripping watching Tiffany's cunt swallow the oversized dildo. She withdrew the whole toy, then poured more lube on the beaded area.

"Why'd you stop?"

Joey didn't answer as she lined up the toy and buried the dildo again while slowly penetrating her other hole.

"Holy fuck!" Tiffany exclaimed. "Oh, yes, Joey. Fuck me harder. Give me more. Please?"

Joey slid both parts in slowly until neither was visible. She pulled them out slowly and moved them back inside.

"Oh, my God. That feels so good! Oh, God, Joey, yes!"

Joey couldn't stand simply watching any longer. She continued to slowly thrust the toy as she moved to the head of the bed. She climbed up and straddled Tiffany's mouth, which instantly closed around her throbbing clit before licking inside her pussy. Joey rubbed herself on Tiffany's mouth as she bent over to watch the toys continue to stretch her.

They were silent as they focused on what the other was doing to them. The sound of Joey's screen door slamming didn't immediately register, but Mel's voice certainly did.

"What the fuck?" She looked away from Joey bobbing on Tiffany's face but couldn't tear her gaze away from the toys up Tiffany's pussy and ass.

"Who is that?" Tiffany called as Joey scrambled off her and slipped an oversized T-shirt on.

"No one," Joey said.

"Is it Mel?"

Mel shook her head, and Joey shrugged.

"Please, Joey…Mel…somebody. I'm so close. Someone finish fucking me."

Joey reached for the toy, but Mel pushed her hand away. She grabbed the base of the toy and pulled it out, then plunged them back in, twisting the toys slightly as they entered and as she withdrew them yet again.

Joey shook her head in amazement. Of all the things she and Mel had done together in their lives, this had to take the cake. Still, it wasn't Tiffany's fault Joey had forgotten she was coming over. She placed her fingers on Tiffany's huge, coated clit and rubbed while Mel fucked her faster and faster.

"Oh, yes! Oh, fuck yes! I'm going to come!"

Mel pushed the toys as deep as they could go and felt Tiffany's cunt and ass sucking them deeper as she came again and again. Joey felt Tiffany's clit pulsing with each climax. She continued to rub until Tiffany cried out once more.

"No more. Please no more. Oh, my God, I can't take anymore."

Mel was all smiles as she continued to stare between Tiffany's legs.

"See why I couldn't say no last night?" Joey asked.

Mel nodded.

"What?" Tiffany said.

"Nothing," Joey said.

"You weren't talking to me. Is Mel still here?"

Joey's eyes got wide, but Mel simply said, "Yeah, babe. I'm still here."

"Did you watch? Was it hot?"

Neither answered, and Tiffany asked, "Did you help? Oh, Mel, tell me you fucked me, too."

Mel blushed a deep red but said, "Yeah. I was moving the toy in and out of you."

"Oh, man," Tiffany said, apparently undisturbed. "You sure know how to fuck a girl."

Before they could say anything, she continued, "But I know those were Joey's fingers on my clit. I recognize them now. Thank you both. I've never come that hard before. Can we do it again sometime?"

"Sure thing," Mel said. She pulled the toys out of Tiffany and bent to lick her wet cunt.

"That feels nice. I like not knowing who's doing what. But I have to tell you, I have nothing left in me."

"That's okay," Mel said. "I just wanted to taste you."

"And?"

"You're delicious."

"Kiss me so I can taste it."

Mel did as she was asked, and Joey actually got hot watching her with her tongue in Tiffany's mouth. She sure as hell wasn't attracted to Mel, but seeing someone else with Tiffany was arousing. The girl was beyond hot, and Joey could easily watch her get fucked often.

"Do you two ever mess around?" Tiffany asked when Mel broke the kiss.

"God no!" they said in unison.

"But you're both really good-looking."

"You're talking nonsense now," Joey said, finally taking the towel from Tiffany's eyes.

"I guess we won't be surfing after all," Mel said.

"I've got to get going," Tiffany said, apparently undaunted that she was still lying spread eagle in front of them. She watched Mel staring at her pussy.

"You sure?" Mel asked.

"I might have time to please you if you'd like." Tiffany smiled.

"Thanks. Maybe some other time. Joey, I'll meet you across from The Shack then?"

"Sure. I'll be there in a few."

"I'll see you later, Tiffany." She left Joey and Tiffany alone.

"Are you ever going to untie me?" Tiffany asked.

"Oh, yeah." Joey untied her ankles.

"The cuff key is on the dresser."

Joey unlocked the handcuffs and watched as Tiffany moved her hands and feet, getting the circulation back in them. Her body was perfect, and she was almost sad that Tiffany would be putting clothes on to cover it. She kissed her hard and closed her hand on a shapely breast.

"What was that for?"

"Because you're too fucking hot. You just lay there and let my best friend have a go at you and you didn't care."

"Why would I care? She knew what she was doing, and it was hot with both of you fucking me." She moved her hand between Joey's bare legs to find her still wet and hard. "Didn't you enjoy it?"

"I thought it was awesome."

"Clearly." She lifted Joey's shirt and sucked on a nipple. "Do you ever masturbate?"

"What kind of question is that?"

"I was just wondering. I think it would be sexy as hell to watch you masturbate."

"That's not going to happen, dear." She closed her eyes at the sensations Tiffany's fingers were causing. They rubbed her clit, then filled her, then moved back to her clit.

"You're about to burst, aren't you?"

"Uh-huh."

"I want you to come for me."

"Oh, God, yes."

Tiffany stopped and sat up on the bed.

"What are you doing? You can't stop."

"Finish for me."

Joey was in no shape to argue. She lay back on her bed and rubbed her clit frantically until a powerful orgasm tore through her.

Tiffany took her hand and sucked it clean.

"What the fuck was that for?" Joey asked.

"I wanted to watch you. Is that a crime?"

"You're full of surprises, young one."

Tiffany got up and dressed quickly. "Thanks for this afternoon. It was even better than I'd imagined."

"It was pretty awesome. But do me a favor. Don't go letting yourself into my house again, okay?"

"Yeah. That was stupid. I'm sorry." She kissed Joey. "I guess I'll see you around, huh?"

"I like sex with you. I hope you know that."

"I do. And I hope we get to do it again. And again. And again." She laughed. "But I'm not looking for a relationship any more than you are. Don't forget that."

"I'll keep that in mind." She walked Tiffany to the front door and watched her walk off down the street.

CHAPTER FOUR

Joey parked next to Mel's van and crossed over to the water. She paddled out next to her.

"So that was interesting," Joey said.

"Yeah. But fun."

"It was kind of cool, both of us getting her off."

"She sure seemed to like it."

"You didn't seem to mind yourself, stud."

"She's just so…I don't know…"

"Fuckable," Joey said.

Mel laughed. "Yeah, she is. I like how she just wanted to come and didn't care how she got there. But it was a little weird stepping into your little episode or whatever."

"That wasn't me. I walked in from work to find her like that."

"No shit?"

"No shit! I was totally pissed at first. But then I realized she was just lookin' for a lay, and I could totally relate to that."

"Well, good for you. She seems like she'd be fun to have around."

"You know, I have to say, I kind of figured you'd be feeling a little guilty. I mean, you and Bess and all."

"She dumped me."

"Huh? When?"

"This afternoon. She said she thought we were getting too serious too fast."

"Hey, man. I'm sorry. I know you really liked her."

"It's all good. And yeah, there's no way I would have touched Tiffany if Bess hadn't cut me loose. But since she did, I figured why not jump on a chance like Tiffany?"

"Well, I was surprised enough when you were fucking her, but when you kissed her, I really thought you'd feel terrible."

"Nope. It felt great and I felt alive. That Tiffany's one hell of a kisser, by the way."

"Tell me."

"You're going to hurt her. You know that, right?"

"I don't think so. I think we'll have a good time and that's about it."

"We'll see."

❖

Joey paddled off and watched the swells, waiting for the perfect wave. She caught one after another, and soon all thoughts of Tiffany and Mel were gone as she communed with the ocean.

Finally, tired and hungry, she paddled back to Mel.

"That's it for me," she said.

"I hear that. You want to grab a couple of burgers?"

"Sure."

They dried off quickly as the fog rolled in earlier than usual.

"Damn, we got off the water just in time," Joey said.

"That's weird for this time of year."

"Well, let's get inside The Shack where at least we won't have this wind to contend with."

They stowed their boards in their respective vehicles, then Joey turned to survey the parking lot.

"Hey, that's her car." She stared toward the lot on the side of the building.

"Whose car?" Mel looked over, then shook her head at the sight of the Dodge Charger. "You're worse than a fucking stalker."

"No. I didn't plan to run into her here. Luck is just on her side tonight."

They walked into the restaurant, and Joey honed in on the beautiful blonde. She was sitting at a table with Brenda and her partner, Liz. Joey didn't like how close Brenda was with the interloper. She led the way to the table.

"What brings you to the lowly Shack?" she asked.

"They're the best burgers in town," Liz said.

"True that." Joey turned to the blonde. "I don't believe we've met."

Brenda exhaled heavily. "Joey Scarpetti, meet Samantha Brewer. Samantha, this is Joey Scarpetti. She's on my crew. And this is Mel O'Brien, who's also on the crew."

Mel waved awkwardly, but Joey extended her hand and studied Samantha Brewer. Her blue eyes were bloodshot, her skin red and splotchy. This was clearly a very upset woman, and Joey, while remotely curious, was decent enough not to pry.

"It was nice meeting you," she mumbled as she and Mel crossed to a vacant booth.

When they finished their burgers, they walked out of The Shack and into the rain.

"What's up with this?" Joey asked.

"Weird," Mel said. "They weren't calling for rain."

"You sure? Maybe you looked at the wrong forecast."

"Very funny. Damn. We're supposed to pour more concrete tomorrow. We can't do that if it's raining."

"We don't need any rain delays. I need the work."

"Don't we all?"

It was raining harder, and they were getting drenched and chilled. They said their good nights and went their separate ways.

Joey could still smell Tiffany as she climbed into bed. She smiled at the thought of her, but her smile quickly faded as she thought of the tormented look on Samantha Brewer's face at The Shack. What could have happened that had her crying in public? And why didn't Brenda and Liz take her home?

She was perplexed but convinced something wasn't right about Ms. Brewer. As long as she didn't cry anymore, Joey was still planning on bedding her. But her curiosity about Samantha was beginning to grow, as well as her distrust. She was convinced she was a spy, and she was probably playing the role of sympathy monger to try to melt the hearts of the good lesbians of Maybon Tir. Joey hoped Brenda would be able to see through her act, but she wasn't so sure about the other residents.

The last thought she had before sleep was of those pained blue eyes, bloodshot and damp.

She woke to her alarm at five fifteen the next morning to hear rain pounding her roof. She turned off her alarm, rolled over and pulled her pillow over her head, promptly falling back to sleep.

❖

"You're still asleep?" Mel stood over Joey's sleeping form. "It's damned near ten o'clock. You can't still be snoozing."

"I'm not now." Joey rolled onto her back. "Is it really ten o'clock?"

"Indeed." She handed Joey a cup of coffee from Nature's Bounty.

"Thanks." Joey sat on the edge of her bed. "You know, I'm starting to think locks on my door might be a wise investment."

"Bullshit. While you were playing sleeping beauty, I was at the library."

"Holy fuck, you need to get laid more. The library? Seriously?"

"What the hell has that got to do with getting laid?" She shook her head. "Whatever. I was doing a little research for you."

"What kind of research do I need?"

"On one Samantha Brewer."

"No shit? Who's the stalker now? But I love it. What did you find out?"

"She came out to daddy dearest after college, and he disowned her, so she moved with her partner to the Bay Area and took a job at a prestigious law firm in San Francisco."

"Okay, so you were right about that stuff. Why is she back here? And where's this partner? And why run a day care when she could be bringing in big bucks as an attorney?"

"Patience, Grasshopper. I found an article about her partner, a Dee Henderson. She was making money in real estate."

"What happened to her? Brenda mentioned something about Samantha just losing a partner."

"She was killed in the storm they had up there a few months ago. She was driving home from showing a house, and a tree got blown over and crushed her Audi. She died instantly."

"That sucks," Joey said, truly saddened.

"Big-time."

"Did you find out anything else?"

"Like what she's doing here?"

"Yeah, like that."

"There just happened to be a blurb about her in the *Pride* edition of the lesbian newspaper up there. She decided to move back here because she's always loved the area, and staying in San Francisco would be too painful."

"What about the day-care center?"

"Nothing about that. Just that she thought living in a community of kindred spirits would help heal her soul. There was no talk of what she'd do when she got here. She sure painted a pretty picture of Maybon Tir, though."

"Wonder if more dykes will move here then."

"Hard telling. It's not like they don't know we're here."

"True. Wouldn't it be cool if we became a truly self-sustained city?"

"I believe that was Mildred Braun's dream."

"We do pretty well. But we still rely on Somerset for things."

"There are only a few thousand of us here, Joey. As we grow, we'll be able to have the supply and demand we need to function independently."

"You really paid attention in econ, didn't you?"

"You knew exactly what I was saying. Don't go trying to work your party boi image on me."

"So what are we going to do today? This weather sucks."

"I was hoping you'd want to hit the garden."

"In this weather?"

"You won't melt," Mel said. "Besides, with the ground moist, it'll be easier to pull weeds."

"True. Okay, let me get dressed and we can go get some food and hit the garden."

They stepped outside, and the rain had turned into a deluge. Water flowed like a creek down the street in front of Joey's house.

"What the hell is going on?" Joey said.

"I don't know. It wasn't this bad earlier."

They climbed in the truck, and Joey managed to navigate them to Good Eats, a café on Main Street.

"Hey, Suze!" Joey called to the owner and cook.

A large black woman came out of the kitchen to join them.

"The place is rockin', huh?" Joey looked around the empty diner.

"You two are the only fools out in this weather."

"We're heading to the garden after food."

"Don't bother. This weather's not fit for woman nor beast. I'm sure the garden will wait. Now what'll you have?"

They ordered their breakfast and were sipping coffee when Brenda came in, dripping from head to toe.

"Where have you been?" Mel asked as she sat down.

"Stopped by the site. It's like a giant mud puddle over there. And this rain's not supposed to stop any time soon."

"Looks like a four-day weekend." Joey sighed.

"At least," Brenda said.

"Shit!"

"Tell me. We're going to have to bust our asses to make deadline now."

"Does that mean OT?"

"We'll see."

"Hey, not to change the subject, but were you and the missus able to comfort the poor Ms. Brewer last night?"

"Damn it, Joey. Let it go. You don't see her going out of her way to get to know you, do you?"

"She seems a bit preoccupied. I just need to get her mind on more pressing matters."

"No, you need to get your mind off her."

"No can do."

"Shit." She stood. "Well, I saw your truck here, so I thought I'd stop and tell you no work at least till Monday. Enjoy your time off."

Suze brought their food as Brenda left.

"What the hell are we going to do with a four-day weekend?" Joey asked.

"Road trip?"

"Where to?"

"We could drive down to Santa Brigida and hit some of the women's clubs there."

"That's not a bad idea." She grabbed her cell phone and started dialing.

"You calling Jett?"

"But of course."

Jett was one of their roommates from college who had gone on to graduate school in Santa Brigida, then stayed there as a physical therapist.

"Hey, Jett, it's your favorite blasts from the past. Mel and I are headed your way tonight and wondered if you'd mind us crashing for a couple of nights. We just need to get out of town. Let me know."

Joey dropped Mel at her house and went home to shower and dress. She found a black golf shirt hanging in the closet so she put that on and tan cargo shorts. She grabbed an overnight bag and threw some things in and was at Mel's house by two o'clock.

She found Mel sitting on the couch, elbows on her knees, phone to her ear.

Joey left her to go to the kitchen to grab a beer. She walked back to the living room to see Mel's arm outstretched. She handed her the beer and got another for herself.

"Fuck!" Mel slammed the phone on the couch.

"What's up?"

"Bess wants to get together and talk. She misses me."

"Damn. You split up yesterday and she already misses you? You really are a stud." When Mel didn't respond, she went on. "So what are you going to do? Are we canceling our road trip?"

"Hell, no. I told her I was going to be out of town and I'd get with her when I got back."

"So what was the 'fuck' for?"

"She told me she wants me to have fun but that she still thinks of me as hers and to keep that in mind."

"Whatever. That's her problem, right?"

Mel took a drink of beer.

"Right?" Joey repeated.

"I don't know."

"Damn it, Mel. Just yesterday, you told me you felt free and alive. Now you're saying you want to go to Santa Brigida with me and avoid trouble? What are you—schizo?"

"No! I guess I'm just confused."

"See what relationships do to you? She dumps you then tries to guilt you into not having fun without her. It's not worth it."

"She's totally messing with my head. I don't know what to do."

"Okay, so here's the deal. I road trip with my single friend. My friend behaves as a single woman and whatever happens, happens. Who knows? Maybe it'll be a chaste road trip."

"Yeah, right." She finished her beer. "Let's get going. We'll take the car."

Mel owned a 1980 Camaro Z28 that she kept in great shape. It was much more reliable for a road trip than the truck or the van. They got in, cranked a nineties radio station, and cruised down Highway 101.

An hour and a half later, Mel turned into the parking lot of Flannels, a women's bar since the early seventies. The parking lot was fairly full for happy hour. Joey looked over at Mel.

"Are you ready to have some fun?"

"You know it."

"Good. You're not still all forlorn over Bess?"

"Who?"

"Excellent answer."

They approached the front door and Joey saw a bright yellow Mustang.

"That looks like Tiffany's car."

"You've got that kid on the brain. You know she can't be here. She's not twenty-one. Or did you forget her age, old-timer?"

"Very funny. I don't think about her age. I just saw the car and it looked like hers is all."

They showed their IDs to get in the front door and were laughing about being carded as they made their way to the bar. They got a pitcher of beer and were walking toward a booth when Mel slapped Joey's arm and pointed to a couple of women kissing against one booth.

"Check out that ass," she said.

Joey stopped in her tracks to admire the fine shape of the young woman in the microskirt. She wouldn't mind a turn with her. She nodded to Mel, and as they were walking past, the couple broke for air. The one with the ass turned and smiled.

"Hey, Joey. Mel."

"Hey, Tiffany," Mel said. Joey just stood there.

"What are you two doing here?"

"Looking for a good time," Mel said.

"Aren't we all?" Tiffany thrust out her chest and rubbed it against the young butch who had her arm around her.

"Well, have fun," Joey finally said and turned to keep walking.

"Why don't you join us?" Tiffany asked.

"Maybe later," Joey said and moved on.

They sat down and poured themselves beers.

"Jealous?" Mel asked.

"Of?"

"Yeah, right. You're jealous that she's mackin' on someone else."

"Tiffany? Oh, hell no. I wasn't jealous when you fucked her. Why would I be jealous someone else is kissin' her?"

"That's different."

"I don't see how."

"Well, for starters, you know me and know I'm not interested. Also, you fucked her while I did. I'm not some young unknown butch making time with her."

"Look, I don't care who kisses her or fucks her or anything else. When we have the chance, we'll get together again. I don't plan to keep my stuff just for her. Why shouldn't she make the rounds, as well?"

"You should have seen your face. You can't hide it."

"You're imagining things. I just wonder how the hell she got in."

They finished their pitcher and started on a new one.

"Want to shoot some pool?" Joey asked.

Before Mel could answer, Tiffany slid into the booth next to Joey.

"Hello again. You know, it's seriously okay if you come join us. They're nice people."

She grabbed Joey's hand and placed it under her skirt. Joey bit her lip at the feel of the smooth flesh under her fingers. She forced her thighs open and ran a finger along her slit.

"That feels nice," Tiffany said.

"Oh, Jesus, you two," Mel said. "Get a room."

"Why?" Tiffany slipped her foot out of her sandal and ran it between Mel's legs.

"Very funny." Mel moved her foot.

"You two just look so delicious." Tiffany leaned back and spread her legs more.

"Just because I know Joey wants to know…what happened to the woman licking your tonsils earlier?"

"Why, Mel, I think you might care." She placed her foot on Mel's thigh and teased the leg of her shorts with her toes.

Mel cursed to herself as a blush started at the base of her neck.

"No chance, young one. I just think it's interesting that you were with her and now you're here with us."

"Do you see the way that black shirt makes Joey's blue eyes pop? Or have you any idea how fine your ass looks in those shorts? You two are positively devourable. I couldn't stay away long."

"I'm glad you didn't." Joey had a finger deep in Tiffany.

"Jesus, you two. People can see you."

"Hey, Tiff, you want to shoot some pool?" Joey quickly drew her hand from under Tiffany's skirt as her lanky friend spoke.

"Sure. I'll be your partner." To the others, she said, "Grab your pitcher. Come sit with us. We just moved to the longer table along the wall. There's plenty of room."

She stood and stared at Joey and Mel.

"What?"

"Now. Grab your beer. Come with us."

They followed her to a long table with chairs along it. Several of the chairs were occupied and several more had drinks in front of them. They chose two seats on the end and settled in to watch some pool.

CHAPTER FIVE

Two women came up and sat with Joey and Mel.
"You're Tiffany's friends, aren't you?"
"I'm Joey and this is Mel."
"Nice to meet you. How do you know Tiffany?"
"We've known her since she was a kid," Mel said.
"She's pretty cool," a tall brunette with generous breasts said.
"Who is?" Tiffany walked up to join them.
"You," the woman said.
"Aw, you're so sweet. Have you guys met? Joey, Mel, this is Amanda and Sara."
Joey stared at Amanda's chest before looking up to see her smiling at her. She smiled back.
"We were just getting acquainted."
"Good." Tiffany winked at Joey before walking back to the pool table.
"So do you two go to school here?" Joey asked.
"In a way. I teach at the local elementary school."
"And I'm a chiropractor," the redhead named Sara said. "What do you do?"
"We work construction." Mel appraised Sara as she spoke.
"That explains the tight bodies," Amanda said.
Mel blushed, but Joey just smiled.
"I'm glad you like what you see."
"Very much."

Tiffany walked up behind Sara and draped her arms around her shoulders, her hands rubbing the top of her breasts.

"I'm thirsty. Anybody want anything?"

"I'll get this round. What is everyone drinking?" Joey stood. She took their orders and raised an eyebrow when Tiffany asked for a Pepsi.

"What? I don't drink."

"Then what's the point of coming to a bar?" Joey fought the urge to point out the fake ID she must have used to get in.

"You don't have to drink to have fun in a bar," she said.

Joey just stared at her, then turned to get the drinks.

"I'll help you," Tiffany said. "I think Amanda wants you," Tiffany said as they approached the bar.

"I think we're all just getting warmed up."

"I have a feeling tonight's going to be a lot of fun."

"I'm planning on it."

They got back to the table, and Joey was disappointed to find Amanda not there. She looked around the room and saw her standing by the jukebox. She sauntered over and handed her a drink.

"Play some Skynyrd," Joey requested.

Amanda leaned into her. "I was thinking something slower."

"Slow is nice."

Amanda pushed some buttons, and she and Joey joined the others.

The music started, and Tiffany grabbed a reluctant Mel and led her to the dance floor. Joey laughed until Amanda grabbed her.

"I thought we were waiting for a slow song."

"I thought we'd start with something faster."

Joey relaxed and watched Amanda gyrating with the beat. She and Mel stood awkwardly and watched when Tiffany and Amanda started moving against each other.

"Not bad," Mel said.

"As long as they don't expect me to dance with you, I'm fine watching."

Joey enjoyed watching as breasts rubbed breasts, then Tiffany swayed her hips while bending her knees and danced down Amanda's body. While on her haunches, she licked at Amanda's crotch, then slowly danced back upright.

The two separated, and Joey watched Amanda move to Mel and found Tiffany as her partner.

"Did you enjoy that?" Tiffany whispered in her ear.

"Very much."

"I'm glad you're not the jealous type."

"Far from it."

"Do you like Amanda?"

"She seems nice enough."

"Would you let me watch you fuck her?"

"It seems to me you'll be too busy with your friend to be worried about what I'm doing. Where is she anyway?"

"She's running the pool table."

"She's not much of a dancer?"

"Not really."

The song ended, and Tiffany wandered back to the table. Joey danced the next couple of songs with Amanda, then pleaded thirst, so they made their way back to the table.

There were many more people milling about the table when they got there. Their seats had been taken, so they stood with Mel and watched the crowd.

"Is it just me, or does everyone here seem sexually charged?" Mel asked.

"It's definitely not just you."

They watched as one woman walked among several others, pausing to kiss each one deeply and grope or be groped along the way. At the table, one woman sat in another's lap, and they openly had their hands in each other's shirts while they made out.

"Face it, you landed with a fun group tonight," Amanda said.

"I guess," Joey said.

"Do you like me?" Amanda wrapped a leg around her.

"Of course."

Amanda moved over to Mel and kissed her, open-mouthed.

"What was that for?" Mel asked.

"I felt like it." To Joey, she said, "What would you do if I decided to fuck Mel tonight?"

"I'd find someone else."

"I love how nonchalant you are."

"Life's too short."

"I agree."

"Where'd Sara get to?" Joey asked Mel.

"She's making out over there."

Joey turned and saw Sara all over a husky butch with a shaved head.

A slow song started, and Amanda led Joey back to the dance floor. She laced her fingers behind Joey's neck and pressed into her as they danced.

"You've got the tightest body," she said.

"I rather like yours, too."

Amanda took a step back and pressed her breasts together. They looked like they would spill out of her blouse. Joey put her hands back behind her neck and placed her own hands on Amanda's ample chest. She bent and kissed the creamy tops that were displayed by the shirt.

She kissed up Amanda's neck and finally claimed her mouth. Her crotch spasmed when their tongues met, and she felt her clit swell as Amanda's talented tongue teased hers. The song ended, but they stayed on the floor, melded together, lost in their kisses.

Joey finally realized the song was over and took Amanda's hand to lead her from the floor. They got back to the table to find Sara in Mel's lap and the two of them kissing while their hands roamed all over each other.

"That Sara gets around, huh?"

"We all do." Amanda shrugged.

"Yeah? Well, you've stuck pretty close to me most of the night."

"I just want to make sure I get the first shot with you."

"I'm thinkin' that could be arranged." She pulled Amanda to her and kissed her again. She cupped her ass and pressed their pelvises together. "Do you have somewhere we can go?"

"I think we're going to the post party."

Joey cringed inwardly. She'd had enough teasing and couldn't wait to get Amanda to bed.

"Post party?"

"Mm-hmm. We generally take the party over to Malia's. She's got a big place down by the water."

"Not that the weather's too conducive for a swim."

"We'll be too busy to think about swimming."

Joey liked the sound of that and was leaning in for another kiss when Amanda was spun away from her. Tiffany had closed her mouth on Amanda's and fished a breast out of her top. Joey was on fire watching Tiffany fondle Amanda's firm, pale mound.

While she watched, Sara sidled up behind Tiffany and slid her hand under her short skirt.

"Holy fuck, they're hot." Mel's voice sounded far away.

Joey could only nod, never taking her eyes off the show.

"People are talking about getting out of here," Mel said.

"Yeah. Something about a post party," Joey mumbled.

"If this is how they act in public, I can't wait to get them to a private party," Mel said.

Sara joined them then and slipped her fingers in Mel's mouth while she kissed Joey. Joey's head was spinning from the intensity of the kiss. She normally wouldn't take Mel's sloppy seconds, but everyone seemed up for grabs that night.

The kiss ended when Amanda pulled Sara away and kissed her while Tiffany kissed Mel. Joey shook her head. She loved the freedom the women seemed to have. There was no possessiveness, no jealousy. It was all about having fun. She was suddenly looking forward to the post party.

Joey and Mel drove behind Amanda and Sara to the party.

"Man, did we ever luck out this weekend, huh?" Mel said.

"No doubt. There's no way we're not getting laid tonight."

"I'm curious to see who we end up with, though. I mean, I'm really into Sara, but you saw how things went down. One minute I'm kissing her, the next someone else has their tongue down my throat."

"Well, I'm not about to give up a chance to do Amanda. I don't care who else she kisses on."

"I don't know. She seemed to be enjoying Tiffany a hell of a lot."

"Who wouldn't?"

"To be honest, I wouldn't mind another go with her."

"I don't own her."

"Yeah, I get that after tonight."

They turned off the main road and down a long driveway that curved in front of a Grecian-looking mansion. Cars were parked all along the drive.

"Holy fuck. We're not in Kansas anymore," Mel said.

"No shit. Did you meet this Malia person at the bar?"

"Would I know if I had?"

"Good point."

Mel parked her car next to Amanda's. Amanda and Sara walked up to them holding hands. They took Mel's and Joey's and hurried to the front porch to get out of the rain.

"This porch is bigger than my whole house," Joey said.

"It's a nice place, isn't it?" Amanda said.

"That's an understatement."

"Come on. Let's get inside." Sara opened the door, and they stepped into an entryway that continued the Greek motif. Ten pedestals lined the walls, and each held the bust of a Greek god. The floor was white marble covered with a charcoal throw rug that was wet and dotted with mud.

Amanda led them through the entryway and down a long hall. At the end of the hall was a room the size of a basketball court. It took Joey a minute for her eyes to adjust to the darkness, but she was able to see that there was no furniture in the room, just thick mats all over the floor. The room was filled with women in various stages of undress performing various sexual acts on one another.

Joey was aroused as she took in the groups of women. There were twosomes, threesomes, and more. Women had their mouths on every possible body part, oblivious to who might be watching them. She thought for sure she'd died and gone to heaven.

Amanda took the group to the far end of the room where several people were already occupying mats.

"Shouldn't we find our own space?" Joey asked.

"We share." Joey looked down when she heard Tiffany's voice. She saw her naked, lying on her back with her legs open. Amanda dropped to her knees and buried her face between Tiffany's legs.

Joey was only vaguely aware of Sara and Mel collapsing on some neighboring mats. She was engrossed in watching Tiffany moving against Amanda. She noticed Tiffany playing with her nipples and thought, rather than just stand there, she might as well help out.

She lay next to Tiffany and took a nipple in her mouth. She felt the hardened nub grow as she licked and sucked it. She felt her shorts being unbuttoned and looked down to see a voluptuous blonde she'd seen at the bar fumbling with her zipper. Joey allowed the woman to slip her shorts and boxers off and run her fingers along her pussy. She moaned as the woman filled her and deftly moved her fingers inside. She kept her mouth on the nipple but watched as Amanda leaned over and kissed the blonde.

Tiffany grabbed Joey's hand and placed it between her legs while Amanda crawled up to kiss Joey. Their kiss was interrupted when Tiffany lifted Amanda's blouse over her head. Joey unhooked Amanda's bra and gasped as her large breasts fell free. She bent to take one in her mouth while Tiffany greedily sucked on the other.

Tiffany's cunt was slick and hot, and Joey loved the feel of it around her fingers. She was being smothered by Amanda's tit. All was right in her world until she felt her own cunt suddenly untouched. She looked down and saw the blonde stripping off her skirt. The blonde lay back down, sliding one leg under Joey and one over, rubbing their clits together as she moved Joey's hand out of the way and began licking Tiffany.

Joey went to work getting Amanda's slacks down and off and reached her hand between her legs. She found her wet and ready and easily slid three fingers deep.

"Oh, yes, that's it." Amanda spread her legs wider.

Joey disentangled herself from the blonde and took Amanda in her mouth. She licked the length of her and sucked her lips before entering her again. She lapped at her tight cunt, loving her musky flavor. As Joey continued to fuck Amanda with her tongue, she felt hands on her hips and someone pulling her. Next she felt a tongue on her hard clit and looked down to see Tiffany's mouth on her. She was dizzy with need, her whole body on fire. While she continued to lick Amanda, she saw Sara kiss her and Mel grab one of her large tits to suck.

While Mel suckled Amanda, she reached her hand over and slipped her fingers inside Tiffany. Joey absently wondered where the blonde was, then saw her head between Mel's legs. Joey felt fingers playing with her holes and was shocked to see Sara's hand busy there.

Joey reached her hand out and slipped her fingers inside the blonde. She plunged her fingers inside her while rubbing her clit with her thumb. She was dripping juices, and Joey was soon coated. She moved her thumb to the blonde's nether hole and slipped it in while she continued moving in and out of her pussy.

She moved her tongue to Amanda's clit and slipped her free hand inside her. She glanced up and saw hands on Amanda's chest but neither knew nor cared whose they were. She continued to ride Sara's hand as she fucked Amanda and the blonde. The sensations were overwhelming to her, and she could feel herself rapidly approaching her climax. She tried to hold back and wait for at least Amanda, when she felt teeth on her clit and the flick of someone's tongue. That was all it took. She flew into oblivion, soaring through the fog of pleasure and finally landing on the other side just in time to feel the blonde's cunt convulse around her fingers and hear Amanda cry out as her orgasm hit.

Joey tried to slide up Amanda's body to kiss her, but Tiffany pulled her to her and kissed her, then released her as she cried out in ecstasy. Joey was lost as she heard women crying out all around her. She felt like she was only getting started, like her orgasm had only been an appetizer.

She looked around and saw Mel kissing Amanda while she had her fingers inside Sara. Sara's face was between the blonde's legs, and the blonde was kissing Tiffany, who had her fingers in Mel.

Joey lay beside the group, trying to catch her breath, and suddenly a large breast belonging to a woman she'd never seen before ended up in her mouth. She sucked it greedily as she felt someone slowly slide a dildo inside her. It was huge, and she felt herself stretching to take it all. She continued to suck the huge tit and reached over to find Tiffany's pussy available for her fingers. She was on her knees then, and the woman took the dildo out and entered her from behind, moving the toy deeper inside her. Tiffany reached down and rubbed Joey's clit while Joey fucked her. Joey felt her pussy tighten around the toy as she climaxed hard, shooting her come down the length of the toy just as Tiffany came on her fingers.

The after party continued into the wee hours of the morning. Joey lost track of how many women had ridden her tongue and how many times she'd climaxed. She was satiated and exhausted when she finally found a spot to fall asleep.

CHAPTER SIX

Joey awoke the next morning and rolled over, finding herself next to a young brunette she didn't recognize. She propped herself up on an elbow and looked over the group, searching for Amanda. She was horny and hoping for a little morning fun.

She saw Amanda three people over on the other side of Tiffany. The brunette rolled over to face Joey, who took a long look at her before deciding not to wake her. Instead, she crawled over to a pile of clothes and fished through them for hers. She dressed quickly and grabbed her phone from her pocket to text Jett and let her know they were alive.

She saw she had five texts from Brenda. Each one warned of the flooding in their community, and each one was direr than the one before. She'd been trying to reach Joey and Mel most of the night to have them help with sandbags to save some buildings.

"Shit," Joey muttered. She gathered Mel's clothes and stepped over bodies until she reached her. The sight of her best friend naked in the light of day made her uncomfortable, but she nudged her with a foot to wake her.

"Hey, Mel. Mel. Wake up." She threw the clothes at her.

Mel opened an eye and seemed to realize she was naked as she scrambled to cover herself.

"What the fuck?"

"We've got to get going. Get dressed."

Mel didn't ask any questions, she simply put on her clothes. Joey stood with her back to Mel and surveyed the room. A slow smile spread across her face as memories of the previous night filled her.

She felt a hand on her ankle and looked down to see Tiffany looking at her. She opened her legs.

"Please?"

"I wish I could, sweetheart, but Mel and I have to hit the road. You might want to check in with someone in Maybon Tir. Apparently, there's widespread flooding. You want us to check your grandma's house?"

"It should be fine. It sits up high. Thanks, though."

Joey just nodded as Mel joined her.

"I wish you two didn't have to leave." Tiffany lightly stroked between her legs.

"Me too," Mel said. "Wait, why are we leaving?"

"Come on. I'll explain in the car. See you back home, Tiffany." Joey led Mel through the maze of bodies and out of the room. The house seemed eerily quiet, and Joey was happy to get outside.

"What's going on?"

Joey told Mel about Brenda's messages.

"Shit! I hope we're not too late."

"We're not the only ones in town who can fill sandbags. We just need to get our asses back and help with whatever we can. I texted Brenda and let her know we'd be there in a couple of hours."

The ride home was much more subdued, the sound of the wipers replacing the sound of the music blaring the day before.

"What do you think would have happened if we stayed?" Mel finally said.

"What do you mean?"

"In Santa Brigida. Do you think all that sex would have continued all day and night again?"

"Hard telling. Man, last night was something, though, right?"

"No doubt. That was mind blowing."

Joey was lost in thought for a moment. "I wonder if Ms. Samantha Brewer's ever done anything like that before."

"How can you have her on the brain after having sex with God knows how many women last night?"

"I don't know." Joey shrugged. "She's never far from my mind, for some reason."

"Damn, I feel sorry for her if you ever really get to know her. If you're this obsessed now."

"I'm not obsessed."

"No?"

"Whatever. She's a hot woman and I want a shot at her."

"Bullshit. She's off limits and you won't be told no."

"That might be part of it."

As they approached their exit, Joey texted Brenda to ask where they should meet.

"She says to meet her by the community church. Apparently, the river has overflowed and the water's up to the church steps."

Mel turned her car down Rio Street but quickly came to a stop as the road was now part of the rushing river.

"Shit. I can't make it down this road."

"Let's go get the truck."

Mel backed up and flipped a U-turn. She had just gotten out of the way when the now familiar Dodge Charger came barreling around the corner.

"What the fuck?" Joey spun in her seat in time to watch the car get washed down the street.

"Oh, shit! Call 911!" Joey jumped out of the car and ran as far as she could. She stopped briefly, mortified, as the nose of the car sank below the surface. Adrenaline driving her, Joey dove into the water and rode the current down to the car. She held on to the vehicle and looked through the driver's window to see Samantha slumped over the steering wheel, blood pouring from her forehead.

Frantic, she pounded on the window to no avail. Samantha clearly couldn't hear her. She tried the handle on the door, but it was locked. The car was sinking slowly, and Joey cautioned herself not to panic.

She needed something with which to break the window. A branch floated by, and she grabbed it, pummeling the window with the blunt end. It neither broke the window nor got Samantha's attention.

"Damn it!" She let the current take the log away and treaded water, trying to come up with another plan. Finally, an idea came to her, and she swam to where the shore normally would be. Fighting the current, she dove down and felt along the bottom for a large rock that made up the embankment. She found one and, after surfacing to catch her breath, was able to dive again and dislodge it. She carried it to the surface and treaded water again, trying to even her breathing.

Finally ready, she held the rock under one arm and swam with powerful strokes out to the car. She steadied herself again and lifted the rock above her head and brought it down with all her strength. She thought she felt the window give but could see no evidence of it. She repeated her actions, again using all her strength to force the rock into the window. The window shattered and Joey continued to pound until it gave way. Joey quickly peeled the glass back and leaned in the car.

Water was rushing through the window as she struggled to unlock Samantha's seat belt. She was tired and cold, and her fingers weren't cooperating. The water was over Samantha's chin before Joey finally got the belt unbuckled.

Joey managed to get Samantha out through the window, then used the lifeguard skills she'd learned years before to swim with Samantha to the shore. She carried her to the center of the road and was only then aware of the sound of sirens. She saw two ambulances and a fire truck parked by Mel's car. Paramedics in wetsuits raced to them and put Samantha on a stretcher. As they wheeled her off, a second set approached.

"Are you all right, ma'am?" someone called.

She nodded as she remained sitting in the water in the middle of the street.

"We've got a stretcher for you."

Joey shook her head.

"We can't leave you here." A woman offered her a hand up.

Joey stood and allowed another paramedic to wrap a blanket around her shoulders. She stared at the gurney.

"I don't need that," she said to the paramedics.

"Just let us check you out for hypothermia."

"Seriously? It's summer. It's raining, but it's warm out here. The river was cold, but I'm fine. I just need to get home."

The two female paramedics had been with Joey in the past and knew better than to argue with her.

"Thanks for your help, but I'm good to go now," she said before climbing into Mel's car.

"You sure you're okay?" Mel asked.

"I'm fine."

"Good. Then I won't feel bad saying I'll kill you if you ruin my upholstery."

Joey laughed and stayed wrapped in the blanket for the drive home.

❖

"Oh, shit! Did you text Brenda?" Joey called from her bedroom after her shower.

"Of course," Mel said.

"Thanks." Joey walked out dressed in jeans and a T-shirt. "I suppose we should go see what we can do to help, huh?"

"I think you've done enough, Wonder Woman."

"Funny."

"Seriously, you're going to be so sore already. You don't need any extra exertion."

"If we need to help, we need to help. This is our town."

"Brenda knows how to get in touch with us. She knows we're here."

"We can't just sit here and listen to the rain."

"What the hell is your problem? Just relax already."

"I can't."

"Why?"

"I don't know. I'm all keyed up."

"I'm exhausted after last night, and I didn't even dive into a rushing river to save a damsel in distress this morning. You've got to be fried."

"I wonder how she's doing." Joey collapsed onto the couch next to Mel.

"Would you like to go check on her?"

"I don't know." Joey was torn. She didn't want people to think she was just seeking glory, but she did want to know how Samantha was doing.

"Let's go." Mel stood. "We're taking the truck. I'm not about to move my car again until this weather mellows out."

Joey grabbed her keys, and they rushed out to the truck. The rain was still coming down hard and showed no signs of stopping. The water in the street in front of her house was now flowing with a decent current.

"You realize we're nuts to be going anywhere," Mel said. "Who knows if we'll be able to get back home."

"We'll be fine," Joey said as they drove off. "It can't last forever."

"It only has to last another day or so and our community will be under water."

"You're such an alarmist."

"We'll be like the lost city of Atlantis."

"Yeah. That's exactly how it'll be."

They drove to Somerset and pulled into the hospital parking lot. It, too, was like a large pond with standing water everywhere. They found a space near the front door next to Brenda's car and waded inside, their feet soaked.

"We're looking for a Samantha Brewer," Joey told the woman at the desk.

"She was just brought in an hour or so ago," Mel said.

"Brought in?" the woman asked.

"Yeah, by ambulance," Joey said.

"You might try the ER," the woman said. "It's down the hall and to the right."

They found Brenda in the waiting room of the emergency room.

"I would have thought you'd be in there with her," Joey said as they sat down.

"Liz is closer to her, so she's in there."

"How's she doing?"

"She's going to be fine."

"Then why the long face?" Mel asked.

Brenda looked from one to the other.

"There's more involved."

"Like what? You said she'll be fine. What else is there to worry about?"

Before Brenda could answer, Liz walked into the waiting room, a huge smile on her face. She hugged Brenda as tears rolled down her face.

"Everything's going to be all right," she said.

Joey and Mel looked at each other, confused. They looked back to the others, just separating from their hug.

"What the hell's going on?" Joey asked.

"The baby's going to be fine," Liz said.

"Baby?" Joey and Mel said in unison.

"I didn't tell them," Brenda said.

"Obviously," Liz said.

"She's four months pregnant," Brenda said.

"Pregnant?" Joey was still trying to absorb the information.

"We told her it was you who saved her," Liz said.

Joey felt claustrophobic. The desire to see Samantha was gone, replaced by a need to get as far away as possible. The last thing she wanted was to get involved on any level with a woman who was expecting. Babies were not her thing.

"Well, we just wanted to make sure she was going to make it," she said. "I guess we'll be heading home now."

"I know she'd love to see you," Liz said.

"That's okay. We should get going."

"What? We drove here in this weather and now you don't want to see her?" Mel said. "Oh, no, you don't. Get your ass in there now."

"Come on," Brenda said. "You started this whole obsession thing."

"I'm not obsessed."

"What's the matter? A little baby has Joey Scarpetti scared?"

"I'm not scared." Repulsed was more like it, but she didn't feel like sharing that.

"Good, because I know Samantha would like to see you."

"Great. Now she wants to see me when I have no desire to see her anymore."

She followed Brenda down the hall to Samantha's alcove in the Emergency Department.

"Look what floated in on the tide," Brenda said.

Samantha's face lit up at the sight of Joey. She ran her hands through her hair as if putting herself together.

Joey noticed nothing, however, save the slight belly bump under the blankets. How could she not have seen that before?

"You saved my life," Samantha said.

"I couldn't very well watch your car sink and not do anything about it."

"You don't have to be an ass about it." Samantha's smile faded.

"I'm sorry." Joey was confused and uncomfortable. The discomfort of the baby warred with the attraction to the woman and left her lost. "I just, well, I guess I don't know what to say."

"Well, thank you for saving us."

"You had me pretty scared. I couldn't imagine losing you before I really got to know you."

"There's the Joey we all know and love," Brenda said.

"Well, I'd like to make you dinner sometime soon to show my appreciation, if you don't mind."

"That's really not necessary."

"It may not be, but I'd like to."

Joey looked into Samantha's deep blue eyes and felt a definite stirring. She allowed her gaze to roam lower, over her full lips, down to her sizeable breasts and lower, where she stopped. And stared at her belly.

Samantha put her hands over her stomach.

"Thank you for saving her."

"Her?"

"I don't know that for sure, but I can just feel it."

Joey only nodded, decidedly uncomfortable again.

"So what do you say about dinner? I should be moved into my new place in Maybon Tir by the first of the month. Will you come over?"

Joey was torn but felt her head nodding on its own. "Sure. That sounds great. Where will you be living?"

"I'm moving into Mildred Braun's place."

"You are?" She thought it odd that Tiffany hadn't mentioned that.

"Escrow just closed. Anyway, Brenda has your number, so I'll call you when I get all moved in, okay?"

An evening with Samantha sounded wonderful to Joey. An evening with Samantha and baby didn't appeal quite as much.

"Sure," she heard herself say.

"From what I've heard of Joey Scarpetti, I expected you to march in here all cocky and not let me forget you were the hero of the day. What's going on with you?"

"She's a little ill at ease over the baby."

"Don't worry," Samantha said. "She's not yours."

Joey laughed, further charmed. The baby may have scared her, but the woman was appealing more to her as they spoke. "I was fairly certain of that."

"So will you relax already?"

"I'll try."

"Good. Now I don't mean to be a lousy hostess, but I'm tired and am going to nap for a bit until they kick me out of here."

"Yeah, sure," Joey said. "It was good seeing you. I'm glad you're all right."

"Thanks again for saving me."

"No problem."

"Liz and I'll be in the waiting room when you wake up," Brenda said.

They left Samantha to get some sleep and joined the others.

"How's she doing?" Mel asked.

"She's pregnant," Joey said.

"Yeah, I got that. Outside of that?"

"She's doing very well," Brenda said. "That gash on her forehead was something, though, wasn't it, Joey?"

"Gash?"

"You didn't notice?"

"To be honest, I didn't notice much except her belly."

"I call bullshit," Mel said.

"Okay, and maybe her eyes and her lips and her boobs," Joey admitted.

"Yeah, maybe her boobs," Mel repeated.

"She's moving into Mildred's place," Joey told Mel.

"Where's Tiffany going?"

"That's a good question."

"We'd better get home while we still can," Mel said.

"With you here, who's running the show in Maybon Tir?" Joey asked Brenda.

"Things are about as shored up as they're going to get. All we can do now is hope for an end to the rain."

"Are there any old timers we should check on?" Joey asked.

"They've all been accounted for or moved to safety, if necessary. You two just go home and stay out of trouble."

Joey and Mel walked out to the truck.

"What are you going to do about your obsession now?" Mel asked.

"She's still fucking hot. Except..."

"Yeah. How big is that 'except'?"

"I don't know, Mel. I honestly have no idea."

CHAPTER SEVEN

The deluge continued through the weekend, and it took the whole next week for the jobsite to dry out enough for the crew to get back to work. The workers had finished pouring concrete for the playground and the toy shed and were taking their midmorning break when the Charger pulled up.

"Don't look now," Mel said.

Joey watched the car pull to a stop and the driver door open. She watched as the shapely calf appeared, followed by the rest of her tan leg and tight ass in khaki shorts. She continued to ogle as Samantha finished climbing out of the car. Samantha flashed a bright smile their way and waved before wandering off to find Brenda.

"She's so fuckin' hot!"

"She's easy on the eyes. I'll give you that," Mel agreed.

"No kidding."

"How're you handling the pregnancy idea?"

"She's not that far along. I could still enjoy that body, I'm sure."

"That's the spirit." Mel shook her head at Joey.

"Hey, what's she doing here?" Joey motioned with her head to the yellow Mustang pulling onto the site.

"She's gotta be looking for you."

"You've done her, too."

"Yeah, but you two have a special bond."

"Whatever."

Joey slid off her tailgate to greet Tiffany, but instead of walking toward her, Tiffany joined Brenda and Samantha. Samantha greeted her with a hug.

"Oh, now it's getting good," Mel said.

"What the fuck? She's kicking her out of her house. Why would Tiffany be excited to see her?"

"She's not exactly kicking her out. And you said Tiffany was only staying there until it sold."

"Break's over," Brenda yelled.

Joey and Mel walked back to the building to start hanging sheetrock. Tiffany walked over to join them.

"Damn, you two look hot when you're butchin' it up at work."

Mel laughed and Joey smiled.

"What business do you have with Ms. Brewer?" Joey asked.

"She bought my grandma's house."

"So I've heard."

"Which is kind of why I'm here."

"Kind of?"

"Okay. It is why I'm here. I need to move out this weekend. I don't have a lot of things there, but I was wondering if I could borrow your truck to move."

"I don't loan out my truck, Tiff."

"Please? I promise to be extra careful with it."

"No way. However, I'll be happy to drive my truck and help you move your stuff."

"You will?" Tiffany hugged her. "Thank you so much."

"No problem."

"I'll even have beer on hand for you."

"Where am I moving you to—Somerset?"

"Nah. We're just going to move my stuff to Nora's Storage here until I move into the dorms," Tiffany said. "Okay. I should let you guys get back to work. Especially since Brenda's looking over here."

"So I'll see you Saturday morning. What time?"

"Ten o'clock?"

"Sounds good."

Tiffany walked off, and Joey and Mel hung another piece of sheetrock before Samantha joined them.

"Excuse me." Mel started to walk off.

"Oh, wait," Samantha said. "This is for both of you."

Mel stopped and turned back, avoiding eye contact with Joey.

"What's up? How are you feeling?" Joey asked.

"Much better. I even get the stitches out tomorrow." She motioned to her forehead.

"I'm glad to hear that. You're looking great."

Samantha smiled brightly.

"Are you quite certain I can't excuse myself?" Mel asked.

"Quite." Samantha laughed. "This Sunday, I'm moving into my new house. Brenda, I'm sure, will tell you, I'm looking for any and all volunteers I can find since I can't do much lifting myself. To show my appreciation, there'll be a barbecue with all the fixings at my new place. I know you've already done so much for me"—she smiled at Joey—"but I'm asking for your help, if you possibly can. And free food and beer after. All you can eat and drink."

"That sounds great." Joey beamed. "We'll be there."

"Thank you. I look forward to it."

Joey drooled over Samantha's figure as she picked her way through the construction site debris on the way to her car. Samantha turned and waved again before climbing in.

"Earth to Joey," Mel said. "We have work to do."

"Yeah, yeah." Joey turned back to the sheetrock.

"And by the way, thanks a hell of a lot for volunteering me for Sunday. Did it ever occur to you that I might not want to spend my day helping a pregnant lady move?"

"No, it didn't actually. But thanks for asking."

"God, you exasperate me sometimes."

"Whatever. Free food and beer. Pool party. What's not to like about that scenario?"

"She didn't say anything about a pool party."

"Are you kidding me? This group hot and sweaty after moving her all day and you don't think we'll be getting in the pool?"

Mel didn't say anything; she just grabbed another sheet and motioned at Joey to help her lift it.

"What the hell's your problem? You know you would have volunteered anyway."

"Maybe, but next time, let me do it myself."

"So I suppose this means you're not going to help me with Tiffany on Saturday?"

"I think you'll be able to handle Tiffany just fine without my help."

"Fine. I will. Are you PMSing or something?"

"Let it go."

"I will if you will. Jesus."

❖

They worked in silence for the next couple of hours, the only sound that of the nail gun. When it was time for lunch, they sat on Joey's tailgate.

"Hey, man, you okay?" Joey asked.

"Yeah. Sorry I blew up. I figure you're right. I'd have been helping on Sunday anyway."

"And Saturday?"

"You can call me if you need me for that, okay? Otherwise, I'll hang back."

Joey stared hard at Mel.

"What's going on? What aren't you telling me?"

"Nothing. It just ticks me off at how twitterpated you get over Samantha. I don't get it. You don't even know her."

"But I plan to."

"Yeah, I know. It just feels different than usual. I can't put my finger on it."

Joey shrugged. "Beats me. Me in search of a bedmate's never irritated you before."

"Like I said, there's something different this time."

"That, my friend, is your overactive imagination."

"Maybe so."

❖

Friday night, Joey and Mel went to Kindred Spirits, the local tavern. The place was packed with locals shooting pool, throwing darts, and enjoying one another's company. Joey and Mel had some beers and relaxed after their hard workweek by holding one of the pool tables until close to midnight when they ran out of takers.

Mel laid her pool cue on the table. "I think it's time we call it a night."

Before Joey could respond, two women approached them.

"We've been watching you shoot pool. You're pretty good. Are you up for a challenge?"

Joey looked at the women, both in short shorts and tank tops. One had auburn hair pulled back in a ponytail while the other wore her blond hair short and spiky.

"You're not from here, are you?" Joey asked.

"No. We're from the Bay Area. We're just here on vacation," the blonde said.

"Where are you staying?" Mel asked.

"At The Tidewater."

"Y'all have a cottage, huh? Those are pretty nice." Joey leaned against the pool table and assessed the women. Both were slightly sunburned, and the color looked good on them. They were a few inches shorter than Mel and her. They were slim with small breasts that formed perfect tents under their shirts.

"They're really nice. And reasonable. Especially for being right on the water."

"I'm Joey. And this is Mel." She extended her hand to the blonde.

"My name's Morgan. This is my friend Kennedy."

"Nice to meet you." The four shook hands with Morgan holding Joey's a little longer than necessary.

"So what's the challenge?" Mel's gaze roamed over Kennedy's body.

"Winners top losers," Morgan said matter-of-factly.

"Whoa!" Joey said. "We don't do the tag-team thing."

"What?" Kennedy asked.

"We don't play together," Mel said.

"That's too bad." Morgan pouted, then shrugged. "But we'll still play you for tops. I top Joey if we win and Kennedy tops you."

"I admire your spunk," Joey said, "but I can't imagine a couple of city girls beating us in pool."

"Do you accept the challenge? Or are you two too butch to bottom?"

"That won't be an issue since we won't lose," Mel said.

"I'll take that as acceptance then. Two out of three. Let's see who breaks."

Joey took her place behind Morgan and licked her lips as Morgan bent over to shoot the cue ball. It banked off the far end and rolled back, inches from the edge.

Morgan turned around, happy with her shot.

"Are you enjoying the view?"

"Most definitely." Joey ran her cue stick up Morgan's leg.

Morgan watched its progress and did nothing to stop it. When it reached the point where her legs met, she looked up at Joey.

"You're going to be fun, aren't you?"

Joey lowered her stick and stepped toward Morgan. She stared into her hazel eyes before lowering her mouth to taste Morgan's.

"Break it up, you two. We still need to lag for break." Mel forced her cue stick between them. "There will be plenty of time for that later."

Joey's cue ball was the only one that passed Morgan's and just barely did. With the winning lag, she watched Morgan rack the balls. She admired her as she leaned in, making sure the triangle held the balls flush. Joey reached out with her cue stick and pulled Morgan's top down, affording herself a view of pert breasts. "Nice."

Morgan stood and lifted her shirt, showing off her tits.

"Can you see them better now?"

"Oh, fuck!" Joey looked around but realized Morgan's back was to everyone but their group. "Yeah, I can."

"Now will you focus on pool?"

"Yeah, right." Joey turned to Kennedy. "How about yours?"

Kennedy took Mel's hand and ran it under her shirt, placing it on a breast.

"No one needs to see mine but Mel."

Joey watched as Mel kissed Kennedy hard on her mouth and could see Mel's hand working under Kennedy's shirt.

"You gonna watch them all night or break?" Morgan asked.

Joey broke and knocked in three solids. She proceeded to run the table. After sinking the eight ball, she stood and smiled at Morgan.

"That's one."

"And only one," Morgan said. "Kennedy, come up for air. Your turn to rack 'em."

Joey watched as Morgan meandered toward her. Morgan wandered behind her and pressed into her back, kissing her neck. She had her fingers on Joey's upper thighs and pulled her into her crotch.

Heat seared through Joey's body. She took one of Morgan's hands and moved it the inch it needed to press into her clit.

"You don't waste time, do you?" Morgan placed her hand back on Joey's thigh.

"Why should I?"

"Because being teased is so much fun."

Morgan turned Joey around and kissed her, mouth open and tongue searching.

Joey kissed her back, light-headed as the blood drained from her head, pooling in the nerve center between her legs.

"Joey? Break already," Mel interrupted them again.

"Damn, your timing is lousy," Joey told her.

"The sooner we win this game, the sooner we get past teasing and on to the good stuff. Now break."

Joey broke again and knocked three stripes in, but her focus was gone, and she didn't sink anything on her follow-up shot.

Morgan went next and ran the table. "That's one apiece."

Joey smiled at Morgan. She was so cute and feisty. She halfway wanted to throw the next game just to see what Morgan would do if she was topping her. Not that the bet mattered much to Joey. She knew they'd win and she'd call the shots, which would mean a free-for-all fuckfest. She couldn't care less who drove. She just wanted to get this woman alone where she could fully enjoy her body.

As Joey racked the balls, Morgan squatted behind her and licked her inner thighs. She hiked up her shorts leg and boxers and licked inches from Joey's wet pussy. Joey leaned over the pool table and let her continue.

"I'm not going to make you stop in case you wondered," Joey said. She felt Morgan stop and stood, pulling her to her and kissing her.

"You don't really give a shit who watches you do what, do you?" Joey asked when the kiss ended.

"Not so much."

"Okay, go break." She patted Morgan's ass.

Morgan broke and kept control of the table until she scratched. Mel took over and knocked in all but two of their balls. Kennedy cleared the rest of the solids but missed on the eight ball. Joey dropped the two striped balls with ease and called the eight ball in the corner pocket. She had to bank it and shoot without much force so the ball would angle just right.

Joey blocked out everyone and every sound in the bar as she lined up her shot. She was far too competitive not to give it her all. The cue ball hit the eight ball right where she wanted it. She stood and watched as the eight ball rolled toward the corner. And slowed. And teetered into the hole.

She and Mel high-fived each other, then turned to Morgan and Kennedy.

"So," Joey said, "do y'all want another round or shall we head to the cottage?"

"We don't need anything more to drink. Let's just get out of here." Morgan took Joey's hand.

Chapter Eight

Once in the parking lot, Joey pressed Morgan against her truck and kissed her, running her hands over her body. Morgan reached into her pocket and held out her keys, which Kennedy grabbed. Aroused to the point of shaking, Joey fumbled with her keys and finally got the door open for Morgan. They continued to kiss until Morgan finally pulled away and climbed in.

Joey followed Kennedy to the cottage and went back to kissing Morgan as soon as they were parked. She lifted Morgan's shirt and bent to take a hard nipple in her mouth. She sucked and tugged on it while Morgan tangled her fingers in Joey's hair.

"You smell like sunshine," Joey murmured, planting kisses first on one breast and then the other. "So fresh and clean."

Her breathing was heavy as she toyed with the button on Morgan's shorts.

"We should go inside," Morgan whispered.

"Fuck it. I want to take you here."

"A bed would be much more comfortable."

"What?" Joey finally registered what Morgan was saying. She knew she'd have much better access to that tight body outside of the confines of the truck. "Yeah, you're right. Let's get inside."

They hurried in the house, where Joey could hear Mel and Kennedy behind a closed door. Morgan shed her clothes as she led Joey down the hall to her room. When she got there, she turned to face Joey, completely naked. Joey closed the door behind her and drew Morgan to her for another kiss. She ran her hands over Morgan's soft, naked skin, clasping her tight ass and spreading her cheeks as she held her close against her.

Morgan took one of Joey's hands and placed it between her legs, moving against it. Joey shuddered at how wet and swollen she found Morgan. She walked her back against the bed and sat her on the edge.

Joey knelt and gently held Morgan's legs apart. She gazed at the creaminess on display and watched as she buried two fingers inside her, knuckles up. She turned them over and pulled them out.

"Oh, God, yes, Joey. Fuck me." She sat up and watched as Joey fucked her.

Joey repeated the motion, sliding three fingers in, then taking them out. She lowered her mouth and licked Morgan's swollen clit, slowly and deliberately, heady from the taste of it. She moved her fingers in and out of her while she licked the length of her.

"Holy fuck, you feel good." Morgan lay back on the bed as Joey moved her mouth to her opening, flicking her tongue around it before entering her. She licked inside her while she stroked her clit, pressing into it as she rubbed.

Joey reached her free hand up and cupped a small breast, alternately kneading it and twisting the nipple. She continued to fuck her as Morgan began to move against her in earnest, bucking and writhing. She felt Morgan's hand on the back of her head, holding her face against her as she cried out, covering Joey's face in come.

Joey licked her clean and kissed her way back to Morgan's mouth, where she firmly planted hers. As they kissed, Morgan began to unzip Joey's shorts.

"Who said I was through with you?" Joey asked.

"I need to touch you."

"Maybe I'm not ready for that." Joey was wet and throbbing but didn't think Morgan needed to know that. She looked around the tiny bedroom, and her gaze landed on the dresser. "Do you have any toys here?"

"Maybe."

"Get them."

"I only have one." Morgan climbed off the bed. She opened the top dresser drawer and pulled out a harness with a long, thick dildo in it.

"Now you're talking," Joey said. Aware of Morgan's attention glued to her, Joey slowly took her shirt over her head and folded it, laying it on the dresser. She kicked off her sandals and had her shorts unbuttoned when Morgan stepped to her, closing her mouth on Joey's breast.

"I said no." Joey pulled away. She stepped out of her shorts and boxers and watched Morgan's appreciative gaze working over her body. She stood, desire flooding her, wanting to feel Morgan on her and in her, and reached to take the harness. She got it on and grabbed Morgan again, kissing her hard as she maneuvered the cyber skin cock inside her. She arched her hips and plunged it deeper, pulling it out slightly before filling her again.

They continued kissing and Morgan held tightly to Joey's shoulders and Joey continued to thrust the toy deeper and deeper. Joey closed her hands over Morgan's breasts, squeezing them and pinching her nipples. She backed away from Morgan, pulling the toy all the way out. She stood there, cock at attention, and gently eased Morgan back on the bed.

She stood in front of her and maneuvered the toy to Morgan's mouth. Morgan looked up at her and ran her tongue along the tip. Joey smiled at her as she watched Morgan take the tip in her mouth and suck it, then lick it some more. She grabbed hold of the shaft as she continued to suck and lick the tip.

The sight of Morgan working with her mouth got Joey even hotter. She desperately needed release but was determined to take Morgan again and again until she was exhausted before she'd let her have her. She moved Morgan's hand away from the shaft and gasped as Morgan deep throated her.

"How does it taste?" Joey asked when Morgan had finally licked and sucked it clean.

Morgan stood and kissed Joey. "That's how it tastes."

"Delicious. Now on the bed on your hands and knees."

Morgan complied and Joey knelt behind her, once again lining the cock up with Morgan's pussy. She slowly pushed the whole thing inside her, then withdrew it until only the tip was inside. Again, she filled her slowly and pulled back out.

"Why are you teasing me? Please fuck me."

Joey withdrew the toy all the way and rubbed it between Morgan's legs along her slit and clit, back and forth.

"Did you say something?" She laughed.

"I'm sorry." Morgan was rewarded with a full pussy again. This time, Joey left it in and thrust repeatedly, the tool buried to its base inside Morgan. She bent over Morgan, pressing her breasts into her back as she fucked her. She reached her hand around and rubbed Morgan's engorged clit.

Morgan mewed, and Joey felt the slightest tremble. She pulled out and rolled Morgan on her back.

"Why did you stop? I was so close."

"I wasn't ready." Joey smiled. She bent over and took Morgan in her mouth. She sucked her clit and lips, coating her own lips with evidence of Morgan's arousal. She licked her pussy and sucked her clit between her teeth.

She felt the pressure Morgan was putting on the back of her head and continued her ministrations until Morgan's writhing was fast and furious. Once again, she stopped what she was doing.

Morgan whimpered, her eyes showing the obvious discomfort she was feeling. Joey kissed her hard and lined her cock up again. She eased it in Morgan's waiting cunt and buried it as they kissed.

Joey felt Morgan move her hand between her legs, and she pulled it away. Instead, she moved the tool in and out of her while she sucked and bit one nipple and twisted the other. Morgan's nipples were so taut, Joey knew they must have been painful.

She finally released her grip on them and moved herself to a kneeling position. She put Morgan's legs over her shoulders and watched as her cock moved in and out of her tight hole. That sight, combined with the slurping sounds and the amazing smell of sex, had Joey wanting to rub her own clit. She needed to come as badly as Morgan did. *All in due time.*

Morgan again moved her hand between her legs, and Joey swatted it away.

"Please. I need to come. Touch my clit."

"No. You know the rules. I make the calls."

Joey continued to bury the toy to its hilt with each thrust. She made her thrusts shorter and faster. She smiled as Morgan arched her hips to take each one. She laughed as Morgan raised her head and looked at her, eyes pleading with her to release her, but still Joey continued to push in and out.

Joey stared down at the shiny morsel peeking from its hood, begging for attention. She wanted to feel it throbbing as Morgan came for her. She looked at Morgan, hair matted to her head, tongue flicking in and out of her mouth, alternating with her biting her lower lip. She had her hands on her breasts, frantically playing with her nipples, but nothing was getting her off.

Joey slid the toy all the way in and held it pressing into the deepest parts of Morgan. She stared into Morgan's eyes.

"Do you want to come?"

"Yes, oh, God, yes."

"I don't believe you."

"Oh, God, Joey. Please let me come. Please."

"I'm not convinced."

"What do I need to do?" She was almost in tears.

Joey just laughed and ran her thumb over Morgan's swollen clit, feeling it pulsating as Morgan exploded with the force of the orgasm, ejaculating down the toy and drenching Joey in the process.

Joey stayed inside Morgan as she collapsed on her, exhausted, yet aroused beyond what she thought possible. Morgan's chest heaved as she tried to catch her breath and Joey sucked on a salty nipple, refusing to let her relax.

"Mmm," Morgan murmured.

Joey slid the toy out of Morgan and stood to remove the harness. Morgan lay on the bed watching. When Joey was naked, she lay back with Morgan, who kissed her and ran her hand over her body. She cupped and teased Joey's breasts, sucking and licking them, while Joey rolled onto her back, legs open.

Morgan moved her hand between Joey's legs, and Joey moaned when she felt her fingers teasing her pussy.

"No more teasing. I want you to fuck me. Now." Joey knew she'd gotten through to her when she was suddenly filled. "Good girl."

Morgan continued to move her fingers inside Joey as she slid down her body and finally put her tongue on Joey's clit. Joey knew it wouldn't take much. Try as she might, she couldn't hold off. The more Morgan licked, the more the hot chills coursed through her body and finally crashed together, resulting in an explosion that rocked her body.

"Wow, you're easy," Morgan teased her.

"Don't go spreading that around." Joey laughed.

"I want more time with your body."

"I'm not going anywhere."

Morgan resumed her licking and sucking, and this time, Joey was able to relax and enjoy the feelings. She propped herself up and watched Morgan's mouth moving on her. The sight moved to further excite her.

"You know what you're doing."

Joey was rewarded by feeling several fingers inside her, moving in and out at a fast pace. She lay back on the bed. "God, yes. That's it."

Morgan stopped what she was doing and grabbed the harness.

"Easy there, little sister," Joey said.

"Oh, relax." She slid the dildo out of the harness and moved it inside herself. Joey thought things had taken an odd turn, but she never complained about watching a woman please herself. She felt her clit swell even more and swore it would burst as she watched Morgan's pussy swallow the toy over and over.

Joey was surprised when Morgan pulled the dildo out of herself and plunged it deep inside Joey, offering that sweet combination of pleasure and pain. Joey fell back on the bed again.

"Holy fuck, I didn't see that coming."

Morgan twisted the toy one way and then the other before pulling it out, then slipping it back in.

"Do you like it rough?" She quickly pulled the toy out, then drove it deep before pulling it out again.

Joey's head was spinning at the sensations. She enjoyed feeling the fuck in her very core. The sight of Morgan's naked body kneeling beside her fanned the flame higher, and she knew she was close again.

Morgan used her thumb on her other hand to press Joey's clit into her pubis and moved her thumb in circles while she continued with the toy.

Joey felt the pressure building and closed her eyes as the waves shot through her. She relaxed and rode the explosion to its conclusion, only then daring to open her eyes and look at Morgan, who was madly rubbing her own clit as she watched Joey.

Morgan fell back on the bed, and Joey found the strength to remove the dildo and plunge it inside Morgan.

"Come for me again, baby," she whispered, watching Morgan's eyelids close halfway as she continued to work her swollen clit.

"Help me out, baby. I wanna get you off." Joey moved the toy in and out of Morgan.

Morgan rubbed faster, eyes closed. Joey stared at Morgan's fingers working their magic. Morgan finally cried out and Joey let go of the toy, watching Morgan's cunt pulling it in and releasing it again and again as the orgasm took her.

Joey rolled to her back and lay there catching her breath. Morgan snuggled against her, her skin slick against Joey.

Joey fought to keep her eyes open. It had been a long workweek with the crew busting their asses to make up for lost time. The night had been fun and eventful, but she was fading fast. She peered at her watch and saw it was almost four.

"Oh, shit," she mumbled. "I need to get going."

She climbed over Morgan and sat on the edge of the bed. She grabbed her shorts, reaching into the pocket for her phone.

"Why? You can stay here."

"No." Joey texted as she spoke. "I'm not much for staying over."

"But think of the fun we could have in the morning." Morgan dragged her fingernails down Joey's back.

"I have too much to do tomorrow. I'm really sorry." She stared at her phone.

"Who did you text at this hour?"

"Mel. I need to see if she's going home with me or staying."

"Maybe she's more the staying over kind."

"Touché."

"How long are you going to give her to respond? She might be busy." She reached a hand around Joey and ran a finger along her clit.

"Oh, no, you don't." Joey stood and dressed. "I need to get going. I really enjoyed tonight. When do you go home?"

"We leave Sunday. Can I see you tomorrow night?"

"I don't know," Joey said. "I'm helping a friend move, and I don't know how long that'll take."

Morgan picked up the phone Joey had left on the bed.

"What are you doing?"

"I'm entering my phone number. If you want to get together tomorrow night, you can call."

"Thanks." Joey hoped she sounded less annoyed than she felt. If she'd wanted Morgan's number, she would have asked for it. She took her phone back and put it in her pocket. She kissed Morgan and left Mel to fend for herself.

CHAPTER NINE

The blaring of her ringtone woke Joey with a start. She rolled over and looked at the phone. The number was blocked. She glanced at her watch and saw it was ten forty-five.

"Shit!"

The ringing stopped, and Joey figured it must have been Tiffany. She momentarily wondered how she got her number but forgot about it as she quickly showered and pulled on baggy shorts and a T-shirt.

She hopped in her truck and headed to the Braun place. She knocked on the door and a very disheveled Tiffany answered the door. She was wearing old gym shorts and a loose-fitting shirt. Her hair was a mess.

"Are you working hard?"

"Funny. I waited until the last minute, so I'm frantically packing things now." She stepped back to let Joey in.

"Well, if you're running late, why did you call me?"

"I didn't call you. I don't even know your number."

Joey paused, wondering who it could have been. She shrugged and set her mind to helping Tiffany. "What do you need me to do first?"

"Those boxes over there"—she motioned along the wall—"are ready to go. If you could start loading them, I'll keep packing."

"I thought you said you didn't have much."

"I have more than I thought I did."

"You've only lived here a month."

"So I made myself at home. Now are you going to help me or what?"

Joey took her time loading the six boxes into her truck. When she was through, she walked down the hall and found Tiffany in one of the bedrooms looking down at a bed full of sex toys.

"Is it break time?" Joey asked.

Tiffany swirled around, beet red. "You weren't supposed to see these."

"It's not like I haven't seen this kind of thing before." Joey walked over to the bed and held up a pair of nipple clamps. She looked down at the various sizes and shapes of dildos, vibrators, and butt plugs spread before her.

"Still. You haven't seen mine."

"Well, I have now. And I'm impressed at your collection. Especially given your tender age." She picked up a thick purple vibrator and turned it on. She ran it along Tiffany's breasts. "I really do think it's break time. What's our hurry?"

"I have to be out of here today." She took the toy from Joey.

"It's only noon." Joey picked up another toy and pressed it into Tiffany's crotch.

"The storage place closes at five." She threw the toy on the bed.

"I don't know why you're fighting it." Joey picked up a slender butt plug. "You know you want to."

"You're incorrigible."

"Why, thank you." Joey nipped at her lips.

"We really don't have time."

"Oh, I think we do." Joey slid her hand up Tiffany's shirt and closed over her breast. "Oh, yeah, I definitely think we do."

"Joey, please."

"I love it when you beg." She kissed Tiffany hard on her mouth and was rewarded with a passionate kiss in return.

"You know what I meant." Tiffany was breathless when the kiss ended.

"Shh, don't talk so much. We don't have time for idle conversation." Joey laughed.

"I'm going to be so angry if we don't make it to the storage unit on time." Tiffany was stepping out of her shorts. She lifted her shirt over her head and stood naked for Joey's enjoyment.

"Your body is fucking hot!"

"I'm glad you like it. Are you going to take those clothes off?" Tiffany pushed some toys out of the way and lay on the bed.

"No. I'm going to fuck you senseless, then we're going to get you moved." She ran her hand between Tiffany's legs and found her swollen and creamy. "See? I knew you wanted it, too."

She continued to move her fingers in and out of Tiffany until they were coated. She took the butt plug and slipped it in Tiffany's pussy, covering it with better lube than money could buy. She placed the tip of it against Tiffany's rosebud and pushed, easing it in. She kept her gaze on Tiffany's face, watching her eyes grow wide as she slid the toy in farther. She pulled it out and slipped it back in a couple of times until she buried it to its base and left it.

Joey grabbed the thickest dildo she could find and rubbed it along Tiffany's hardened clit, pressing it into her. She moved it down to her opening and stared. "Can this really fit in you?"

"There's only one way to find out," Tiffany said hoarsely.

Joey grinned as she ran the toy in the juices that were spilling from Tiffany. She placed the tip at her pussy and twisted it slowly as she moved it inside of her. Joey watched in amazement as Tiffany spread wider to swallow the toy. Joey only pushed it partway in before pulling it back out. She twisted it back in again, urging it deeper. She did this several times, with Tiffany groaning louder each time. She finally had the whole toy inside Tiffany, fucking her deep.

Tiffany had her legs wide and moved her hips around on the bed as she reveled in the fucking. "That feels so fucking good."

"It looks pretty fucking hot, too." Joey couldn't take her gaze away from the area between Tiffany's legs. She finally moved her focus from the disappearing dildo to the clit protruding from its hood.

Joey bent over and dragged her tongue along the hard morsel and felt Tiffany's hand on the back of her head. She continued filling Tiffany with the dildo while she licked greedily at her clit. She moved her tongue all around it for a few moments before Tiffany pressed her face into her and she thought she might suffocate. She felt Tiffany stiffen and heard her cry out, a harsh, guttural scream that shook the room.

When she relaxed her grip on Joey and Joey could breathe again, Joey slowly removed both toys from their respective orifices and lay them on Tiffany's belly. "You and these need to get cleaned up so we can finish."

"I'm a pile of Jell-O. I'm not going anywhere for a while."

"Yeah, you are. I'll take these few boxes out to the truck. I'll be right back."

Joey returned from her last trip to find Tiffany still on her back. "Seriously? This is the thanks I get?"

"I only have a few more things to pack."

"Well, get them packed. You said you had beer?"

"Yeah, there's some in the fridge."

"When I finish one, I'd better come back and find you working."

Joey had worked up quite a thirst and quickly downed a beer. She grabbed a second one and wandered back down the hall. She found Tiffany up and packing the toys in a box. "Were you going to put some clothes on?"

"I want to shower first, and I don't have time."

"You need to get dressed or I'm going to have to have you again."

"That's not an option."

"Seriously, Tiffany. Your body is smokin'. I can't concentrate with you all naked."

"There's nothing for you to concentrate on."

Joey drew a ragged breath, frustration and desire consuming her.

Tiffany just laughed and handed her the box of toys. Joey took them to the truck and came back to find Tiffany folding clothes into another box. She watched Tiffany's leg muscles flex as she bent to pick up an arm full of clothes. She groaned inwardly as Tiffany's ass cheeks spread slightly when she bent over to place the clothes in the box.

"I can do that. You go shower."

"I've got it."

"No. You don't understand. I'm telling you. I'm not strong enough to be around you naked. I'm being perfectly honest."

"You're really cute when you're horny."

"I'm always horny."

"You're always cute."

"It's nice that you think so, but please go shower."

"You started this."

"Yeah, but you're the one bitchin' that we don't have time. And now you're gonna flaunt that body in front of me when I can't do anything with it."

"Oh, you're welcome to do whatever you like with it. When we're all through. Now would you just relax while I finish getting the last of the boxes ready for you?"

Joey took her beer out to the pool area and sat in the sun. Every muscle in her body was tense, every inch between her legs aroused. She wanted to devour the length of Tiffany, from the lips on her face to the ones between her legs. And she didn't want to leave a spot not sucked.

She tried to block out thoughts of Tiffany, so she closed her eyes and took a long pull on her beer. She was starting to relax when her phone rang. She got it out of her pocket to see the blocked number again.

"Screw 'em." Joey figured if they didn't want her to know who was calling, she wasn't going to answer.

The ringing stopped and she waited, but there was no indication of a voice mail. As she slid the phone in her pocket, she told herself she should answer it next time and tell whoever it was to grow some balls and let the number be seen. Especially if they expected her to answer. But she knew she wouldn't. She refused to answer if no number showed.

She finally finished her beer and decided to see what Tiffany was up to. It was only two o'clock. She was hoping Tiffany had more packed so if she was still naked, Joey could do something about it. She walked back to the bedroom to find several more boxes sealed, but Tiffany was nowhere to be seen.

She grabbed a box and started down the hall when she heard the shower running behind one of the doors. She decided to hurry and get the truck packed so maybe she could sneak into the shower with Tiffany.

Joey came back for the last box and found Tiffany slipping back into her clothes. "Damn. I'm too late."

"For?"

"I was going to join you in the shower."

"We still have to get all those boxes out of your truck and into storage."

"We have plenty of time, but as long as you're dressed, let's get going."

They got to the storage unit and Tiffany attempted to grab a box from the truck.

"Do you mind?" Joey said. "That's my job."

"I was just trying to help."

"You've helped enough for one day."

Tiffany laughed and opened the unit. "The boxes will all go back in that cleared area, okay?" She motioned to the right rear portion of the unit.

Joey went to work and had the truck unloaded in no time. She leaned against a box to catch her breath when Tiffany walked up to her and kissed her.

"What the hell was that?" Joey asked.

"Have you ever done it in a storage unit?"

"Oh, no. No, no, no. We're not doing anything here. Let's get you home."

Tiffany ran her hand along Joey's crotch.

"But I've never done it here. And I want to."

"Yeah? Well, I have issues with spiders and rats crawling over me while I'm having sex. Call me crazy."

"You sound like a girl."

"Whatever. We're not doing it here."

"Fine. Be that way."

"Now where am I dropping you off?"

"Well, I'll be staying with some friends, but I was thinking we could go back to my grandma's place and go swimming or something."

"Or something?" Joey pulled her close, sucking at a tit through her shirt.

Tiffany lifted her shirt, exposing her bare breast.

Joey looked around her to the door of the unit. "What's going to happen? No one's going to come by."

"You don't know that." Joey lowered her mouth and sucked an erect nipple.

"I love your mouth on me."

Joey released the nipple and sucked Tiffany's neck. She was interrupted when Tiffany's phone rang.

Tiffany stepped back and fished her phone from her pocket. "Hello?"

Joey couldn't help but hear her conversation.

"Not yet, but almost. I'll definitely be out of there today. No, I promise." She had a big smile on her face. "Of course I'll help you tomorrow. I'll see you then. Bye-bye."

Joey's ears had perked up by that point.

"Who was that?"

"Samantha Brewer. She's moving into my grandma's house. That's why I had to be out."

"You're helping her tomorrow?"

"Of course. I'd do anything for her. She's such a sweetheart." She sidled up to Joey again. "Now where were we?"

Joey was uncomfortable, and she didn't like it. Something about Samantha Brewer calling Tiffany made her feel strange. She was sure she wasn't jealous as she didn't believe she felt that emotion. Also, just the mention of Samantha had her cooling her jets toward Tiffany.

Confused and determined not to blow an opportunity, she pushed Samantha Brewer out of her mind and focused on the young woman offering her lithe and limber body to her.

"I think we were going to your old place for a final dip in the pool," Joey said.

They locked up the storage unit and climbed back into Joey's truck for the short drive back to the house.

Once again, Joey followed Tiffany around to the back of the house where the pool looked incredibly inviting after all her manual labor on such a hot day. She stripped out of her clothes and jumped in, reveling in the feel of the cool against her burning skin. She surfaced, treading water, and looked up at Tiffany, still standing poolside.

"What are you doing? Get in here," she called.

Tiffany stayed where she was and looked down at Joey. She slowly removed her shirt, affording Joey a view of her pert breasts with nipples already at attention. She pushed her breasts together and ran her hands all over them. She pinched her nipples, all the while staring at Joey.

Joey swam to the edge and folded her arms on it to hold herself up, enjoying the show Tiffany was putting on.

Tiffany stepped out of her shorts and stood over Joey, who was looking up between her legs.

"Are you coming in?" Joey asked.

"Are you?" Tiffany sat on the edge, one leg on either side of Joey.

Joey ran her hand along Tiffany's inner thigh and spread her lips. She ran her finger the length of her before slipping two fingers inside and dragging her thumb over her clit. "I love how you're always ready."

"Always." Tiffany scooted closer to Joey.

"That concrete has to be hot," Joey said.

"Yeah, it's a bit uncomfortable." Tiffany laughed.

"Well, get in the water." Joey backed away from her and watched as Tiffany eased herself into the water. She sank underneath and reappeared in the shallow end, droplets of water decorating her bare flesh.

"Better?" Joey asked.

"Very." Tiffany swam over to Joey. She put her arms around her. "But I'm still hot."

"Sweetheart, you're always hot. Hell, you're on fire." She kissed her, fiercely and passionately, her mouth open and tongue darting into Tiffany's mouth.

Tiffany returned the kiss in kind, holding tightly to Joey, pressing the length of her body against hers as her tongue kept pace.

Joey used her powerful arms to swim the two of them to the shallow end, never breaking the kiss. Once standing, she ran her hand down Tiffany's body, caressing the firm swells of her breasts and cupping the cheeks of her ass. She ground her own pelvis into Tiffany's, craving more contact. She moved her knee between Tiffany's legs and moved it against her.

Tiffany's arms closed more tightly around Joey as their kissing intensified. Joey could barely get her hands between them to play with her breasts again. As she flicked her thumbs over her nipples, Tiffany moaned into her mouth.

Joey walked them to the steps and sat Tiffany on the top one. The water barely covered it, so it was cool enough for Tiffany to sit comfortably, yet dry enough that Joey wouldn't drown. She knelt on a lower step and put Tiffany's knees on her shoulders as she dipped to run her tongue between her legs. Her lips were swollen and creamy and her clit hard and throbbing.

Her musky flavor had Joey's head spinning. She licked voraciously at her pussy, burying her tongue as deep as she could, then licking forward to her clit. Over and over, she repeated the process, dizzy from the tastes and scents. She wanted to spend forever between Tiffany's legs, feasting on everything she found there.

Tiffany placed her hands on Joey's shoulders, fingernails scratching her as she thrust her hips in rhythm with Joey's tongue. The sharp pain urged Joey on, and she licked with greater fervor. Finally, she felt Tiffany's nails dig deeply into her, and she continued to lap at her rigid clit until Tiffany cried out as she shuddered and reached her climax, then slowly floated back to the present.

The cool water did nothing to soothe the burning in Joey's crotch. She waited until Tiffany was coherent to take her hand and lead her to a lounge chair. Joey lay back and spread her legs. Tiffany apparently didn't need to be asked twice. She buried her fingers inside and bent to suck Joey's hardened clit.

"Fuck me harder, baby," Joey pleaded.

Tiffany slipped another finger in and plunged them as deep as she could. She did this repeatedly as Joey arched her hips to take more.

"Roll over for me," Tiffany said.

Joey happily obliged and raised up on her knees so Tiffany could enter her from behind. She felt wonderfully full, and when Tiffany reached around and stroked her clit, she had to bite her lip to keep from coming too soon. She held off as long as she could, relishing in the sensations Tiffany was creating, but finally, she could hold off no longer. Her whole body tensed before the thunderous burst of energy overtook her and she let herself go to enjoy the ride.

"Holy fuck, that was intense," Joey breathed.

"I thought you were gonna break my fingers." Tiffany laughed as she withdrew her fingers so Joey could roll over.

"Damn," was all Joey could manage.

Tiffany got up and walked into the house. She came back out with a cold beer and placed it against Joey's cunt.

"What the fuck?" Joey yelled, moving away from the beer.

"Just thought you might need to be cooled down."

"You're a funny girl." Joey took the beer and chugged half of it. "Thanks. That's delicious."

Tiffany sat at the foot of the lounge chair and opened her soda. She took a long a sip. "You're a lot of fun, Joey Scarpetti."

"Thanks. You're not so bad yourself."

"Do you ever suppose you'll settle down?"

"Whoa there, little sister. I thought we had this covered."

"Oh, no! Not with me. I don't mean that at all. I just meant in general."

Joey flinched when Samantha Brewer's face floated through her mind. She shook her head violently.

"What?" Tiffany said.

"Nothing." Joey tried to sound nonchalant. "It's just the thought of monotony, I mean monogamy, gives me the heebie-jeebies."

Tiffany just stared at her.

"What about you?" Joey asked.

"Me? I have no idea. I'm much too young to worry about a lifelong partner."

"And I'm not?"

Tiffany just shrugged.

"What's that supposed to mean?"

"You're older than I am, but I don't know. I suppose I can't see me settling down when I'm your age, either."

"Just how old do you think I am?"

"I figure you're in your late twenties, maybe early thirties."

"Let's stick with late twenties."

"Okay." Tiffany laughed.

Joey tipped her beer bottle and finished its contents, then stood.

"Last one in is a rotten egg." She ran and did a cannonball into the pool.

Tiffany just shook her head.

"What?" Joey asked.

"If I'm a rotten egg, does that mean I won't get eaten again?"

"Don't count on it." Joey laughed and dove underwater, waiting for Tiffany to join her.

CHAPTER TEN

"I swear to God, all you do is sleep anymore." Mel shook Joey's shoulder.

"What the hell are you doing here so early?"

"It's not early. It's nine o'clock, and we're supposed to be helping your lovely Ms. Brewer, remember?"

Joey threw her arm over her forehead and stared at Mel, still too groggy for anything to sink in.

"Seriously. Get your lazy ass up, woman!"

Consciousness finally made an appearance in Joey's clouded mind. "Oh, shit! We're late!"

"Ding, ding, ding!"

"Shut up." She rolled to a sitting position.

Mel picked up some clothes from the floor and threw them at her. "Get up. Get dressed. Let's go."

"Those are dirty." Joey threw them back on the floor. "You sure are excited for someone who didn't even want to do this."

"I figure since you committed us, we may as well be there."

"Give me a sec. I need to take a quick shower."

"Are you kidding me? We're going to go *move* her. You know, work up a sweat and get stinky while creating sore muscles?"

Joey ignored her and grabbed some clean clothes. She left the room and returned, clean and dressed, ten minutes later. She had her work boots on when Mel finally handed her a cup of coffee.

"About time you give up the java," Joey said.

"You didn't deserve it."

"How was moving yesterday?" Mel asked as they walked to the truck.

"It was fun. She didn't have a whole lot of stuff to move."

"Fun?" She shook her head. "Why doesn't that surprise me?"

"Honestly? Nothing should surprise you anymore."

"That's what I'll be thinkin', then you drag me to Santa Brigida, and I end up in an eight-way."

"Okay. That was fuckin' hot."

"Yeah. Surprising but hot."

"Where am I going?" Joey asked.

"I thought you knew."

"Oh, shit." She dug into her pocket for her cell phone.

"Where the fuck are you two?"

"Good to talk to you, too, Brenda. Hey, where are we going?"

"We're on our way to the Braun place with the first load. Just meet us there." *Click.*

Joey stared at the phone, then shoved it back in her pocket as she turned down a street to take her to Samantha's new home.

"We're going to the Braun place?" Mel asked.

"Yeah. I guess we missed the first loading."

"You almost sound upset."

"I promised we'd be there. I fucked up."

"We have all day for you to show off your butch self to Ms. Brewer."

"That's not the point." Joey growled.

"What the hell is with you when it comes to this woman? You don't even know her, yet you're all over the board when it's time to deal with her."

"She's different."

"Why? Because she's prego?"

"Whatever."

"Don't tell me you like her?"

"What? You sound like a middle schooler."

"Deny it."

"Of course I want to take her to bed. Who wouldn't?"

"That's not it. There's definitely something different here."

With Mel's words hitting too close for comfort, Joey was relieved when she pulled up in front of the house she'd spent hours at the day before. They walked up the front steps, and she rang the bell that sounded all around them.

Samantha opened the door in a beige tank top and long denim skirt.

"Sorry we're late." Joey's gaze roamed over the vision in front of her. "We weren't sure where we were supposed to be. I called Brenda, and she told me to just meet them here. I hope that's okay."

"That's fine." She stepped out of the way for them to enter the empty house. "I tried to call you a couple of times yesterday to let you know what the plans were, but I never got a hold of you, obviously."

Joey stared, dumbfounded. "That was you with the blocked number?"

"Oh, I see, you were screening my calls." Samantha laughed, warming Joey to her core.

Joey shrugged. "I tend to do that."

"No worries. Come on in and have some coffee and pastries. The first load should be here shortly."

Joey was amazed at the barren floors and walls. "When did this place get emptied out?"

"This morning," Samantha said. "Tiffany Swanson got all her stuff out of here yesterday, and her family had the movers load Mildred's stuff this morning."

"Mildred?" Joey at once felt Samantha the interloper again and didn't think she had the right to call the community's founding mother by her first name. "Did you know her?"

"Of course. She was good friends with my partner's family. She was actually instrumental in getting us together."

Joey's gut was in knots. She was getting madder by the minute and couldn't explain why. Suddenly, the pastries that had moments ago looked inviting now tempted her as much as rocks would. She walked through the kitchen and out to the pool area without a word.

"Well, that's one way to win her heart. Act like an ass, then storm out without a word." Mel joined her a few minutes later.

"Fuck you."

"Look, Joey. I get it. You're sweet on her. But you need to get a grip because you can't have your moods bouncing all over the place if you plan to make time with her. I may not get your obsession with her, but I still feel obligated to tell you you're blowing it."

"I just don't like how she acts like she's one of us. She's not."

"She's just moving here. We all had to move here at some point. We were all the newbies, but the community embraced us. There's no reason not to embrace Samantha."

"I'd love to embrace her." Joey grinned.

"Well, you're not going to get a chance if you don't act like you've got some manners."

"It's hard."

"Why? What's the big deal?"

"I don't know. One minute I'm cool with her and jonesing for a roll with her, and the next, she's pissing me off."

"Man, you've got it bad."

"Fuck you," she said again.

"You're the one who's fucked." Mel laughed. "But you won't be if you don't pull your head out. Now get in there and have something to eat before we go to work."

Joey followed Mel back into the kitchen and helped herself to a bear claw and a cup of coffee.

"Thanks for this," she managed.

Samantha leaned against the stove and studied Joey.

"What?" Joey felt uncomfortable under her scrutiny.

Mel wandered out of the room, leaving them alone.

"You don't like me much, do you?"

Joey shrugged.

"When I first showed up in town, you were all about making sure I saw you and knew who you were. And now, you leave in the middle of conversations, you don't answer my calls…"

"Not fair. I didn't know those calls were from you," she said defensively, then softened her tone. "I would have answered if I'd known."

"I appreciate that." Samantha's tone was soft. "I do hope we can be friends. I'd like to get to know you better."

Joey found it hard to breathe. The warm morning air was dry, and the temperature had shot up ten degrees. She didn't trust her voice, so she simply nodded.

"Truck's here!" Mel called.

Joey turned toward the front door but felt the warmth of Samantha's hand on her arm. She looked back at her and felt herself getting lost in her sapphire eyes.

"I really do appreciate you being here to help me," Samantha said.

"My pleasure." Joey smiled at her, then hurried out the front door to help the rest of the crew.

The first two U-Hauls were unloaded quickly, and boxes and furniture were left in various rooms of the old house. When it was time to head back to Somerset to pick up more things, Samantha placed a hand on Joey's arm again.

"Why don't you and Mel stay here and help me get things arranged?"

"It's really not fair to make the rest of them do all the work," Joey said.

"But I can't stand to see this place in such disarray, and I can't move things by myself."

"Mel!" Joey called.

Mel walked in from the front porch. "What's up?"

"We're staying."

"You stay if you need to," Mel shook her head, "but I'm going to help these guys."

"No, Samantha wants us to stay and move stuff around here while we wait for the next load. She can't move this shit by herself."

Mel looked from Joey to Samantha, who simply nodded. "I guess that makes sense. Okay, I'll stay."

The rest of the gang took off, and Samantha led Joey and Mel down the hall to a back bedroom. As she walked past the room she'd been in with Tiffany the day before, Joey looked in, only to see emptiness. It was almost as if this was a different house altogether.

"This is the master bedroom," Samantha said.

Joey looked around the room, which consisted of a broken-apart bed frame and mattresses against one wall, a dresser in the middle of the room, and boxes piled all around it.

"Since I need this room to sleep in tonight, I'd really appreciate some help getting it together."

"Where do you want the dresser?" Joey asked.

"Up against that wall." She pointed to the wall with a window that looked out onto the pool.

Joey and Mel picked up the piece of solid oak furniture and carefully walked it over to the wall. They looked back at Samantha.

"I guess I can start unloading these boxes."

"What about your bed?" Joey asked.

"Let's move these boxes out of the way and set up the bed in the middle of the room."

Joey and Mel made quick work of the bed. Once the box springs and mattress were on, Joey lay on it to make sure it was sturdy.

"Don't mind her," Mel said. "She'll do just about anything to get in a woman's bed."

"So I've heard." Samantha laughed and Joey blushed, then rolled over onto her back and locked her fingers behind her head.

"It really is a comfortable bed." She looked at Samantha. "Maybe you'd like to join me?"

"I'm quite aware how comfortable it is." Samantha laughed and sat on the edge of it.

"I need more food," Mel said, leaving the room.

"Are you happy to be in my bed?" Samantha asked.

"Are you happy I am?"

"I have to say you look damned good in it."

Joey lay there staring at her, frozen with indecision. Her crotch clenched and her heart raced. This is where she should pull Samantha on top of her and kiss her. Clearly, she wanted it. Instead, she rolled over and climbed off the other side of the bed.

"You don't know who you're messing with." It came out gruffer than she'd intended.

"Who are you kidding? Your reputation precedes you, Joey Scarpetti."

Joey stood looking at her, trying to read her eyes. "And my reputation doesn't scare you?"

"Honestly, I don't believe everything I hear."

"Maybe you should."

"Maybe I want to find out for myself what you're like."

Joey was confused. Was she serious? Or toying with her? And why did not knowing piss her off so?

"Maybe you will." Joey shrugged and left the room. She found Mel in the kitchen.

"Did you two enjoy yourselves?" Mel asked.

"Very funny."

"Why am I even here?"

"To help get me moved in," Samantha said from the doorway.

"Sorry," Mel mumbled. "I didn't hear you coming."

"No worries," Samantha said. "Now how about we get back to work?"

They moved more boxes from the living room into the other bedrooms and put together various pieces of furniture. The front room was cleaned out by the time the next load pulled up. They helped unload and stayed behind again.

Joey watched Samantha walking down the hall toward the front room. She was the epitome of sexy. The way she swayed her hips just so, the way her breasts bounced just slightly as she walked. Even the sight of her bare feet on the hardwood floors was sexy as hell.

"You're staring," Mel whispered.

"I'd be crazy not to."

"You've got it bad."

"The question is, does she?"

"Am I to assume I'm the topic of your conversation?" Samantha smiled as she joined them.

"Just look at Joey and do you really have to ask?"

Joey wanted to make a snide remark but didn't want to dampen the arousal she was feeling. Her gaze met Samantha's, and her stomach fluttered. She wanted this woman in the worst way.

Samantha walked past her, brushing against her as she did. Joey's body tingled from head to toe. Once again, she fought for air.

"Let's get these boxes moved," Samantha said.

Joey watched as she bent to lift a box. "What the hell do you think you're doing?"

"It's not heavy."

"Still…"

"Relax."

Samantha bent her knees and picked up the box, then dropped it as she cried out in pain.

"What the fuck?" Joey was beside her in a heartbeat. She stood with an arm on either side of Samantha, unsure of what to do. "Are you all right?"

Samantha stood and placed her hand on the small of her back. "I'm fine, just tweaked my back a bit."

"Are you sure?" Joey was beside herself. "You sure it wasn't the baby? She's fine, right?"

"Calm down," Samantha said softly. "Thank you, but everything is fine. I just lifted wrong. I'll be okay."

"Maybe you should sit down." Mel motioned to a couch in the middle of the room.

Samantha nodded and sat. Joey continued to hover. "Shit, woman. What were you thinking?"

Mel left and returned with a bottle of water. She handed it to Samantha, who took a long drink.

"Thank you," she said. "My back is already feeling better. Now let's get back to work."

The day progressed with no more incidents. By four o'clock, the final trip back from Somerset was complete, and the whole crew helped Joey and Mel finish putting boxes and furniture where they belonged.

Joey looked around and noticed Samantha was missing. She wandered through the house, finally looking in her bedroom. She peeked out the window and saw Samantha out by two generously sized barbecues. Samantha turned and saw Joey and waved. Joey turned away from the window and hurried outside.

"Should you really be standing out here in the heat barbecuing? Why don't you go relax and let me take over?"

"You've done enough today. Why don't you get your suit on and get in the pool?"

"I really can't let a lady barbecue while I swim. That's not okay."

Samantha rested her hand on Joey's arm. "You really are a sweetheart. But I've got this."

"Now there's a pair to draw to." Tiffany walked up behind them. "Are you two up to no good?"

"She was trying to take over the barbecue, and I was trying to get her to change into her suit and get in the water."

"Come on, Joey." Tiffany tugged on her arm. "Let's go get changed."

"Go on."

"I really wouldn't feel right," Joey insisted.

"What if I promise I have friends coming over to do the barbecuing for me? I'm just getting it ready."

"You promise?"

"I do."

Joey allowed Tiffany to lead her back into the house. They cut through the crew drinking beer in the kitchen, and she grabbed her backpack that had her suit in it. They wandered down the hall until they came to Tiffany's old room. Tiffany closed the door behind them.

"What are you doing?"

Tiffany quickly stripped and pressed herself into Joey, kissing her.

Joey pulled away. "No. I can't. This doesn't feel right. I can't do that here."

"You did more than that here yesterday."

"That was different. I feel disrespectful."

"Now that's something I never thought I'd hear from you." Tiffany shrugged. "But whatever. Suit yourself. Let's get out to the pool."

Joey quickly pulled on a pair of trunks and a tank top over a sports bra. They made their way back to the kitchen where Joey started telling people to get their suits on and hit the water. She helped herself to a beer and followed Tiffany back outside.

Samantha turned and smiled at them, watching as Joey set her beer down, then dove in the water and swam to her side of the pool. She held herself up on the edge and eyed Samantha.

"So where are these friends who are going to help you?"

"They'll be here any minute."

"Then will you be getting in the water?"

"If it means getting closer to you, I believe I will."

"You talk a good game."

"You should know."

"I back up my talk with action."

"And you're so sure I won't?"

"I haven't figured you out yet."

Samantha laughed and walked inside the house.

Joey climbed out of the pool and sat on a lounge chair, drinking her beer. She watched Tiffany splash around in the pool, but the sight of her in a skimpy bikini wasn't holding her attention. Soon others were on the patio and in the pool. Mel finally showed up with another beer and a bottle of tequila. She took a swig and handed it to Joey, who upended the bottle for a few seconds before chasing it with beer.

Brenda and Liz wandered over to join them and took turns with the tequila.

"Did you enjoy having a whole day with Samantha?" Brenda asked.

"We were working," Joey said.

"And flirting," Mel added.

Joey gave her a dirty look as she took the bottle of tequila again. The warm fluid flowed down her throat and spread comfort throughout her body. She had the feeling she was going to be more than a little inebriated before the night was over. She finished her second beer and went to get another.

She ran into Samantha in the kitchen. Samantha was at the island chopping fruit. Joey walked up behind her and wrapped her arms around her. She nuzzled her neck.

Samantha leaned back and rubbed her hands along Joey's muscular forearms. "I love how strong you are."

Joey pressed her lips to Samantha's neck.

Samantha turned in Joey's arms and faced her. Joey smiled and leaned forward to briefly touch her lips to hers. "Tequila." Samantha smiled.

"Guilty." Joey kissed her again, longer this time, enjoying the feel and taste of Samantha.

"That's enough for now." Samantha broke free. "Will you do me a favor and take one of those ice chests outside? It's heavy because I filled it with beer and ice. I'd rather people not come traipsing in and out of the house after swimming."

Joey looked forlorn.

"Present company excluded, of course," Samantha added.

"Thank you." Joey kissed her briefly, then grabbed an ice chest and, determined not to let on how heavy it was, strained every muscle in her body as she carried it outside.

Joey jumped back in the pool and surfaced just as Samantha walked out of the house in a blue one-piece bathing suit with a sarong wrapped around her waist. She thought she'd never seen a sexier woman. Samantha held her head high as she greeted the crew and seemed to float as she walked among the group. She stopped and stood over Joey. "How's the water?"

"It's great. Are you coming in?"

"In a minute." She walked off to talk to some others, and Joey enjoyed the view from the rear.

"I don't think you should be thinking about her like that."

Joey turned around to see Tiffany treading water.

"Aw, come on, Tiff. Surely, you're not jealous."

"If I was going to be jealous, it would be of her looking at you. I'd do her in a heartbeat."

Joey's crotch was on fire at the visions that created. She'd love to watch that for a while, then join in. "If that happens, will you call me?" She laughed.

"It won't. But if it did, I would."

"So if you aren't going to make a move, why shouldn't I?"

"She's not like us. She's not the play-around type."

Joey looked back at Samantha talking in a group. She'd sensed that already, yet Samantha had been plenty playful that day. And if she wasn't into messing around, Joey asked herself why she was still in hot pursuit. Sure, she was good-looking, but she also seemed smart and funny. Traits Joey never really paid attention to in the past. But Samantha wasn't like anyone from her past. And she liked that.

Samantha looked over at her and winked. It was almost imperceptible, but Joey saw it. Apparently, so did Tiffany.

"You may have met your match, Joey."

Joey said nothing as she got out of the pool and grabbed her towel.

CHAPTER ELEVEN

Joey was relaxing, lying back in the lounge chair with her eyes closed when a shadow covered her. She opened her eyes to see Samantha standing over her.

"Are you coming in?" she asked.

"Sure." Joey stood and followed her to the edge.

Samantha got a mischievous grin before she shoved Joey, sending her flying into the water. When Joey surfaced, she saw Samantha laughing. She swam to the edge. "You're lucky you're cute."

"Is that right?"

"Indeed."

Samantha dove over Joey and into the water. As she came up for air, Joey stared at her, thinking her more beautiful than ever with her wet hair flowing down her back and her suit clinging to her curves.

"What?" Samantha swam over to Joey.

"Just admiring the view."

"You like the view, huh?"

"I do." She leaned in to kiss Samantha, who pulled away.

"Not in front of everyone."

Joey didn't care about the rest of the people around them. "Why not?"

"I'm not like that."

"Whatever. Either you want me to kiss you or you don't."

"I'm not into PDA."

"Are you embarrassed you want me?"

"Joey, please. I'm not used to wanting anyone. It's been a rough few months for me, and I can't believe I'm suddenly finding myself attracted to someone. Much less the town player."

Joey's head was foggy from desire, so Samantha's words weren't making a lot of sense. She was convinced Samantha was just playing her.

"Well, I'm not into on-again, off-again women."

"You're not listening to me."

Their conversation was interrupted when Brenda and Liz swam over to them.

"Seeing the two of you together scares me a little," Brenda said.

"Apparently, it scares her, too," Joey said.

Samantha rolled her eyes, and Joey just glared at her.

"Did we interrupt something?" Liz asked.

"I guess not." Joey swam off.

Brenda swam after her and followed her out of the pool. "I thought I told you to stay away from her."

"She's been coming on to me, if you must know."

"I doubt that. And even if she is, you need to be careful. She's not what you're used to."

"No one around here seems to think I can handle a class act." She drained her beer.

"Check your track record, my friend."

"Look, I'm just out for a good time."

"And she's not one of your good time gals."

"I'm beginning to see that."

"Let it go, okay?"

"Why not tell her to let it go?"

"Because you're like a dog with a bone. Even if I tell her to back off, you won't now that your mind is set on her. So I'm imploring you to leave her alone."

Joey shrugged and sat on a lounge chair, watching Samantha's trim figure cut through the water as she swam laps. Brenda shrugged and walked off, jumping back in the pool.

Mel walked up and handed Joey another beer.

"How's it goin'? I saw you and Samantha getting chummy in the pool."

"She's a tease."

Mel took a long drink. "I think she likes you."

"Whatever."

"I mean it. I see the way she looks at you."

"One minute, she's hot. The next, she's cold. I don't need that shit."

"Maybe she just wants to take it slow."

"That's not my style." Joey knew, although she hated to admit it to herself, that if she really had a shot with Samantha, she'd take it as slow as Samantha wanted. And that thought made her even less comfortable with the situation. Then she reminded herself she didn't believe Samantha was truly interested.

"Just take it easy. See what happens."

"Why does she irritate me so much?"

"Hate to say it, my friend, but I think you like her."

Joey glared at her, even as she felt the truth in her heart.

"Let's get some food," Mel said.

Joey got up on unsteady legs and walked to the long table set up next to the barbecue. She grabbed a hamburger and hot dog and some potato salad and walked back to her chair. She was eating when Samantha walked up.

"Mind if I join you?"

"I don't know. Sharing a chair might make people talk. You surely don't want that."

Samantha didn't answer. She simply looked at Joey imploringly.

Joey scooted back and let her sit down. They ate in silence for a few minutes, as the whole pool area quieted while everyone ate.

"This is really good." Joey stared at her plate.

"Yes, my friends are from the Bay Area. They own a barbecue joint up there."

"Impressive."

"Joey," she said quietly. "There's something about you. I can't begin to explain it, but I really like you. I know that's not a good idea, but I'm drawn to you."

"Maybe you just like that I saved you. How about we agree to that and just leave it?"

"It's not just that. That was just the excuse I needed to let you in. I've been attracted to you since the first time I saw you at the jobsite. But I have to admit, you scare me."

"Me? I'm harmless."

"I'm sure there's a trail of broken hearts out there proving otherwise."

Joey felt the icy fortress she was hiding behind beginning to melt. She wanted to be angry, to feel anything but attraction to Samantha, but she couldn't help it. Much as she hated to admit it, she really liked that she liked her. She looked up so their gazes met.

"I'm really not that bad."

"I guess I'll find out, huh?"

"Are you really sure you want to?"

Joey finished dinner and led Samantha back in the water, enjoying the closeness of her. Others joined them and talked and splashed with them, then swam off, but Joey and Samantha stayed together.

Slowly but surely, people took their leave, until it was only Brenda, Liz, Joey, and Mel drying off with Samantha.

"I'm afraid to see your kitchen," Liz said. "We should probably help you clean up."

"No need," Samantha said. "My friends will have it spotless, I'm sure. I wish they could have stuck around, but they had someplace to be tonight. It was so nice of them to come over."

"They made a killer dinner," Mel said.

Joey looked around and realized the pool area was clean of trash. "Wow, they did a great job cleaning out here."

"They're amazing," Samantha agreed.

"Well, we should probably get going," Brenda said. "Joey, Mel, you guys want to join us at Kindred Spirits?"

"Sounds good to me," Mel said.

Joey looked at Samantha, who seemed to be examining her feet. "You all go on ahead. I'll meet you there," Joey said.

"Are you sure?" Liz asked. "Why don't we follow each other?"

Joey looked from Brenda to Liz. "You guys head on. I promise I'll be there in a few."

"You'll be okay?" Brenda asked Samantha.

"I'll be fine. Thanks."

"Okay then. Come on, Mel. We'll see you in a little bit, Joey. Samantha, thank you again for everything."

"Are you kidding?" she said. "Thank you for all the work you did this morning."

"I hope you don't mind me staying," Joey said when they were alone.

"I wanted you to."

"You might have told them that."

"It didn't feel right."

Joey stared at Samantha and tried to imagine what she was feeling, but it wasn't possible. She'd only loved once and that ended in pain, but she knew it was different. And now, for her, it was all about the immediate attraction and instant gratification. Try as she might, she couldn't imagine losing a partner in a horrible accident and then finding herself attracted to someone else. She wondered what Samantha was feeling. "Do you feel like you're cheating?" she blurted.

Samantha looked at her for a moment before answering. She seemed to be measuring her words. "In a way, I suppose I do." She shook her head. "It's complicated."

"I've got to tell you, I find that to be the most overused phrase in the English language."

Samantha laughed softly. "I suppose it could be. But this really is complicated. I'm not ready to offer my tender, bruised heart to another. And I don't offer my body unless my heart goes with it. But I do like you. And find you very attractive."

"So you're saying no shot?"

"I don't think I'm saying that."

"I'm hearing no loud and clear."

"Not no, Joey. Just not yet."

"Well, I guess I should be going then."

"No, stay." The words tumbled out. "I'll make some coffee and we can talk."

Talking was not Joey's favorite thing to do with her mouth. But she wasn't ready to leave. She tried to tell herself that if she stayed, she might still be able to get Samantha to bed, but she knew it wasn't true. She just wanted to spend more time with her. The thought terrified her even as she lowered herself to the couch.

"You don't need to make coffee." She patted the couch next to her. "Sit."

"I'll feel better if I do." Samantha wandered back to the kitchen. Joey took a deep breath and cautioned herself to tread lightly.

Something besides coffee was brewing, and she was confused and scared and excited at once. She wanted to stay. She wanted to flee. She leaned back against the sofa and closed her eyes, trying to make sense of it all.

"Did you fall asleep?" Samantha was back with two steaming cups. She handed the coffee to Joey and set her tea on the table.

"No. I was just thinking."

"Happy thoughts?"

"I couldn't tell you. None of my thoughts make a lot of sense to me right now."

"I'm sorry. I wish I could make this easier."

"It is what it is." Joey shrugged and sipped the coffee, taking away the chill from the night.

"Who are you, Joey Scarpetti?" Samantha stared at her intently.

"I am who I am. What you see is what you get. No more, no less."

"Talk about overused phrases. How about you say something with meaning?"

"I'd rather talk about you. I can't believe someone as beautiful and lovely as you came from Old Man Brewer."

Samantha flung herself against the back of the couch. "Oh, no. *Must* we discuss him?"

Joey immediately felt more comfortable. Finally, a topic she could handle.

"Yeah, we must. Does he know you're living here? In this hated community? Will he still do everything in his power to cripple us and make us go away?"

"I'm not my father's favorite person. I assume he knows I'm here for a couple of reasons. I assume he still keeps tabs on me, and there's no way I could have lived in Somerset even for a few weeks without it getting back to him."

"So your living here doesn't help our cause?"

"It neither helps nor hurts in my opinion."

"Are you sure it won't hurt? His anger at you could result in greater measures to get rid of us."

"Maybe I'm delusional, but I really don't think he hates me that much. Besides, what else could he possibly do to close down our town?"

"What was it like growing up as his kid?"

"He was strict. But with three older brothers, I was definitely a daddy's girl."

"That must have hurt when he disowned you."

"How did you know about that?"

"I hear things."

"I guess that wasn't exactly top secret information."

"No. So did it piss you off when he turned his back on you?"

"I felt betrayed. I guess he did, too."

"You deserved to feel that way."

"And he didn't?"

"You didn't do anything wrong."

"We're not from his generation."

"Are you defending him?" Joey felt her ire rise.

"Not in the least." She was silent for a moment. "Oh, maybe I am. I'm over hating him for it. He's a misguided old man."

"A misguided old man who spews hatred and untruths in an effort to hurt others."

"Don't hold back, Joey. Tell me how you really feel."

Joey relaxed against the couch again. "I'm sorry. He's just not my favorite person."

"Well, you do have every right to feel that way."

"What happened? How did it go down? Did you just come out to him and he freaked or what?"

"Something like that. I still don't believe he didn't have an inkling, but when I told him Dee and I were lovers, he lost it."

"Do you think it was mostly because of his public image?"

"God, I hope not. I've wondered, but I can't allow myself to think I mean less to him than his stupid political career."

"Either way, he's a fool."

"Thank you."

An awkward silence fell, and Joey grew increasingly ill at ease. "You're probably tired," she said lamely.

"You're still trying to run away from me?"

"Well, there's really no point in staying."

Samantha set her cup on the coffee table and took Joey's from her. She placed it next to hers and moved over so she was right next to Joey.

Joey's heart raced at the closeness of Samantha. Moisture pooled between her thighs when Samantha leaned over, pressing her breasts into her. She tried to back up but had nowhere to go. She leaned away, but still Samantha's lips found hers.

The meeting was gentle yet firm, soft yet unyielding. It was tentative yet deliberate, and Joey was at a loss to defy it. She kissed back, reining in her desire to lay Samantha back and climb on top of her. She kept her hands in her lap as Samantha deepened the kiss, probing Joey's lips with her tongue. She opened her mouth, and her breath caught as their tongues met. The kiss was feeding her desire, urging it onward, yet she was acutely aware that things wouldn't end as she'd like.

Samantha's hands were in Joey's hair, on her jaw, and finally on her chest. Joey wanted to rip her shirt off to feel Samantha on her bare breast but continued to show restraint. Said restraint waivered significantly when Samantha grabbed one of Joey's hands and placed it on her full breast.

Joey pulled her hand back as if it hurt.

"What's wrong?" Samantha asked.

"You can't do that to me. You can't tease me like that."

"I didn't mean to tease you. I thought you'd like it, and I know I wanted it."

"But see? You're not ready for more, and I'm not used to stopping once we've reached a certain point."

"So we can't even play around?"

"I can't. Not yet."

"Fair enough," Samantha said easily and leaned in for another kiss. Joey stood.

"I think I'd better be going."

"I've upset you."

"No, not really. I just…respect you, I guess. And if I stay, I'll be tempted to try to go further than you're ready for. And that would ruin everything. And I don't want to do that."

"I'm sorry, Joey."

"Please don't apologize. You've done nothing wrong. And so far, neither have I. I'd just like to keep it that way."

Samantha stood and took Joey's hand, leading her to the door.

"When will I see you again?"

"I suppose that's up to you."

"This is a two-way street."

"I know. I'm sorry. I'm trying not to be an ass, but I'm not thinking too clearly right now."

"Are you okay to drive?"

"Oh, yeah. It's not alcohol-related."

Samantha nodded. "You're welcome to stay the night. I'd love to have you hold me."

"I'm not ready for that."

Samantha laughed at the irony. Joey cracked a crooked grin.

"Are you going to the bar?"

"It's closed. I'm just going home."

"Will you call me?"

"I don't have your number. But I promise the next time I see a blocked number on my phone, I'll answer it."

"Why don't we plan on dinner tomorrow? Be here at six and I'll have spaghetti ready."

"That's a dangerous proposition," Joey joked. "Cooking spaghetti for an Italian takes major guts."

"I make a mean spaghetti."

"We'll see. I'll definitely be here to check it out." She kissed Samantha.

"Thank you," Samantha said, "for everything."

"No. Thank you. I had a great time."

Samantha glanced at her watch.

"Sweetie, it's almost three. You either need to go or stay, but you've got to do something since you have to be at work in a few hours."

Joey paused at the pet name. She felt surprisingly warm and comforted. Not what she'd expect. "Okay, okay. I'm out of here. I'll see you tomorrow."

She drove home with a smile on her face that she just couldn't get rid of.

CHAPTER TWELVE

Joey was dog-tired when she pulled up to the site the next morning. She put on her tool belt and walked over to where Mel and Brenda were talking.

"You look like shit," Mel said.

"Thanks."

"You never joined us at the bar," Brenda said.

"No. I lost track of time. What are we working on today?" She ignored Brenda's glare.

"You and Mel start laying carpet in the big room." She pointed to her left. "That's the only thing I want you to lay."

"She's so subtle," Joey said to Mel.

Brenda stormed off, and Joey and Mel walked over to a roll of carpet leaning against a far wall.

"I can't believe this place is almost done," Joey said.

"I know. Grand opening is in two weeks. Samantha must be excited."

"I'd imagine." Joey made a mental note to talk to her about the day-care center that evening.

"You don't have your usual 'I just got laid' strut going on today," Mel said as they rolled out the carpet.

"Just because I didn't go to the bar doesn't mean I got laid."

"What time did you get home?"

"Around three."

"And you're going to tell me you two just talked? I know you better than that."

"But you don't know her!"

"Whoa. Easy there. I think I found the exposed underbelly."

"What's that supposed to mean?"

"You're just a little defensive. I think Samantha may be your weakness."

"Fuck you."

"Nice comeback." Mel laughed.

"I'm tired, and I'm not in the mood right now."

"But you were in the mood last night. So spill. What happened?"

"Nothing. We talked."

"About?"

"Her dad mostly."

"Are you fucking kidding me? You finally get the woman of your dreams alone and you talked about the man you hate more than anyone else?"

"He's still her dad."

"So nothing happened? No bullshit?"

"No bullshit. Nothing happened."

"Did you at least make out? Cop a feel? Don't disappoint me here, Romeo."

Joey's mind flashed back to the feel of Samantha's breast under her hand. She quickly shook the image out of her head.

"We kissed a little. Nothing major."

"I can't believe you crashed and burned."

"I didn't!"

"Sounds to me like you did."

"You don't get it."

"So explain it to me."

"She's not like the rest." Joey stood and looked at Mel. "Plus she's got a lot of shit she's dealing with."

"So what does that mean? You're giving her time? Space? What?"

"It means she's not ready to jump into bed yet."

"And you stuck around anyway? What the hell? You really do like her, don't you?"

"There's something about her. I'll say that."

"Damn. I never thought I'd see the day."

"Cut the crap. I don't need it."

"I'm happy for you in some warped, twisted way. I think you may have met your match."

"We'll see." Joey knelt back down and began to tack the carpet.

❖

By the time they were through for the day, Joey was exhausted and sore.

"You wanna catch some waves?" Mel asked as they loaded their tools.

"Not today. I think I'm gonna go home and take a nap."

"You have plans tonight?"

"As a matter of fact, I do."

"You gonna not sleep with someone again?"

"Do you think this is easy for me?" Joey whirled on her. "You think this is some laughing matter?"

"Turbo down. I'm just giving you shit. You don't have to be so sensitive. It's just so unheard of for you."

"Right. And who knows how long it'll last. Chances are, I'll get bored and tired of waiting." She hoped she wasn't telling the truth.

"So answer me this, lover boi, if she's not putting out, are you still allowed to get it elsewhere?"

The question stopped Joey cold. She hadn't thought about that. Nobody had said anything about commitment or anything. Just that they weren't sleeping together. She was about to answer that she could still sleep with someone else when it occurred to her she had no desire to do so. Regardless of what had or hadn't been said.

"I suppose I could."

"But will you?"

"I don't know."

"Damn, woman. You've got it bad."

"So it would seem," Joey admitted.

"Hey, all bullshitting aside, have fun tonight." Mel slammed the side of her van shut.

"Thanks. I'll see you tomorrow."

❖

Joey was groggy when she turned off the alarm from her nap. It took her a second to realize she had to be somewhere. She checked the time and saw that she had an hour until she had to be at Samantha's.

She took a quick shower and put on her khaki cargo shorts and black polo shirt. She hopped in her truck and headed for the liquor store for a bottle of wine. As soon as she parked, she realized the error of her ways, so she drove instead to Petals of Desire, the local flower shop.

"Joey Scarpetti in, my shop?" Delta, the owner, exclaimed. "Why, I never thought I'd see the day."

Joey smiled at the harassment. "Since I'm not too familiar with this, maybe you could help me out?"

"Sure thing, darlin'. What do you need? And more importantly, who's the lucky lady?"

"I just want to get some flowers. Nothing major. No roses or anything like that. Just a nice summer bouquet to take to a friend's house for dinner."

"Nothing major. Don't you be tellin' stories to Delta. I know better. I could see it when you walked in here."

"Really, it's just a nice gesture is all."

Delta cast a measuring sideways glance at Joey. "I'm just trying to figure out why I haven't heard any mention of this. This kind of thing usually tears through Maybon Tir."

"Seriously." Joey was trying not to lose her patience. "There's nothing to hear. Now will you help me out?"

"What's your lady's favorite color?"

"I have no idea."

"Well, Josephine, you'd better find that out. And soon. That's important to know."

Joey cringed at the sound of her birth name and quickly made another mental note. This one was to find Samantha's favorite color. She thought of describing the colors of her house but figured that would give too much away to the nosy flower peddler.

"Those are pretty." She pointed to some bright yellow sunflowers.

"They certainly are. But they don't really send any message from the heart, if you know what I mean."

"I'm not trying to send a message, Delta. I just want to bring flowers. So what can you do with those?"

Delta pulled a few sunflowers and added some daisies, finally putting some salal leaves in for contrast.

"That's really pretty," Joey said.

"I hope the lady likes them."

"I'm sure she will."

Joey paid Delta and glanced at her watch. Only five minutes to get to Samantha's. She thanked the gods that Maybon Tir was such a small town. She arrived with a minute to spare and knocked on the door.

Samantha answered the door in a long yellow tank dress that hung to her calves. She smiled when she saw the flowers Joey brought.

"That is so sweet of you."

"Well, I didn't want to show up empty-handed. And I didn't think a bottle of wine would be appropriate."

"Thank you for realizing that." She kissed Joey's cheek and invited her in.

"You look amazing," Joey said. "That color is great on you."

"Why thank you. It happens to be my favorite." She motioned to the sunflowers she was holding. "But I'd imagine you already knew that?"

"That was just luck," Joey admitted. She sniffed at the air. "I'm impressed so far. Dinner smells wonderful."

"I hope you like garlic."

"With a last name like Scarpetti, I'd better."

"Even though you didn't bring wine, I bought some Chianti. I hope you'll enjoy it with dinner."

"That would be great. Thanks." She followed Samantha to the kitchen and poured herself a glass of wine while Samantha busied herself with putting the flowers in a vase.

"I'm impressed yet again," Joey said. "You've lived here one day and you already know exactly where the vases are."

"I spent today unpacking and organizing the kitchen. The vases go under the kitchen sink, so there you go."

Joey nodded and sipped her wine.

"How was work today?" Samantha said over her shoulder as she stirred the sauce. "You weren't too tired, were you?"

Joey stared at Samantha's back, admiring her figure and the way the dress clung lightly to her shapely ass. She walked over and leaned into her, lightly brushing her neck with her lips.

Samantha set the wooden spoon down and turned, linking her hands behind Joey's neck. "You just gave me chills."

"In a good way, I hope." Joey bent and kissed her lips, tenderly at first, but Samantha tightened her grip and wouldn't let her back away. Joey ran her hands around Samantha's waist and down her back until she was cupping her ass, pulling her into her as their kiss grew more passionate. Electricity coursed through her, and she lost her resolve to go slow. Her tongue pressed against Samantha's lips and slid quickly into her mouth. She continued to knead her ass while she ground her own hips into her. She moved one hand to the back of Samantha's head, where it tangled in her soft hair, pulling her mouth closer yet.

Joey was lost in the kiss and dizzy when Samantha finally pulled away. She rested her forehead on Samantha's as she fought to catch her breath.

"Well, it's good to see you, too," Samantha breathed.

"Sorry about that." Joey took her hands off Samantha and moved back to the island to get her wine.

"No need to apologize. It was wonderful."

"Yeah? Good. I didn't know. I mean…I'm sorry. I guess I'm just confused."

"I'm sorry I'm not making this easy." Samantha leaned on the island opposite Joey and looked into her eyes. "It's just that it feels so right and then feels so wrong."

"I kind of get that." Joey nodded slowly. "Unfortunately for me, there's nothing wrong feeling about it."

"And I get that. I wouldn't blame you if you said you never wanted to see me again."

"I'm afraid I can't do that."

"Really?" Samantha smiled. "I like to hear that."

"I guess I'm going to see this thing through, whatever that means."

"I wish I knew what it meant, too."

Joey kept hearing Mel's voice in her head asking if she had to be faithful. Part of her wanted to toss it out there, just to be sure, but she didn't want to bring up anything that might blow her chances.

She finished her wine and poured another glass. "Do you miss drinking?" she asked Samantha.

"Sometimes I wish I could have a glass of wine. But I'm not that big of a drinker, so it's not a huge deal for me." She turned to the oven when the alarm went off and pulled a loaf of garlic bread out.

"Oh, yum. Now you're talking," Joey said. "Is there anything you need me to do?"

"You can grab the salad out of the fridge. That would be great."

Joey did as instructed and set it on the island. Samantha grabbed two plates and put heaping piles of noodles on them, then smothered the noodles in sauce. She put two slices of bread on each plate and carried them to the table. Joey served the salad into the two bowls on the island and joined Samantha at the table.

"I'm starving," she said.

"I figured you must be after working construction all day."

"Speaking of that, it's really coming along. I understand the grand opening is in a couple of weeks."

"I know. You guys got it built fast."

"Do you already have kids signed up for it?"

"I do. I have teachers and about twelve kids. We'll see how it goes."

"We have that many kids who need day care in Maybon Tir?"

"You'd be surprised. Plus I have some friends from Somerset who are going to bring their kids."

Joey tried to think of who had young kids in town as she scooped up her spaghetti on her fork and twirled it into a spoon. She swore her taste buds had orgasms at the taste of the sauce. "Oh, my God. This is delicious." She quickly scooped up some more.

"I'm so glad you like it. I hoped it wouldn't disappoint."

"Seriously. This is as good as my grandma's, and she was full-blooded Italian. Where did you learn to make sauce like this?"

Samantha was silent for a minute. "Dee's mother was Italian."

"Dee?" Joey asked before her memory kicked in. "Oh, your partner. Got it."

The silence was heavy and awkward. Joey searched for something to say but couldn't come up with anything that she didn't think sounded lame.

"At any rate, I'm glad you like it."

"Very much."

"It's okay to talk about her, you know," Samantha said.

"I know." Joey weighed her words. "But I kind of feel like I'm with her woman, and that feels strange. Does that make sense?"

"It makes perfect sense. Now you know how I feel, to a degree."

"Yeah. So it's not like…I mean…oh, hell, I don't know what I mean. I guess I know she's part of this…whatever it is we're doing, but at the same time, I don't like to be reminded about her. I don't mean to sound cold."

"You don't. And I don't like to remind you of her. But she was a very large part of my life and still is, in some ways. We need to acknowledge that if we're ever going anywhere with this."

Joey nodded.

"Wow, not exactly the mood I was going for with the wine and the spaghetti," Samantha finally said.

"I'm trying to shake it off."

"Tell me more about your work today. What did you do?"

"Mel and I laid carpet. The whole place is carpeted now. It looks really good, if I do say so myself." She smiled.

"I'm so impressed that your crew can do everything from foundation to finish. Brenda's very lucky to have such a talented group working for her."

"It's fun building things. It's a rush to start with a plot of land and watch a useable building go up."

"I bet. Where did you learn construction?"

"Mel and I hired on with Brenda right out of college. She was nice enough to teach us all the tricks of the trade."

"She speaks very highly of you both."

"Don't let her know you told me that." Joey laughed. "She likes to pretend we're just pains in her ass. Myself, especially."

"I think she just likes to put on a good show of bravado as much as you do."

"Funny, I don't think we're anything alike."

"You both think you have images to uphold."

"I'm not doing much about my image right now."

"No, you're not. Does that bother you? Will you tell people we're sleeping together?"

Joey stared thoughtfully at Samantha. "That never occurred to me. I've never had to lie about it before."

"And now?"

"No, I won't say that. We're not. And it's not like you're just jerkin' me around and deserve to have rumors spread. You've got valid reasons why we're not in bed yet, and I respect that."

"You're a special woman, Joey Scarpetti, even though you do your damnedest to make people think otherwise."

"I don't really. I just don't care what people think, so I don't correct misconceptions."

"I don't know about that. I think you like your bad boi image."

Joey grinned, feeling the blush start on her chest and work its way up.

"Aha! I knew you couldn't deny it."

Joey pushed back from the table and stood, collecting plates.

"That's not necessary," Samantha said.

"Sure it is. You cooked; I clean. That's fair."

Samantha helped her clear the table and joined her in the kitchen. "At least let me do the dishes."

"Nope. Go get a chair and get comfy while I get these done."

Samantha leaned against the island and smiled as she watched Joey make short order of getting her kitchen clean. "Do you cook?"

"Hardly." Joey laughed. "I mean, I can if I have to, but I really don't have any reason to."

"Not even for yourself?"

"No, I generally eat out."

"I've heard that about you."

It took Joey a minute to catch what she'd said. "Touché."

"Sorry, I couldn't resist."

"No problem. Did you at least hear I was good at it?"

It was Samantha's turn to blush. Joey turned and smiled at her. "You mess with the bull…"

"Lesson learned." Samantha grabbed a dishtowel and started drying the pots and pans as Joey washed. "We're a pretty good team."

"That we are." Joey set the last clean pot in the strainer.

Samantha left it there as she put the towel down and took Joey's hand. She led her back to the couch and sat leaning against her.

"You're very easy to spend time with."

"As are you. I could get used to this."

"Except for the going home part?"

"Oh, no." Joey laughed. "Going home is one of the things I do best."

Samantha playfully swatted her on her arm. "So I shouldn't take it personally that you won't stay the night."

"Not at all. That's about the only thing you have in common with the other women in my life." She pulled Samantha to her and kissed her.

Samantha broke the kiss. "Just so I know, how many other women are there in your life?"

"You mean now? I meant in general."

"Okay, but I mean now."

"There aren't any other women."

"Don't bullshit me."

"I'm not the type to keep women around for long. I thought you knew that."

"But surely you've got some that you're sleeping with."

"Not at the moment. I kinda thought I'd take a break from that and see where this goes."

"I appreciate that. More than you could know. But I don't know that I could ask that of you."

"Okay. You're confusing me again. You mean the idea of me sleeping with someone else doesn't bother you at all?"

"Of course it does. I don't even want to think about it."

"Then don't tell me it's okay to do."

"But you have needs. I get that."

"Look, let's just get this out in the open. Either you like me or you don't."

"I do. Very much."

"Then you don't want me sleeping around. Even though you may get why I would, you wouldn't be okay if you found out I was."

"I'd have to be."

"No. You think you would, but deep down, you'd resent it."

"I suppose you're right. But that makes me a horrible person, doesn't it?"

"Not as horrible as if you tell me it's okay to do something, then get upset when I do it."

"So what are you saying?"

"I'm saying let's make some rules here. You don't date other women and I don't sleep with other women. Fair?"

"And you won't resent me?"

"I'll try not to. So far, it's okay."

"It's only been two days."

"Oh, my God! Is that all?" Joey laughed.

"You are such a brat!" Samantha leaned Joey onto her back and lay across her. "I don't know what I'm going to do with you."

"I have several suggestions."

"I'm sure you do." She kissed Joey as she hiked up her dress so she could straddle her.

Joey was lost in the kiss until she ran her hands down Samantha's back and down to her bare ass cheeks. She started to move her hand around to the front but stopped herself.

"You can't do that." She squirmed out from under Samantha. "That's not right."

"But my dress was in the way."

"As far as I'm concerned, all our clothes are in the way. But you can't go offering stuff to me that I can't have."

"I'm sorry. I wasn't thinking."

"It's okay." Joey tried to calm her racing heart. "Just please be careful."

"So what are we allowed to do?"

"Kiss. That's it. Until you give the go sign, there's nothing but kissing because anything beyond that is too painful for me."

"I wish I didn't want you so desperately."

"You're not helping."

"I get confused, too, Joey."

"I'm sorry. I really am. But if you want me to respect your wishes, you need to respect my boundaries. Don't go waving the candy in front of me, then tell me I can't have it."

"Fair enough," Samantha said.

"Now walk me to the door and tell me good night."

"I don't want you to go away mad."

"I'm not mad, babe. Just frustrated. And that shouldn't surprise either of us."

CHAPTER THIRTEEN

The next two weeks passed quickly for Joey. She and Samantha had settled into a routine of seeing each other most nights. Joey's libido was in overdrive, and she spent much of the time lashing out at Mel or anyone who happened to be nearby on the jobsite.

"Man, I do wish you'd get laid. You're a royal bitch," Mel said on the day they spent cleaning up the site around the day-care center. It was set for the grand opening the next night, and Brenda and Samantha were at the site making sure everything was perfect.

"You think I don't know that? I can't help it. A deal's a deal."

"How much longer do you think she's gonna wear that chastity belt?"

"I don't know. And it doesn't matter. She'll be ready when she's ready. And not a moment sooner."

"Well, are you at least adding some pressure? Pushing the envelope?"

"Not at all. She's the one who'll decide when it's time."

"You're crazy. But good for you. Although I've missed my buddy lately. I'd feel better if I knew you were at least getting some."

"Me too, Mel." Joey laughed. "Me too."

Brenda used her bullhorn to get the crew's attention. She called them over to her truck where Samantha was standing with her. Joey and Mel moseyed over and said hi to Samantha.

"You look so hot when you're working," Samantha said softly.

Joey looked at her and smiled. "I want to kiss you so bad right now."

Before Samantha could respond, Brenda addressed the group.

"It's Friday night, and I know that means you're probably all heading to Kindred Spirits this evening. But as thanks for all your hard work, Ms. Brewer is buying burgers and beer at The Shack at five o'clock. Everyone is invited." She looked specifically at Joey. "And you're welcome to bring a date."

When the crew had dispersed, Joey stayed behind to talk to Samantha. "Boy, that Brenda's a smooth one, isn't she?"

"She's just trying to protect me."

"What's her interest? Is she more than just the head of this jobsite?"

"I guess I never told you. Liz was Dee's cousin. So I've known them for years."

"Ah, things make a lot more sense now."

"Will you be at The Shack?"

"Sure. I think Mel and I are surfing after work, so it'll be easy to stop by."

"I look forward to seeing you."

Joey studied Samantha's eyes and saw a longing that matched her own. "I'd better get back to work."

"I'll see you a little later then."

Joey walked away, her heart racing. She hated that she couldn't kiss Samantha in front of the others. She was a mess of pent-up energy as she helped the crew finish cleaning.

When the work was done, Joey went home to change and wait for Mel. She had just stepped out of her work clothes when her phone rang. She saw that it was Samantha, so she answered it quickly.

"What are you doing?" Samantha asked.

"Getting ready to hit the waves. What are you doing?"

"Missing you."

Joey braced herself for the waves of nausea that generally accompanied that statement, but there were none. Instead, there was a surge of warmth throughout her body.

"You just saw me." She laughed.

"I know. But I just wanted to make sure you'll be there tonight."

"I told you I would. What's going on? Why the double check?"

"I'm sorry. I'm really nervous for tomorrow."

"You'll be fine, babe. You'll do great. Everyone's gonna love the center." Joey heard the front door slam. "Oh, shit. Mel's here, and I'm not dressed. I gotta go."

"Okay. I'll see you in a few."

"Give me a minute," Joey called down the hall after she hung up. She heard Mel pop the top on a beer as she quickly donned her board shorts and tank top. She walked out to meet Mel.

"Whose ride are we taking?" Mel asked.

"We'd better take yours since I'll probably be going over to Samantha's after dinner."

"Damn, you're whipped."

"Whatever. Let's just go."

They surfed for several hours, but eventually, Joey's attention turned away from the waves and toward the parking lot of The Shack, looking for the Charger to pull up. Mel finally gave up and paddled over to join her.

"Are you gonna surf anymore? Or just stare at The Shack?"

At that moment, the Charger pulled into the lot, followed by Brenda's truck.

"Maybe just one more," Joey said, paddling farther out. She caught a nice eight-foot wave and rode it to the shallow water before jumping off her board. She picked it up and carried it to shore where she sat on a towel and opened a beer.

"You're like a fuckin' school kid with a crush," Mel said when she finally joined her. "Do you ever think of anything but her?"

"Of course I do. But I'm looking forward to seeing her."

"You just saw her a couple of hours ago. And you see her every fucking night."

"What can I say? I like her."

"I guess." Mel downed half a beer. "When are you two gonna make it official?"

"What do you mean? If you're asking when we're going to sleep together, I'm telling you I'm getting tired of that question."

"No, I'm asking when y'all are gonna go public with your coupleness."

"Coupleness? Is that even a word?"

"It is now." Mel laughed.

"I don't know. We haven't really talked about it. I think we both kind of like how things are now."

"You don't mind being her dirty little secret?"

"It's not like I don't have a few of my own."

"True that."

Joey stood and put a T-shirt on over her tank top. She glanced back at The Shack. "Looks like people are showing up. You ready to head over?"

"Sure thing." Mel slipped on her sandals, grabbed her board, and crossed the beach and street to her van.

When their boards were stowed, they walked into The Shack and easily found the noisy group that was their coworkers. They moved over to them and were just saying hello when Joey felt breasts against her back as a pair of arms snaked around her.

"Hi, stranger," a soft voice said.

Joey disentangled herself from the embrace and turned to see Tiffany in short shorts and a tube top, looking much as she had on her birthday. "Hey, Tiffany. How have you been?"

"Not bad. I haven't seen you around much."

"Yeah? I guess it's strange that our paths haven't crossed."

"How are you doing?"

"Not bad. You still staying with your friends?"

"Yep. I get to move into the dorms next month. I'm so excited."

"I bet. That's huge."

"Tell me." Tiffany looked around the restaurant. "So what's going on here tonight?"

"Samantha Brewer is buying us burgers and brews for the excellent job we did building the day-care center."

"Oh, Samantha's here? I didn't see her." She glanced over the crowd again and this time saw Samantha. She waved, then turned back to Joey. "So you wanna get out of here and have our own party?"

Joey stared at the tan, youthful body in front of her. She knew what was under the tube top, and the thought of taking it off with her teeth made her crotch spasm.

"No, thanks. I need to be here. I mean, it's really decent that Samantha's doing this and all."

"Suit yourself. Maybe Mel wants to play." She walked over to Mel, and Joey exhaled heavily. That had been tough. She hadn't really considered leaving with Tiffany, but she sure liked the thought of it. She watched Tiffany and Mel talking and knew Mel would take her home. They'd fuck like rabbits, and she'd go make out with Samantha. She shook her head.

"Penny for your thoughts?" Samantha was by her side.

"They're not worth a penny." Joey smiled. "Has anyone thanked you for doing this for us? Because it's really not necessary."

"It may not be necessary, but I wanted to show my appreciation. You guys really busted your humps to get that done."

The evening progressed with everyone having a blast. Mel and Tiffany were some of the last to leave and then it was just Brenda and Liz and Samantha and Joey.

"I think we should get going," Brenda said. "You need your rest for your big day tomorrow. Joey, did you need a ride?"

"I'll give Joey a lift," Samantha said.

Brenda looked from one to the other, a battle clearly raging inside her. Joey held her breath, waiting for the lecture, but none was forthcoming. "Suit yourself. I'll see you tomorrow night."

They left, and Joey and Samantha walked out to the car. The fog had rolled in and the night was chilly. Joey was tempted to put her arm around Samantha but didn't, knowing she wouldn't appreciate the public attention.

"Where are we going?" Joey asked once they were in the car.

"I'm going to drop you at your place if you don't mind. I'm pretty tired."

"No worries." Joey hoped her disappointment wasn't obvious.

Samantha pulled up in front of Joey's house and turned off the car.

"I'd invite you in, but you don't want to see how messy it is," Joey said.

"That's okay." She turned to look at Joey. "Are you going tomorrow?"

"To the grand opening thing? I hadn't planned on it."

Samantha's face fell.

"Think about it, hon. How would I explain my presence there?"

"But it's huge for me. I'd love to share it with you."

"Well, maybe we can celebrate afterward."

"Or you can be my date."

"What?" Joey was sure she'd misheard.

"I guess I'm asking you out. Kind of role reversal but whatever. Will you be my date to the gala tomorrow?"

"People will start talking," Joey said.

"People are already talking." Samantha laughed.

"Really?"

"Have you not heard? Ever since you walked into Delta's store that day, texts have been flying and tongues have been wagging. There was immediate curiosity as to who Joey Scarpetti's lady was."

"How did they figure it was you?"

"Your truck is at my house every night."

"Oh, yeah. I'm sorry. I know you didn't want people to know."

"I'm ready, though. Why not just confirm what they already know?"

"Fine by me." Joey thought her heart would explode from relief. "So I'll be your date tomorrow." She leaned across the console and kissed Samantha briefly. "I guess I'll see you tomorrow then."

"I'll pick you up at five thirty."

"I'll be ready."

❖

Joey stood in front of her closet trying to decide what to wear to a grand opening for a day care. She picked up her phone to call Samantha to see how formal it would be but decided against it. She was probably already a nervous wreck.

She finally decided on a pair of black silk slacks, a long-sleeved button-down white shirt, and a skinny black tie. She combed her hair, parting it on the side and combing her bangs back, but they continued to fall back into her face. She finally gave up and had just grabbed a beer when her phone rang. "Hey, babe," Joey said.

"Hi there. I'm in front of your house if you want to come on out."

Joey put the beer back in the fridge and took a deep breath. She was about to make her big debut. She felt like she was coming out all over again.

She slid into the car and had to laugh at Samantha's dress. It was a long black sleeveless number with a white stripe that started at her left breast and cut down to the right side of her waist, then back across and down to just below her left hip, then back toward her right knee. It was slit up to her mid thigh. "We couldn't have dressed more alike if we'd tried."

"Very true. I guess black and white is our theme tonight."

"You look stunning."

"Thank you, sweetheart. And you look quite dapper."

They drove in silence to the day-care center, and it seemed surreal to Joey to see all the cars in the parking lot and the place lit up. "It looks pretty darned good," she said.

"It really does."

They got out of the car, and Samantha took Joey's hand.

"You sure about that?" Joey asked.

"Positive." Samantha gave Joey's hand a squeeze.

Joey had never been much into hand holding, but Samantha's hand in hers felt perfect. She squeezed back, as much to reassure herself the night was going to go well as Samantha.

"Are you sure about this?" Samantha asked.

"Totally."

They walked in, and Joey felt like Moses parting the Red Sea. The crowd seemed to separate in half, with everyone turning to stare at them. She heard no sound as they cut through the crowd. Joey had never known that many people could be silent at one time. Soon, though, the crowd closed around them, and laughter and chatter refilled the air.

"That was uncomfortable," Joey said.

"The hard part's over now. Let's find Brenda and Liz."

"Seriously? Brenda's gonna want to take me out back when she sees us."

"She'll just have to get over it."

They found Brenda and Liz in a corner, and Joey had correctly anticipated Brenda's response.

"Are you fucking kidding me?" Brenda said.

"You'll just have to trust me on this," Samantha said.

"You, I trust. Her? Not so much." She motioned to Joey.

Joey had no comeback. She knew Brenda deserved to be skeptical. And she wasn't sure what she could say to reassure her.

"I've got to admit, I'm more than a little surprised the rumors are true," Liz said.

"You hurt her and I hurt you. You got that?" Brenda said to Joey.

"Please lay off her," Samantha said. "I'm a big girl."

"Who's endured enough pain. I don't plan to sit idly by and watch you suffer more."

"Look at her for a minute, Brenda," Liz said. "She looks happy again. We haven't seen that since—"

"Sure, she looks happy now. But imagine how she'll look once Scarpetti is through with her."

"You know something?" Liz said. "I think this is the first time I've ever seen Joey holding a woman's hand."

"That should count for something," Samantha said.

"I'm still disgusted."

"Maybe you should listen to Liz and be happy Samantha's happy." Joey finally found her voice.

"Maybe you shoulda listened to me and backed the fuck off."

"Maybe you should chill and not ruin Samantha's evening," Joey shot back.

"She's right," Liz said. "Now shouldn't you be mingling?"

"We should." Samantha turned to Joey. "Are you ready?"

"Lead the way."

"I'm really sorry about that," Joey said when they were out of earshot.

"You have nothing to apologize for."

"I do. If you were with someone besides me, they'd all be thrilled to see you beaming."

"If they care about me, it won't matter that it's you who makes me happy."

"It's because they care about you that it does."

They made their way through the crowd of lesbians, all dressed in their finest to celebrate the new day-care center. Joey knew most of the people there and graciously met the few she didn't. There were several couples from Somerset who had signed up to have Samantha and her staff watch their kids.

When the event was drawing to a close, Samantha moved to the front of the room and took a microphone. "Excuse me," she said and waited for the room to grow quiet.

Joey stood back and watched, enthralled as Samantha thanked everyone for coming and for their support. She promised them their children would have the best care possible. She went on to introduce her staff, and Joey felt a sense of amazement that this totally together, successful woman wanted to be hers. Her heart skipped a beat just thinking about it.

"She looks damned fine."

Joey turned to see Mel smiling at her, Tiffany at her side. "Yeah, she does."

"I hear you two are an item now," Tiffany said.

"Where'd you hear that?" Joey asked sarcastically.

"More people are talking about that than the day-care center," Mel said.

"I don't see you two together," Tiffany said.

"We're an odd couple," Joey agreed. She turned her attention back to Samantha, who was wishing everyone a good night. She hung up the microphone and hurried to Joey's side.

"You were amazing," Joey said.

"I was a nervous wreck."

"No one could have guessed. You're so smooth."

Samantha turned her attention away from Joey to say hi to Mel and Tiffany. "Thank you for coming. I was beginning to think you weren't going to make it."

"We were a little busy earlier." Tiffany winked.

Joey arched an eyebrow at Mel, who simply shrugged.

"I need to go thank Brenda and Liz for everything. They got the place set up and promised to supervise the closing down. I need to get home. I'll be right back."

"Damn, she lights up like a frickin' Christmas tree when she looks at you," Mel said.

"Isn't it cool?" Joey grinned.

"I sure hope you two make a go of it," Tiffany said. "I really do."

"Thanks, Tiff. I appreciate that."

Samantha was back and took Joey's hand. "Are you ready to head out?"

"Sure."

She turned to Mel and Tiffany. "I'll see you two later."

Tiffany hugged Samantha. "I wish you the very best," she said.

"Thank you. I think the center will be a huge success."

"I wasn't just talking about the center."

"Well, thank you again then. I think a lot of people are going to be surprised."

"A lot of us already are." Mel smiled.

Samantha and Joey left the center and entered the foggy night. Joey put her arm around Samantha and pulled her tight. "Are you completely wiped out?"

"Actually, I'm quite invigorated."

"Really?"

"Really. And I thought we'd go back to my place, if that's okay with you?"

"Your place is always okay with me."

CHAPTER FOURTEEN

Samantha parked her car in the driveway and turned to Joey, who saw a desire deeper than any she'd seen before burning in Samantha's eyes.

"You were wonderful tonight," Joey said.

"Thank you for being there for me."

"My pleasure." Joey leaned forward and captured Samantha's mouth with hers. She kissed her long and lovingly, thrilling at the emotions she'd thought herself unable to feel.

"We should probably get inside," Samantha murmured against her lips.

"Yeah." Joey slid her tongue in Samantha's mouth.

"Maybe now?" Samantha laughed when the kiss ended.

"Yeah, now." Joey was light-headed as she stepped out of the car and followed Samantha into the house.

Samantha locked the door behind Joey and took her hand. She led her to the couch and sat next to her, arms immediately circling her neck, pulling her close, and kissing her hungrily. Joey's whole body responded to the kiss, and she had to break away to catch her breath.

"I think it might be time for you to take me home," Joey said.

"But we just got here."

"You're kissing me in a way that promises more. And I'm afraid I just can't take that."

Samantha stood and looked down at Joey. She reached her hands behind her back and unzipped her dress, stepping out of it when it hit the floor.

Joey allowed her gaze to roam over the vision before her, taking in the lacy black bra and panties and yearning for what lay beneath. She longed to lean forward and run her tongue along the crotch of the skimpy panties.

Samantha knelt on the couch, one knee on either side of Joey's hips. She licked at Joey's lips and kissed down her cheek to suck on her neck.

Joey balled her hands into fists at her side, trying to exercise self-control. "We've talked about this, babe. You know the rules. You're being downright cruel right now."

"Just relax," Samantha whispered before nibbling on an earlobe.

"I can't." She gently pushed Samantha away. "You need to stop. Now."

Samantha climbed off her and stood, offering her hand.

"What?" Joey hadn't meant to sound so angry.

"Come with me."

Joey was far from amused at the turn of events. She was hard and wet and losing the battle not to give in to everything she wanted to do. She took Samantha's hand and stood.

"Where are we going?"

Samantha led Joey down the hall to the master bedroom. She lay back on the bed and ran her hands over her breasts and along her slightly bulging belly, moving them lower and separating them to slide down her thighs.

Joey's heart raced as she watched Samantha. She hoped to God Samantha wasn't just fucking with her.

"I'm yours," Samantha said. "Take me."

Joey lay on the bed next to Samantha and allowed her hand to skim the length of her body. She drew her focus away from the perfection to look into Samantha's eyes.

"Are you sure?"

"Very."

"I don't know what to say. I've dreamt of this moment. But now…well, I just want to be sure you're ready."

"I've never been more ready. You've been more than patient, and I see no reason to deny either of us any longer." She pulled Joey to her and kissed her with more desire than ever.

Joey returned the kiss as she moved her hands over Samantha's full breasts. She coaxed the nipples through the flimsy material and was rewarded as they grew at her touch. She kissed Samantha back with every bit of fervor as she slipped her fingertips just under the top of a cup, glancing over the soft flesh underneath.

Joey kissed down Samantha's neck and chest and ran her lips over the tops of her breasts. She folded the cup down and closed her mouth on a nipple. She rolled over it with her tongue while she continued to caress the breast. The softness of Samantha's skin drove her desire upward. She never wanted to stop touching her.

Samantha managed to reach behind her back and unhook her bra, allowing both breasts the freedom they craved. Joey took them in her hands and buried her face between them. She kissed one and sucked the nipple while she slid her hand down Samantha's smooth belly. She moved it between Samantha's legs and gasped at how wet her panties were. She deftly moved the crotch to the side.

Joey rose from the attention she was giving Samantha's breasts and gazed into her eyes. She wanted to watch the look on Samantha's face the moment she first touched her. She wanted to memorize the pleasure and need etched there.

She purposefully slid a finger under the crotch and skimmed the whole of Samantha's womanhood. She glided her finger over her swollen lips and around her hardened clit. She watched Samantha's eyes close as she moved her finger lower again and teased her opening.

Samantha's eyes opened as Joey eased her finger inside, testing Samantha's readiness. Samantha smiled at her, and Joey kissed her as she added another finger. Their kiss grew more passionate as Joey's tongue matched the motions her fingers were making. She ended the kiss and whispered in Samantha's ear. "Are you sure you're okay?"

"Oh, God, yes."

Joey smiled as she kissed down Samantha's body, ending up at the top of her panties. She withdrew her fingers and peeled the dainty undergarment down her legs and tossed it to the floor.

Samantha opened her legs for Joey, who happily positioned herself between them. She ran her hands up Samantha's supple inner thighs while she bent to taste her for the first time. She ran her tongue along her wet opening before teasing her way to her clit. She licked across the top of it, then circled it several times before licking back and burying her tongue inside her. She lapped at Samantha's creamy walls and struggled to lick deeper. She wanted to taste more of her. She was delicious beyond words, and Joey wanted and needed more.

"Come here," Samantha whispered, breaking Joey's concentration. Joey moved up her body and propped herself above her.

"What? Is something wrong?"

"No, my love. Everything you're doing is just right." She kissed Joey as she fumbled to unknot her tie. She cast the tie aside and unbuttoned her shirt with Joey's help. Together they got her shirt and undershirt off.

Joey stood on unsteady legs and stepped out of her slacks and boxers. She stood naked before Samantha, who reached out and placed her hand on Joey's trim stomach.

"You're gorgeous," she said. "Just as I knew you would be."

She guided her hand down and dragged her hand between Joey's legs. Joey couldn't suppress a shiver as Samantha's fingers crossed her nerve center. "You're so wet."

"I'm always wet when I'm around you."

"Step closer."

Joey did and was rewarded as Samantha entered her. Her knees went weak, and she struggled to stay standing as the sensations shot through her body. Samantha moved her fingers inside Joey while she skimmed her thumb over her clit. Joey bent over and kissed Samantha as she ran her own hand down between her legs again. She buried three fingers in Samantha and moved them in and out, plunging them deeper with each thrust.

She was having a hard time concentrating as Samantha continued to play between her legs. She had waited so long to bring Samantha to an orgasm and wanted so desperately to give her that pleasure but wasn't sure she wouldn't come first.

She placed her hand on Samantha's wrist. "You need to stop."

"Why?"

"I'm getting too close. I won't be able to hold off much longer."

"That's wonderful." Samantha's eyes lit up. "Come for me, Joey."

"Ladies first."

Samantha took her hand back and placed it on Joey's hip. She pulled her close and darted her tongue between Joey's legs.

"Holy fuck, baby," Joey said through clenched teeth. Waves of heat rolled over her, and she fought not to give in to the climax just seconds away. She stepped back.

"You taste wonderful," Samantha said. "Get back here."

"I can't." Joey climbed back on the bed and between Samantha's legs. She spread her own legs, hoping that the air might cool the fire burning between them. She ran her tongue along the length of Samantha again, then settled in, licking her clit while she slipped her fingers back inside her.

She reached her free hand up and teased a nipple. She felt Samantha running her hand along her arm as her breathing grew heavier. A moment later, her arm was in a firm grip as Samantha held tightly while the orgasm tore through her body. Joey kept her fingers deep and licked frantically at her clit as she tried to extend Samantha's ride.

Joey smiled to herself as she felt Samantha's body relax. She slowed her licking and sucked Samantha's clit between her teeth.

"No, no." Samantha laughed softly. "I'm much too sensitive for that."

"But I'm not through."

"You are for now."

Every nerve in Joey's body tingled as she climbed up and took Samantha in her arms. She kissed her shoulder and sighed as Samantha nestled against her.

"You were amazing," Samantha said.

"As were you. I want to make you do that over and over."

"The night is young."

"So it is."

Joey felt Samantha's hand between her legs again and rolled onto her back, letting them fall open.

"I can't believe how wet you are." Samantha moved her fingers along every inch.

Joey's clit swelled, pleading for release. She arched her hips, trying to make contact with Samantha, but Samantha seemed intent on spreading her with her fingers and letting one tip tease just inside.

Samantha moved lower and sucked greedily on Joey's nipple, taking the top part of her breast with it. She played over it with her tongue, flicking and licking the erect nipple.

Joey was covered in goose bumps. White-hot chills coursed through her as she bit her lip and experienced Samantha's ministrations. She felt like her clit was three inches long, standing there waiting to be stroked. She fought hard not to reach down and touch it herself.

Samantha finally released her breast and kissed down her belly.

"I love your stomach. You're in such great shape," she murmured against Joey. She kissed lower, then back up. "I could spend all day kissing your belly."

"While I appreciate that," Joey swallowed hard, "there's another part down there just begging for your kiss."

"What part might that be?" Samantha kissed lower. Joey watched her stare at her clit and gasped when she blew on it.

"Oh, shit! That's not fair."

"You don't think you need to be cooled down?"

Joey laughed, as much to keep from crying as in response to Samantha.

Samantha looked up at Joey and lowered her mouth until it was hovering over her. She felt Samantha's breath on her clit and held her own, waiting. Samantha moved her mouth and sucked on Joey's engorged lips.

"Sweet Jesus! You're cruel." Samantha's mouth felt amazing on her. Her finger continued to tease her. But she needed more. And she knew Samantha knew it.

Joey watched Samantha licking and sucking her and was about to swallow her pride and beg when she felt Samantha's fingers plunge deep inside as her tongue finally found Joey's throbbing clit.

"Oh, fuck! Fuck yes!" Joey lay back and closed her eyes, reveling in the shock waves Samantha's tongue was creating. She arched her hips to meet Samantha's thrusting fingers and gyrated against her tongue.

She felt Samantha's mouth close and suck on her, and bright lights exploded behind her eyelids. She felt the storm brewing in her center and mentally coaxed Samantha on until the storm clouds burst open and lightning shot through her body, sending sizzling bolts to her extremities. Samantha continued to lick her, and she felt the clouds forming again. Incapable of thinking, she felt the explosion rock her body again and rode it until her muscles finally unclenched and she lay spent.

Joey felt Samantha's tongue still licking between her legs. "I'm wiped, babe. There's no more."

"But you taste so damned good. I'm not ready to stop, even if you are."

"I'm serious." Joey laughed. "You're not going to get anything more out of me."

"I'm not trying to. I'm simply enjoying myself."

Joey propped herself up and watched Samantha's head bob as she continued to clean her with her tongue.

"You do realize the more you clean, the more you create?"

"So more for me to enjoy."

"Why don't you come up here?"

Samantha joined her, and Joey kissed her while grazing her hand over her body yet again. She nibbled her way down Samantha's neck to her breasts and lovingly kissed all over them. She moved her hand between Samantha's legs and lightly rubbed her clit. "Still too sensitive?"

"Not at all."

Joey pulled a nipple with her teeth and pressed harder into Samantha's clit. She moved her fingers lower and entered her briefly before moving them back to her clit.

"Oh, yes, Joey. That's it."

Joey continued licking and biting Samantha's nipples while her fingers made deliberate little circles. She pressed harder and harder, and soon Samantha's hips were bucking as Joey kept her pattern consistent.

Samantha moved her hand between her legs and placed it on Joey's. They slid over each other at first, but soon Samantha was guiding Joey's hand, using it to fuck herself just where she needed.

Joey allowed her hand to be used by Samantha and was rewarded as Samantha almost crushed her fingers as she pressed her into her clit and screamed. Joey felt her clit throbbing as the orgasm reached its crescendo and subsided.

Samantha rolled over and snuggled against Joey, who welcomed her with an outstretched arm. She pulled her close and held her against her. They lay in comfortable silence for a few minutes.

"Do you need me to take you home?" Samantha finally asked.

Joey lay still, pondering the question. She was quite content to hold Samantha, but she wondered how long that would last. She knew eventually, she'd want to leave. But she wasn't ready just then. "No. I think I'm okay for now."

Samantha raised her head and smiled at Joey. "Well, just let me know."

"Will do." She kissed the top of Samantha's head and allowed herself to relax.

Several hours later, Joey woke to find Samantha had rolled away. Feeling alone and not enjoying it, she rolled over and wrapped her arms around her and fell back to sleep.

CHAPTER FIFTEEN

Joey woke in the morning to an empty bed. She quickly donned her boxers and undershirt and padded to the kitchen, following the scent of bacon and coffee. Finding the kitchen empty, she poured herself a cup of coffee and stepped outside, where she discovered Samantha sitting at a picnic table reading the paper.

"How long have you been up?"

"Not long."

"Why didn't you wake me?"

"You work hard. I thought you needed your rest."

Joey sat across from her and squirmed as Samantha stared. "What?"

"Nothing." Samantha smiled. "I was just kind of surprised to see you in my bed this morning."

"Well, I wasn't going to walk home."

"I told you I'd give you a ride." The smile faded somewhat.

"I'm just teasing, babe. I enjoyed staying with you."

Samantha arched an eyebrow.

"What?" Joey said again.

"I'm just surprised is all."

"Tell me about it." She stood. "Now how do you like your eggs? I'm cooking."

"Oh, no. No eggs."

"Why not?"

"They make me nauseous."

"You don't like eggs?"

"Well, normally I do."

Joey's eyes widened as her gaze fell to Samantha's belly. "Oh, yeah. I guess I'd kind of forgotten."

"I don't buy that for a minute."

Joey sat back down. "I guess now would be as good a time as any to talk about that, huh?"

"So she still scares you?"

"Well, yeah. I mean, I've never gotten into kids."

"It's still a long way off. No one has you signed up for diaper duty yet."

"I know. But…"

"But what?"

"Well…" Joey struggled with what she wanted to say. She was most definitely seeing herself with Samantha for more than a few months. On one hand, that terrified her. Admitting it terrified her more. "Don't you maybe see us together then?"

"I'd like that."

"I just don't know that I'm cut out for a ready-made family."

"As I said, it's not like this is happening tomorrow. Let's see how we do as an 'us' before we go worrying about a family."

"But one's on the way. There's no getting around that."

"You need to be honest with me now, Joey. Is this a deal breaker? I'd rather find out now than when I'm in too deep."

Joey sat silently contemplating the question. She didn't want to give up a shot at something with Samantha. That feeling was unfamiliar enough for her. She was in uncharted territory and wasn't sure how far she was willing to go. Staying with Samantha meant becoming a parent. The thought made her shudder.

"I suppose that answers it then," Samantha said. "I kind of wish we'd had this conversation before last night."

"I haven't answered yet," Joey protested.

"Yes, you did."

"I don't know the answer. If I don't know it, how can you?"

"I think you do know it. Get dressed. I'll drive you home."

"No. I'm scared, Samantha. This whole relationship thing is new to me. Don't be like this. Give me a break."

Samantha blinked back tears. "It's not worth trying."

"I think it is."

"What?"

Joey didn't know where the words came from, but they were out and now that she'd heard them, she knew it was truly how she felt.

"I said I think it is worth trying. I'm not ready to give up. And we'll just deal with the little booger as we go."

"Little booger?"

"Isn't that how big it is now?"

"She's actually about ten inches long."

"No shit? How far along are we?"

"We?"

"I may as well get used to it." The idea of a miniature Samantha coming into the world seemed easier for Joey to focus on, so she held on to the idea and decided to be as positive as she could.

"About five months."

Joey nodded and tried to visualize Samantha with a protruding belly.

"What are you thinking?" Samantha asked.

"Just wondering how you'll look when you're waddling and all."

"You make it sound so wonderful." Samantha rolled her eyes.

"Well…"

"Joey, I'm serious. If the idea of dealing with me when I look like I've swallowed a watermelon or dealing with a baby is that horrible to you, please just say so."

"I've already said I'm staying. Now how about some breakfast?" She stood and walked over to Samantha.

"You know, my body's going to change in other ways, too. And soon."

"Can't we just worry about things when they happen?"

Samantha smiled a wicked grin. "I suppose."

"You're making me nervous."

"And you're making me horny." She reached out and grabbed Joey's waistband, pulling her close. She sucked Joey's breast through her undershirt. "I can't get enough of you."

Joey pulled her up and slipped a hand under her satin robe to cup a breast. She kissed her eagerly as her hands untied her belt. She peeled it back and admired Samantha's body anew.

"We're in broad daylight," Samantha said.

"You have fences and trees. No one can see us." She laid the robe on the picnic table and kissed Samantha again, bending her until she was on the table. She kissed down her body, pausing briefly to kiss her nipples, then traced her tongue down her stomach. She bent over and placed Samantha's legs over her shoulders. She ran her tongue between her legs, swirling it inside her then flattening it over her clit. Her own arousal heightened as she felt Samantha's clit grow.

She glanced up and saw Samantha fondling her breasts, and the sight aroused her further. She doubled her attention on Samantha. She grabbed her hips and held her closer while her tongue moved all over her. She licked and sucked Samantha's swollen clit until Samantha arched her hips and froze, then slowly lowered them again.

"God, baby. I love your tongue."

Joey smiled and continued to lick until the throbbing in Samantha's clit subsided. She kissed up her belly, then stood.

"I feel weird kissing her."

"But you do it so well."

"What? No." Joey laughed. "Not *her*. I enjoy kissing her. I meant Little Booger."

Samantha sat up. "She needs love, too. And maybe she likes your kisses."

"Oh, shit. Do you think she knows what we're doing out here?"

It was Samantha's turn to laugh. "Oh, Joey. You really are too cute."

"I'm also starving. I'll make pancakes."

Samantha put her robe on and went back to her paper while Joey made breakfast. They ate in the sun and finished around ten o'clock. Joey felt herself growing antsy. She was enjoying her time with Samantha but was feeling the need for time away.

"Why don't you get dressed while I do dishes?" Samantha said. "Then I'll give you a ride home."

Joey was dumbfounded at the way Samantha read her. She wanted to protest to be polite but thought better of it. "You wouldn't mind?"

"Of course not. I've still got some prep work to do for tomorrow, and I'm sure you have things to do. One night together doesn't mean you've moved in."

"You're the greatest." Joey kissed her and hurried into the house to dress. When she picked up her slacks from the floor, she grabbed her phone to check for messages. There were several from Mel asking where she was. Apparently, she'd shown up at Joey's an hour earlier and discovered her house empty.

Joey quickly texted her and told her she was on her way. She finished dressing and got to the kitchen in time to dry the dishes so Samantha could put some clothes on.

Samantha met her in the kitchen. "You are such a sweetheart. Thank you for breakfast this morning."

"No problem. I don't mind cooking on occasion."

Samantha wrapped her arms around Joey. "And thank you for staying the night."

"My pleasure. It really wasn't that bad." She pulled Samantha close.

"Wasn't that bad?"

"I'm teasing, babe. I really did enjoy staying here. I was lonely when I woke up and you were gone."

"You always know just what to say."

"Let's hope that's always the case."

"I don't expect perfection."

"Thank God for that."

They laughed and kissed and walked hand in hand to Samantha's car.

❖

"Mel's here early," Samantha said when she pulled up in front of Joey's house.

"She's been here for an hour worrying about me." Joey laughed. "I finally got her text when I was getting dressed."

"Are you guys going surfing?"

"Probably. It's a beautiful day for it."

"Well, have fun. I'll talk to you a little later."

Joey kissed Samantha and got out of the car. She let herself into the house to find Mel on the couch watching cartoons.

Mel stared at Joey, obviously taking in her attire.

"Looks like somebody had a sleepover."

"Indeed. Are we gonna catch some waves?"

"Yeah. Get changed."

Joey was in her room changing when Mel called down the hall. "So is the drought over?"

Joey walked out in her trunks and shirt. "Yes. It's over."

"And?"

"And what?"

"How was she? Was it worth the wait?"

"Ah, shit, Mel. I don't want to talk about it like that."

"What? Ice Princess finally puts out, and I don't get any details?"

"I don't know. I don't feel right talking about it."

"What the fuck? You've got it worse than I thought. And you spent the night. That's damned near a first for you."

"Is it going to be like this all day?"

"Only until you spill. Was she fast like a rabbit or languid like a cat?"

"Let's hit the waves."

Mel followed Joey to the van. "Come on, man. This is me you're talking to."

"It was weird, okay?"

"Weird? You've done some pretty kinky things. What do you mean by weird?"

"I can't explain it. It was just, like, weird."

"You have such a way with words, Romeo. Spit it out. Pain? Blood? What?"

"Not that kind of weird." She climbed out of the van in the parking lot of The Shack.

"Well, then, what?" Mel struggled to keep up with her across the sand.

Joey paddled out in the water without answering. Mel caught up to her and straddled her board next to Joey.

"What?"

"You'll think I'm a total douche."

"I already do." Mel laughed. "So spill."

"It was, like, I don't know."

"Yeah, weird. I got that."

"No, it was intense, you know?"

"How so?"

"Like pleasing her wasn't like a conquest or anything. It wasn't just trying to get her off to prove I could."

"You mean you wanted to please her to actually please her? You did it for her and not just you?"

"Exactly. And it wasn't like two people fucking. There was this connection there."

"Oh, my God! You're not a virgin anymore."

"Very funny."

"I mean it. You finally made love. Pretty amazing, right?"

"Fuckin' a!" She shook her head slowly. "I'm still trying to wrap my brain around it."

"And sleeping with her, I mean after. Did she make you?"

"No. She actually offered to take me home."

"Damn. Sounds like she gets you."

"Yeah, it was an awesome experience." Joey stared off into the distance.

"Hey, I hate to bring you back to earth and all, but have you forgotten her situation?"

"Situation?"

"You know." She motioned at a rounded belly.

"We talked about that this morning."

"And?"

"I don't know, Mel. I'm not ready to be a mom, but I'm not ready to walk away. And she tried to make me leave this morning. She didn't think I'd stick around when it's born, so she told me I should just leave now."

"And you didn't?"

"I don't know. There's something kind of cool about the idea of a little Samantha running around."

"Oh, man! You've got it bad."

"Don't make fun of me. This isn't easy."

"I'm not making fun of you. You're just blowing my mind. Personally, I think it's pretty cool."

"But it's hard, you know?"

"What?"

"Like, reconciling who I've always been and how I see myself and how others see me with what I'll have to become. Part of me can see me hanging with Samantha and the little one, but part of me says that's not for Joey Scarpetti."

"Hate to say it, pal, but people grow up. Maybe it's that time for you."

"Right, but I never planned on doing that. So it's hard to admit it could happen. Does that make sense?"

"You've got a lot to think about, my friend."

"It makes my head spin."

"Well, remember I'm always here for you if you need to voice your thoughts."

"I appreciate that. Now let's catch some waves."

CHAPTER SIXTEEN

Joey stepped out of the shower and heard her phone ringing. She answered immediately when she saw it was Samantha. "Hey, babe."

"Hi there. What are you doing?" Samantha asked.

"Just got out of the shower."

"How was surfing?"

"It was nice. What are you up to?"

"I was wondering if you wanted to come over for dinner tonight."

Joey thought about it for a minute. Dinner would be wonderful. Dessert would be better. Either way, time with Samantha sounded fantastic.

"You know, now that we're out about us, you should let me take you out to dinner."

"That sounds wonderful. Where shall we go?"

There were only a few restaurants in town, but Joey was determined not to go to Somerset for their first dinner date.

"Let's go to Suzette's." She settled on the town's crepe house.

"That would be very nice. What time?"

"I'll pick you up around six."

❖

Joey knocked on Samantha's door at precisely six o'clock, dressed in tan cargo shorts and a green golf shirt. Samantha was laughing when she opened the door.

"What's so funny?" Joey asked.

"I don't know. Something about you knocking amused me."

"Would you expect me to just walk in?"

Samantha cocked her head.

"I kind of think I would."

"I'll remember that for next time."

She stepped in and took Samantha in her arms, crushing her lips in a smoldering kiss. She ran her hands over the yellow chiffon Samantha was wearing, cupping her breasts and teasing her nipple.

"It's good to see you, too," Samantha said when the kiss ended.

"My whole body heats up anytime I'm around you." Joey kissed her neck and sucked an earlobe. "I can't get enough of you."

Joey reached around and unzipped Samantha's dress, stepping back as it fell to the floor. She helped Samantha get her own shirts over her head and kissed her again, walking her back to the bedroom.

They fell onto the bed as hands roamed over each other. Samantha squeezed and pulled on Joey's breasts, then replaced her hand with her mouth as she sucked and played with the tip.

Jolts of electricity shot through Joey. Her nipple was directly wired to her clit and the current that coursed between them was white hot. She felt the burning of Samantha's sucking and knew she was leaving a mark, but Joey didn't care.

Samantha moved her hand down Joey's tight stomach and slipped it under the waistband of her boxers. She found Joey hot and wet for her and quickly slid her fingers inside. Joey struggled out of her boxers and opened her legs wider.

She got Samantha's bra off and ran her fingers over her nipples before moving her hand lower to tease Samantha through her panties. Samantha's crotch was drenched and her clit poked at Joey's hand as she played.

"Get up here," Joey pleaded.

"Hmm?"

"Get these off." She tugged at the undergarment.

Samantha stopped what she was doing and quickly stripped for Joey, who expertly guided her to her face. Samantha lowered herself to Joey's mouth then leaned forward to get back inside her. She ran her hand over Joey's bundle of nerves before easing her fingers back inside. She bent to take her clit in her mouth as Joey's tongue frolicked between her legs.

Joey devoured Samantha's offering, working her tongue over every available inch of her. Joey buried her tongue inside, happily tasting her depths. Her flavor was light yet delicious and Joey couldn't get enough. She pulled Samantha closer to her and craned her neck to get as deep as she could.

She moved her mouth to Samantha's clit and sucked it between her teeth all the while moving her hips to the rhythm of Samantha's tongue. Her focus wavered as she neared her climax, but she fought to stay on task. She continued to flick her tongue until Samantha finally cried out and shuddered over her.

Samantha climbed off Joey and moved between her legs, working her mouth and fingers intently. Her fingers moved in and out while her tongue went back to lapping at Joey's clit.

Joey tangled her hands in Samantha's hair and held her to her as she moved her hips against her. She lost all thought and could do nothing but feel as the waves of orgasms crashed over her, one after the other until she was lost in a sea of convulsions.

When she returned to reality, Samantha moved up to lie next to her.

"A little dessert before dinner, huh?"

"That was nice," Joey said.

"Very."

Samantha propped herself up.

"Are you going to need a nap now?"

"No. Why?"

"Because I'm famished."

"Ah, yes." Joey laughed. "I'm here to take you out for dinner, not have you for dinner."

"Precisely."

They got up and dressed, with Samantha opting for a light blue cotton frock, rather than the now wrinkled yellow chiffon.

"Sorry about your dress." Joey was chagrined. "It looked nice while it was on."

"Thank you, sweetheart." Samantha smiled. "And no need to apologize. It was well worth the wrinkles."

They arrived at the restaurant and stood waiting to be seated. Joey had her arm around Samantha's waist and felt all eyes on her. She felt like part of a freak show.

"Why does everybody have to stare?" she whispered in Samantha's ear.

"When was the last time you brought a date here?"

"Joey and Samantha!" The owner hurried over to greet them. "So nice of Mabon Tir's newest couple to join us."

Joey smiled at her name linked with Samantha's. It sounded good. It sounded right. She pulled Samantha closer.

"Good to see you, Suzie," Joey said, shaking the hand of the tall, thin woman.

"Follow me. I have the perfect table for you."

They walked behind her to the center of the restaurant and were shown to a table for two beside a large white fountain.

"This is perfect," Samantha said as Joey held her seat for her.

They felt like local celebrities as patrons kept stopping by to say hello or to wish Samantha luck on the new day-care center. They finally managed to finish their dinners and split a chocolate mousse crepe for dessert.

"I'm stuffed," Samantha announced as they walked out to the truck. "That was delicious. Thank you."

"My pleasure." Joey pressed Samantha's back against her truck as she kissed her. Samantha opened her mouth and locked her hands behind Joey's neck, pulling her close.

They kissed for several minutes, oblivious to anything going on around them. Samantha came to her senses first.

"That was some kiss."

"Yeah it was. There are plenty more where that came from."

"Hopefully, they won't all be in a parking lot downtown."

Joey looked around. "I'm sorry. I forgot you don't do PDAs."

"It seems to me I was an active participant," Samantha said. "Although, you're right. As a rule, I don't make out in public."

"Well, then let's get home and do it in private."

Joey held the door open for her and smiled as she looked at her. She thought Samantha more beautiful now than the first day she'd shown up on the jobsite.

"You're gorgeous," she said, before closing the door.

"What was that for?" Samantha asked as Joey started the truck.

"I don't know, but it's true. It boggles my mind how beautiful you are."

"Well, thank you, but you're not lacking in the looks department either."

"Thanks for that, but you're stunning. I mean, like, breathtaking."

Samantha simply stared at Joey and smiled the rest of the way home.

"Am I coming in?" Joey asked as she pulled up in front of the house.

"I hope so."

They had barely closed the front door behind them when Samantha was in Joey's arms, leaning her body against her and nibbling her neck.

Joey quickly tilted Samantha's chin and captured her mouth with her own. She ran her hands up and down Samantha's back trying to find her zipper.

"This is a pullover," Samantha said, lifting the dress over her head. She took Joey's hand and led her to the couch. She quickly removed her underclothes and lay on the couch, one leg over the back. She lightly dragged her hand between her legs.

Joey stood watching Samantha's hand.

"Are you sure the bed wouldn't be more comfortable?"

"With your reputation, I find it hard to believe you confine your escapades to the bedroom."

Joey lay across the couch and buried her face in Samantha's pussy. She licked and sucked her swollen lips, then lightly dragged her tongue over her clit.

"You taste so fucking good," she murmured.

Joey teased Samantha with her fingers, tracing her opening and slipping just her fingertips in before pulling them out.

"Please. Don't. No teasing. I need you, baby."

Joey smiled to herself as she finally plunged her fingers deep and licked in earnest at the hardness of her clit. Samantha gyrated her hips against Joey, who kept her rhythm steady. Samantha was moaning, her breathing coming in gasps until finally she stilled and Joey felt her pussy tighten around her fingers, pulsing as she climaxed.

"Your touch is magical," Samantha said when she'd caught her breath.

"You're so easy to please. I love how quickly you come."

Joey sat up and let Samantha stretch her legs over her lap. She ran her hands over the long, shapely limbs.

"I'm glad that's not a bad thing."

"Not at all. It just shows you're always aroused and ready. I love that."

Samantha looked Joey up and down.

"Aren't you a little overdressed?"

"Ah, my sweet, as much as I'd love to get naked with you, I need to get going. You have a big day ahead of you tomorrow."

"What will you be doing tomorrow?"

"I don't know. I haven't heard from Brenda yet."

"I'd love for you to stay, but I understand what you mean. I need to be fully rested for tomorrow."

"Are you excited?"

"Very."

"What made you decide to open a daycare center, anyway?"

"I wanted to move here after…"

"Got it."

Samantha drew a deep breath and continued. "Anyway, I wanted to move back, but wanted to do something that would help the community."

"You could have practiced law here."

"But that wouldn't help the people of the town every day. I wanted to make a daily difference in the lives of the townswomen. I looked into the demographics and realized that a daycare center would work very well."

"Have you always been into kids?"

"I have. I was a camp counselor in my younger days. I've always babysat. I really do love kids."

"Did you always know you'd have one?"

"I don't think so. I used to think my sexuality precluded me. But, obviously, I learned quickly that wasn't the case."

"Well, I hope your first day tomorrow is a huge success."

"It shouldn't be too hard. There aren't a lot of kids yet. It'll be fun."

"Okay. If you say so." She moved Samantha's legs off her and stood. "Walk me to the door?"

"How about you kiss me good night here?"

Joey gazed at her, lounging naked on the couch. She bent over and kissed her.

"I'll talk to you tomorrow. Good luck."

❖

Joey stopped by Passion Petals and picked up a nice summer bouquet on her way to Samantha's house the following evening. When she arrived, she started to knock, but remembered Samantha's invitation for her to walk in. She let herself in and found Samantha at the stove.

"I can't believe you wanted to make dinner after your first day of work," Joey said before kissing the back of her neck.

Samantha turned, her face lighting up at the sight of the flowers Joey brought. She threw her arms around Joey and pulled her in for a kiss.

"I'm energized," Samantha said. "I'm totally buzzed and needed something to do with all this energy."

"I know something we could do to burn energy."

"I'm sure you do." She turned back to the stove. "How was your day?"

"Not bad. Didn't really do much. Surfed, hung out with Mel."

"Did you hear from Brenda?"

"Finally. We're going to build some houses on the north end of town."

"It's nice to see this place growing."

Samantha served up stir-fry and carried the plates to the table. Joey grabbed a glass of water for Samantha and a beer for herself then joined her.

"This looks great," she said as she sat across from Samantha.

"Not to terrify you, but I could really get used to this."

"It is nice. And don't worry. I'm not as scared as I should be."

"As you should be?"

"Well, you know. As I normally would be. Never mind, I'm going to shut up now."

"You don't need to shut up." Samantha laughed. "You're cute when you get flustered."

"Very funny."

Joey cleared the table and started loading the dishwasher. It was a few minutes later that Samantha joined her, wearing a yellow robe.

"You look relaxed," Joey said.

"I'm feeling anything but."

"Is that right?" Joey arched an eyebrow.

Samantha reached into the pocket of the robe and pulled out a slim vibrator. She pulled her robe to the side, revealing one pert breast. The only sound was that of the slight buzzing as she drew the tip of the toy over her nipple.

Joey watched as Samantha looked down at her breast. She held it in one hand and ran the vibrator around and around her nipple, then across the tip of it. She finally looked up at Joey, who stepped forward and untied Samantha's sash, allowing the robe to fall open. She gazed longingly at the shapely body on display.

Samantha walked out of the kitchen and Joey followed. Samantha sat on the dining table and ran the toy between her legs. Joey was mesmerized as she watched the thin purple toy cross her clit then disappear inside Samantha.

Samantha withdrew the toy and pressed it to Joey's lips. She coated her lips with juices then licked her lips, tasting herself before sliding her tongue in Joey's mouth.

Joey's head was swimming. She was more aroused than ever as she tasted Samantha on her tongue. She pulled Samantha to her and kissed her harder. She felt Samantha unbuttoning her shorts and felt them fall to the ground. She felt the slick toy against her thigh as Samantha moved it under the legs of her boxers. When the tip of the vibrator reached her clit, she gasped.

Samantha moved the toy inside Joey and thrust it deep several times. Joey struggled to stay standing. Samantha slowly slid it out and put it back inside herself.

Joey watched as Samantha worked the vibrator, only losing sight as she took her shirts off. She stepped out of her boxers and leaned in to kiss Samantha, who moved the toy back inside Joey while they kissed.

"You're killing me," Joey said.

"What a way to go." Samantha continued to move the vibrator in and out of Joey.

Joey reached between her legs and tried to take the toy from Samantha, who would not relinquish control.

"Just relax and go with it."

Joey was about to protest when Samantha slipped the toy out of Joey and back inside herself. Again, Joey tried to take it.

"Don't you like to watch?"

"I can watch just as easily if I'm holding that." Her voice was husky with need.

"Mm, I love how this feels." She pressed the tip of it into her clit.

Joey stared between Samantha's legs, enthralled by what was playing out. She plunged her fingers inside Samantha and stroked her while Samantha kept the vibrator pressed to her clit.

"Oh, dear God. I'm so close," Samantha mewled.

"Yes, come for me, baby."

Samantha gently pushed Joey away and held the vibrator against Joey's clit again.

"You first," she said.

"Not fair," Joey said through gritted teeth.

"I want to watch you come." She leaned forward and took Joey's breast in her mouth while she held the slippery toy against her clit. She rolled the vibrator around, keeping it pressed to her as she sucked hard on her nipple.

"Oh, fuck." Joey gave up hope of holding out. She held tightly to Samantha as her knees weakened when the climax hit. She struggled to stay upright as her muscles turned to mush, leaving her weak and spent.

"Happy?" she asked.

"Very." Samantha smiled. "Thank you."

Samantha handed the toy to Joey and kissed her as Joey slid the toy inside her then pulled it out and kept it against her clit. She moved the length of the toy against her clit as the tip teased her opening, barely entering before Joey pulled it back again.

Joey moved her mouth away and kissed lower, closing on an erect nipple and sucking hard.

Samantha dug her fingernails into Joey's back and clenched tightly as she screamed. Joey kept the vibrator in place, holding it there as Samantha cried out again and again.

When she was coherent, Samantha took the toy from Joey and sucked it clean. She slid off the table and fastened her robe anew.

"The dining room table? Seriously?" Joey asked.

"This house has quite a few rooms and I figure we need to christen each one."

Joey laughed, realizing Samantha was not only drop dead gorgeous, but a lot of fun as well.

"That sounds like a great idea." Joey kissed her and reluctantly dressed. "Same time tomorrow?"

"Sounds wonderful."

Joey kissed her good night and drove home. She missed Samantha already.

CHAPTER SEVENTEEN

Joey was exhausted the following Friday when she pulled up to Samantha's house. The crew had poured the foundation for five houses that day and she was beat. Brenda had even approved overtime for them so they could finish. Joey didn't even go surfing with Mel after work. She texted Samantha, who left work early to meet her at her house.

Joey stripped and took a hot shower as soon as she arrived, then walked in to the bedroom naked.

"I have nothing to put on," she complained. "This wasn't very well thought out."

"I think you look great like that." Samantha patted the bed next to her.

"I'm sorry, but if I lie down, I may fall asleep."

"Why don't we go out to the hot tub?"

"That sounds wonderful."

Samantha grabbed some thick, oversized towels and followed Joey outside. The fog was already rolling in and there was a chill in the early evening air. Samantha turned on the bubbles, and they sank to their chins in the hot water.

"Oh, my God, this feels amazing," Joey said, positioning herself so one jet could blow on her back and another on her shoulder.

"You really worked hard today, didn't you?"

"You wouldn't believe how hard Brenda pushed us."

"Did you do good work, though?"

"Oh, yeah. Even when we bust our asses, we don't do shoddy work. Everything is perfect."

"I love that about you guys."

"We work hard and we do good work. There's no denying that."

"And now you're exhausted."

"I am. I haven't been this tired in a very long time."

Samantha rested her head on Joey's shoulder.

"Does this hurt?"

"Babe, your touch does anything but hurt."

"Don't encourage me."

Joey laughed.

"Are you trying to see if I can butch up past the exhaustion?"

"Maybe."

"I don't think I could ever pass up making love with you."

Samantha kissed her and settled back against her. Joey took her onto her lap and kissed her again.

"I see you're open for business," Joey said.

"Help yourself."

Joey kissed Samantha's mouth, her neck, and her shoulders. She lifted one breast to kiss lovingly, then the other. Her body forgot its weariness as it was suddenly alive with passion.

"I wish I could describe what you do to me."

"Try."

"I can't." Joey refused to feel pressured to talk about things when all she wanted to do was feel.

She sucked Samantha's neck and nibbled her earlobe. Samantha's breasts floated above the water and were covered with goose bumps.

"Are you cold?"

"Quite the opposite."

"Yes, you are hot." Joey chuckled. She squeezed Samantha's breasts together and kissed the tops of them while her thumbs flicked her nipples.

"Touch me," Samantha pleaded.

"I'm busy," Joey said. "Touch yourself."

Samantha lowered a hand between her legs and moaned.

"Damned bubbles. I can't see," Joey said.

"Just imagine then," Samantha murmured. "Imagine soft, pink, and creamy."

Joey lifted a breast and took a nipple in her mouth, rolling her tongue over it.

"Yes, baby. That's it." Samantha arched her neck and threw her head back, her hand lazily stroking herself.

Joey sucked harder, pulling the hardened nub between her teeth.

"God, that feels good," Samantha said. She took one of Joey's hands and guided it between her legs. "That feels even better."

Joey wasted no time sliding three fingers inside Samantha. She moved her other hand behind her hips and held her closer, so she could get deeper. She wriggled her fingers and dragged them along the sensitive spots inside Samantha.

Samantha rocked on Joey's hand as she moved her own to her swollen clit and stroked it deliberately.

Joey felt Samantha's walls begin to tremor and quickened her pace as she moved in and out. She closed her mouth over Samantha's and felt her groan into it as her pussy tightened around her fingers.

Samantha climbed off Joey and forced her legs open and pressed her hand into Joey's clit. Joey closed her eyes and concentrated on the feelings Samantha was creating. She felt Samantha's fingers stroking her hard underside, her fingertips barely entering her, then pulling out to rub her swollen clit.

"Oh, right there," she whispered. "Don't stop. Please. Yes, oh yes." She bit her lip to keep from crying out as her body shuddered its release.

"Isn't it amazing how we can find energy when we think we have none?" Samantha asked.

"Well, I won't be finding any more tonight. That's for sure." Joey sank in the water.

"You won't be needing any more. I promise." Samantha climbed out of the tub and dried while Joey looked on.

"Suddenly I'm not so sure," Joey said. "I feel another surge coming on."

"Really?" Samantha rubbed the towel between her legs.

Joey got out of the water and grabbed a towel for herself. She quickly dried, then lead Samantha to the bedroom. Samantha fell back onto the bed and Joey was quickly between her legs, running her tongue over her lips and clit while she ran a finger around her opening.

She reached a hand up to pinch and tug a nipple while delving into her waiting pussy with the other. She sucked on Samantha's swollen lips and dragged her tongue over her clit.

"You know just what to do," Samantha gasped, arching her hips to increase contact with Joey's mouth.

Joey smiled against Samantha's clit as Samantha put her hand on the back of her head and held her in place. Barely able to breathe, Joey continued her ministrations, determined to give Samantha another climax.

Samantha screamed loudly as she moved against Joey's face and her pussy clenched around her tongue.

She lay there breathing heavily, offering no resistance as Joey pulled her into her arms and curled behind her. Joey kissed her shoulder before falling into a deep sleep.

Joey woke the next morning to the feel of Samantha's fingers probing inside her.

"Well, good morning to me." She spread her legs and watched as Samantha dipped her head to take her clit in her mouth.

"Oh my God. I'm going to come already." She clasped the sheet below her as the spasms racked her body.

"I've never come that quickly," she said.

"I'd been at it for a while before you woke," Samantha said.

"Then I don't feel quite so bad."

"You shouldn't. I love it when you come for me." She kissed Joey's inner thigh then moved up next to her. "Happy birthday."

"How'd you know?"

"It's a small town, sweetheart."

"Well, thank you for my birthday present." Joey laughed.

"Oh, Joey. That wasn't your birthday present."

"You mean there's more?"

Samantha padded to the dresser and took out a rectangular shaped box wrapped in black paper.

"Black? Really?"

"To mourn the loss of your youth." Samantha smiled as she handed it to Joey, then sat on the bed to watch her open it.

Joey tore open the paper and stared at the cardboard box.

"Open it!"

"I'm trying to imagine what you could have gotten me."

"It's actually something for us."

"Hmm...okay..." She opened the box and looked at Samantha. "More black?"

"Partially. Just take it out."

Joey grabbed a black strap and lifted out a harness with a red dildo hanging from it.

"Oh, my. I like."

"See? This short knobby end goes in you while you wear it." Samantha pointed to one end of the toy.

"Yes, I figured as much." She stood and stepped into the harness, inserting one end of the dildo inside.

Samantha stared at Joey's hard cock and absently stroked herself.

"You look so fucking hot," she said.

"So do you." Joey ran her hand over her shaft.

"I bet that feels good," Samantha said.

"I bet what you're doing does, too."

"It does. I'm so wet for you. Are you ready to fuck me?"

Before Joey could get on the bed, Samantha had climbed up onto her hands and knees, legs spread slightly.

"I want to feel you deep," she said.

Joey knelt behind her and guided the tip of her cock to Samantha's waiting pussy, but she quickly moved it away. She leaned into her, running the length of the toy between her legs, letting the tip glide over her clit to tease it. She leaned back and forth, rubbing it against her.

"It's not nice to tease," Samantha chastised her.

"But it's fun."

"I need you inside me. I want you to bury that thing all the way inside me."

Joey drew the cock back along Samantha and maneuvered it so its tip was pressing against her opening.

"Please. I need you in me."

Joey eased the dildo inside an inch or two, then withdrew it before sliding it in a little further and pulling it out again.

"Seriously? I'm about to rip the toy out of the harness and fuck myself with it!"

Joey just laughed as she plunged the toy in as deep as it would go, her thighs against Samantha.

"Like that?"

"Yes! Do that again, please!"

Joey rocked back and took the cock almost completely out before filling Samantha again. She repeated her actions, slowly at first, but with greater speed as her own body responded to the attention it was getting. Her clit was being rubbed with each thrust and she was struggling for control as she continued to wield the cock.

She bent over Samantha, pressing her breasts into her back and reached around to find her clit slick and engorged.

"Oh, fuck, baby. You feel like you're ready to explode."

"Come with me?" Samantha said.

Joey couldn't answer. She felt Samantha's clit throbbing then lost her ability to focus as her own orgasm robbed her of awareness of anything but the pleasure that washed over her. She collapsed on Samantha, spent from the force of the climax.

"Now you can thank me for your birthday present," Samantha said.

"Mm hm."

"Are you alive?"

"Barely." Joey eased herself off of Samantha, slowly drawing her cock out as she did. She rolled next to her, still trying to catch her breath.

"That was fucking amazing," she managed.

"It was pretty wonderful. And you didn't do so bad for an old woman."

"Was that necessary?"

"Yes, it was." She snuggled up against Joey.

"You're lucky you're cute."

"I'm lucky you think so."

"That I do."

"So what do you have planned for today?" Samantha asked.

"Not a damned thing. Mel will probably want to catch some waves, but that about covers it for me. Why?"

"Just wondering. Hey, maybe I can meet you and Mel at The Shack for dinner?"

"That sounds good."

"Let's get dressed and I'll take you to Nature's Bounty for breakfast."

"Oh man, an omelet sounds great." She swung her feet over the edge of the bed. "Shit! I don't have any clothes."

"That's right. Well, put on your grimy clothes and we'll stop by your place so you can change."

"I'll tell you what," Joey said after she was dressed. "I'll swing home and change and we'll meet for breakfast in half an hour."

"Am I ever going to see your place?"

"I suppose it's inevitable. But I plan to postpone it as long as I can."

"What's wrong with it? Seriously."

"It's a sty, babe. I mean, it's thrashed. Maybe someday I'll clean it and then I'll invite you over."

"Why not let me clean it?"

"That's not about to happen."

"Why not?"

"It's just not. Now let's not argue. I'll head home and we'll meet at the restaurant."

She kissed Samantha and turned to leave.

"Excuse me, but you're forgetting something." Samantha held up the harness and toy.

"That's staying here." Joey grinned. "I won't need it anywhere else."

Chapter Eighteen

A re you about ready for dinner?" Mel asked as she and Joey bobbed on their boards. The waves had died down, and the fog was beginning to edge in from the horizon.

"I'm meeting Samantha for dinner."

"What time? Because I'm getting cold, and the waves just aren't here anymore."

Joey checked her watch.

"Oh shit. I had no idea it was this late. Let's dry off, then I'll have to go."

They sat on their towels with other towels wrapped around them as they stared out at the ocean.

"What's it like being thirty?" Mel asked.

"Seriously? It's like being twenty-nine with a day added on."

"So, no earth shattering, monumental revelations this morning?"

"Please."

"How am I supposed to know? I'm not there yet."

"You really think you wake up one day and you feel different than you have in the past?"

"It could happen. I mean, you've changed a lot in the last month or so, anyway."

"It's not that I've changed, really. I'm still me."

"With a girlfriend."

"Well, there's that."

"And a kid on the way."

"That has nothing to do with getting older, though. That's all about finding the right woman."

"You really believe she's the one, don't you?"

"I wouldn't be with her if I didn't." Joey looked at her watch again. "We should get going."

They got their things and crossed the sand.

"What the hell," Joey said. "It looks like everyone in town decided to have dinner at The Shack tonight."

"No kidding. The place looks packed."

"I wonder what's going on."

They stowed their boards in Mel's van and slipped some sweatshirts on.

"I guess I'll see you later," Joey said.

"I think I'll come inside and say hi to Samantha."

They entered the restaurant to a resounding cry of, "Surprise!"

Joey looked around at the black balloons hanging from the ceiling and took in the crowd that had clearly gathered in her honor. She sought out Samantha and found her beaming at a back table. Joey quickly crossed the room to her.

"You are a devious one, aren't you?"

"Is that a bad thing?"

"No. I just need to keep my eye on you."

"There's lots of you I want on me."

Joey pulled her close and kissed her.

"I'm happy to oblige."

The crowd moved in on them, with everyone wishing Joey a happy birthday. When they finally sat down and ordered burgers, Joey looked around the restaurant and realized every table was taken by her friends.

"Did you reserve the place or something?"

"I did."

"I didn't realize this was the kind of place one could rent out for events."

"Well, they were happy to do this. This town really likes you, Joey."

"Still. This must have cost you a fortune."

"Not really. And I was happy to do it."

Joey stared hard at Samantha, realizing that there was still much about her she didn't know. She knew she came from money and had been a successful attorney, but she really had no idea how well off she was. She wasn't sure how she felt about it.

"What's up, handsome?" Samantha was watching her.

"Nothing. I was just thinking I may have found me a sugar mama."

"Oh, I hope that's not what I am."

"You're not. Although I think you may have a lot more money than I realized."

"I'm not obsessed with money, Joey. So please don't you be."

Joey made good money working for Brenda. She certainly wasn't in the poor house. But she was sure she couldn't compete with Samantha.

"I mean it, Joey," Samantha said.

"No worries." Joey smiled and kissed her.

Brenda and Liz wandered over and the festive mood returned. Soon everyone was eating and drinking and Joey was basking in the love from her community. She and Samantha got separated in the crowd, but Joey kept an eye on her. She loved watching Samantha interact with others. She was so graceful and beautiful, and Joey couldn't help but be proud to be in a relationship with her.

She watched as Samantha worked her way back through the crowd toward her. She opened her arms and embraced her, smiling at the happiness she'd finally found. She held Samantha to her until she felt something wet on her shirt.

"What the hell?" She backed away and looked at the wet spots.

"Oh, my God," Samantha exclaimed, folding her arms across her chest.

"What?" Joey asked. "What's going on?"

Tiffany's mom had been watching from a nearby table and quickly grabbed some napkins. She pulled Samantha into the bathroom, leaving Joey dumbfounded.

Mel was next to her in a minute.

"What was that all about?"

"Hell if I know."

"Is she okay?"

"I hope so. I'm totally lost here. Should I follow them?"

Before Mel could answer, Samantha emerged from the bathroom. "I'm afraid I need to go home," she said.

"What's going on? What happened? Why are our shirts wet? Are you okay?"

"I'm fine, just a little embarrassed and more than a little uncomfortable."

"I hear that." Joey was trying to dry the spots on her shirt. She started toward the door. "Let's go then."

Many of the townswomen had gathered around Samantha and were hugging her and chatting with her. Joey recognized that most of the women were parents. She wondered why they were suddenly drawn to her girlfriend but stood by the door until Samantha finally joined her.

"Do you mind telling me what that was all about?" Joey asked when they were alone in the car.

"I've started lactating."

"Huh? You've what?"

"My breasts are making milk."

"For Little Booger? But she's not due any time soon. Or is she coming early? Oh, shit."

"Calm down, Joey. She's not making her appearance. It's just something that happens."

Joey stared at the swollen breasts that she had just enjoyed the night before.

"What?" Samantha asked.

"So, is this like a one shot deal? Or will it happen off and on now?"

"No, sweetheart. Now that it's started, it won't stop."

"You mean your boobs are going to leak for the next few months?"

"Exactly."

"But…I mean, what about…well, what if I…"

"They're not going to stop leaking. If you touch them, you'll get wet."

"Bummer."

"I told you my body would be going through some changes."

"Yeah, you did. I just assumed you meant your belly would get big."

"Which it has, by the way."

"Just a little." She reached over and rubbed the small bulge.

Once at the house, Samantha took a shower while Joey lounged on the bed.

"I'm sorry I ruined your party." Samantha had tears in her eyes.

"Babe, it was no biggy." Joey sat upright, nervous and uncomfortable. "Please don't cry."

"I'm trying not to, but I feel so bad."

"You shouldn't. I had a great time. And just throwing that party for me was huge. You've nothing to feel bad about."

"But I wanted you to be able to relax and party with your friends." She sat on the edge of the bed and buried her face in her hands.

"And that I did. Babe, you're scaring me. I don't understand why you're so upset."

There was a knock on the door and Joey happily climbed out of bed.

"I'll get that. You get dressed."

Joey opened the door to find Brenda and Liz on the porch.

"Hey, guys. What's up?"

"Can we come in?" Brenda asked.

"Huh? Oh, sure. Um, Samantha will be right out. She just got out of the shower."

She moved aside and let them in.

"Go ahead and have a seat. I'll check on Samantha."

"You don't need to. I'm right here."

Joey turned to see Samantha in a pair of sweats and an oversized T-shirt. Her eyes were dry, and her smile seemed genuine. Joey stared momentarily before regaining her composure.

"Can I get anybody anything?" Samantha asked.

"We really just stopped by to make sure you're okay. That was an abrupt departure earlier."

"My breasts were leaking," Samantha said matter-of-factly.

Brenda looked decidedly uncomfortable and turned to Joey with a questioning look.

"I know, right?" Joey said. "Who knew? I guess it's normal, though."

"I've heard of that," Liz said. "I'm glad that's all it was. Do you need anything from us?"

"No, thank you. I'm sorry to have worried you."

Joey watched the exchange with growing curiosity. She wondered what had happened to the upset woman from a few minutes before. And if she'd be coming back any time soon.

❖

The rest of the weekend was uneventful and Monday after work, Joey hurried to get her tools packed.

"Where's the fire?" Mel asked.

"Samantha has an appointment this afternoon. She gets to find out the sex of the baby."

"No shit? That's kinda cool."

"She really wants a little girl, doesn't she?" Brenda joined them.

"She does."

"Dee wanted a boy."

"I'm not exactly sure what to say to that," Joey said.

"What do you want?" Mel asked.

"Me? I don't know. I guess I've always just assumed it'll be a little girl."

"I don't know that I can see you with a little girl."

"I can't see you with any kid," Brenda said. "But I wish you luck."

"Hey, if I can handle leaking boobs, I can handle anything."

"Yeah, right. She's the one I'm worried about. Having to babysit you and an infant."

"Joey, didn't you have to get going?" Mel said.

"Yeah. I do. Samantha's waiting for me. I'll see you two tomorrow."

She pulled up at the midwife's office and found Samantha still in the waiting room.

"I'm so glad you're not in there yet," she said.

"Me, too. Thank you for being here for this," Samantha said.

"I'm pretty excited, to be honest."

"Really? That's awesome."

The assistant called them back and Joey stood uncertainly.

"Come on, sweetheart. I want you in there with me."

Joey smiled and followed her, surprised at her own level of anticipation. She stood a discreet distance away while Samantha was weighed, then listened intently when the doctor came in and asked Samantha how she'd been feeling. They also talked about how the baby should be developing.

She was amazed when she heard the whirring sound that the doctor said was the baby's heartbeat. And she held Samantha's hand when it was time for the ultrasound. They watched the screen as the baby's head became apparent, then saw the outline of the arm against its belly. The midwife moved the hand piece and froze.

"Do you see that?" She moved so the picture shifted to the bottom of the baby's belly.

Joey strained to make out the details on the screen.

"That's definitely his penis," the midwife said.

Joey's heart skipped a beat. Suddenly, it all became real. There really was a little person inside Samantha. She was at once excited and terrified. She looked at Samantha, who squeezed her hand.

"Congratulations," the midwife said. "You've got a wonderfully developing baby boy inside you.

The midwife froze the screen and printed it, then took several more pictures for them. As she cleaned Samantha's belly, she asked if they had any questions.

"I don't think so," Samantha said, examining the pictures. "Thank you for these."

"You're quite welcome. We'll see you next month then."

She left them alone in the room.

"Are you okay that it's a boy?" Joey asked.

"Of course. As long as he's healthy."

"And she said he was."

"Yes, she did."

Joey walked Samantha to her car.

"Can I take you to dinner?" Joey asked.

"No. I think I'll just head home."

"I don't think I heard an invitation."

"I think I need to be alone."

"Hey, babe, please don't be too upset it's a boy. I know your heart was set on a girl, but you're still going to be a great mom."

"Thank you, Joey. I hope so."

"And I'll teach him to surf and play ball and build things."

Samantha rested her hand on Joey's chest.

"You'd like that, wouldn't you?"

"I think I would."

"You're a sweetheart."

"So, you're going to be okay?"

"Maybe you should come over."

"Great. I'll meet you there."

Joey followed Samantha home after texting Mel that it was a boy. She couldn't get over how excited she was and how much she was looking forward to meeting him in person. The visit had really changed her outlook. She was ready to start handing out cigars.

She walked into the house with Samantha and took her in her arms.

"This has got to be the coolest thing that has ever happened to me," she said. "This little guy is going to be such a stud. It's going to be awesome."

Samantha backed out of the embrace and looked at Joey with a touch of sadness in her eyes.

"Babe? What's wrong?"

"Dee really wanted a boy."

"So I heard." She sank on the couch.

"I don't know. I feel like this should be her baby boy."

"Well, in a way it always will be."

"I don't know how to say this."

"Say what?"

"I don't feel right sharing him with someone else."

"You mean as in me, don't you?"

Samantha nodded.

"Babe, nothing is going to bring Dee back. And I'm not trying to replace her. I'm not her. But I am someone who cares very much about you and that unborn little boy."

"And I know that. But it still feels wrong."

"What? Why? How?"

"I think I tried to move on before I was ready."

"Oh, no. Don't do this. Samantha, please."

"I'm sorry, Joey."

"Samantha, think about what you're saying."

"I know what I'm saying."

Joey lowered her face to her hands, unable to find the words she desperately needed.

"I think you'd better go now," Samantha said.

"This is bullshit!" Joey stood. "Kicking me out isn't going to bring her back. Nothing is. She's gone, Samantha. I'm here. I'm living and breathing and here."

"Good-bye, Joey."

Joey stared at Samantha, anger and sadness welling inside her. Samantha held the door open and Joey left, feeling like she'd left her soul behind.

CHAPTER NINETEEN

Joey was on the phone before she'd even buckled her seat belt.
"Hello?" Mel answered.

"Meet me at Spirits. We're drinking."

"When?"

"Now." She hung up and fired up her truck, fuming at how insensitive Samantha had been. Joey had been patient when she wasn't ready for sex. She'd worked hard to overcome her own fear of the small child growing inside her. Where did Samantha get off kicking her to the curb once Joey had finally settled in to a committed relationship and being a parent?

The parking lot was practically empty, for which she was grateful. The last thing she wanted was to talk to anyone but Mel, who walked in shortly after Joey.

"What's going on?" Mel asked.

"You want a shot, too? Or just beer?"

"Give us a small pitcher and a couple shots of Cuervo," Mel told the bartender, then looked at Joey. "What the fuck is going on?"

Joey took her shot and swallowed it, then ordered another.

Mel picked up the pitcher and glasses and moved to a booth. Joey followed after she'd downed her next shot.

"Trouble in paradise?" Mel asked.

"She fucking dumped me."

"She what? She dumped you? Did you like freak out at the appointment or something?"

"No! That's just it. Damn, Mel. You shoulda been there. That was the coolest thing I've ever experienced."

"Are you shittin' me?"

"No. Okay, so like first, we hear the heartbeat. No lie. You can actually hear its heartbeat. Sounded kinda like a washing machine, but whatever. It was totally cool. Then she did the ultrasound."

"The what? Was something wrong?"

"Heck no. The ultrasound is how we got to see the baby."

"You could see it? What did it look like?"

"Like a baby. We saw the head and the arm and the belly."

"And you thought this was cool?"

"Totally! And then we saw his little wee-wee."

"His what? Did you just say wee-wee?"

"What do you want me to call it? His dick? He's just a baby."

Mel shook her head and laughed. "Okay, so you saw it. So it's a boy."

"I was totally jacked! I was thinking how we could take him surfing and teach him to play football and—"

"Hold on there, daddy-mama. You were really thinking like this?"

"I was. I can't explain it. It suddenly became so real and so exciting."

"Okay, okay. I don't get it, but okay. So how did we end up here?"

"Dee wanted a boy."

"Yeah. So?"

"Well, apparently she feels like she's not being fair to Dee for letting me near the little guy."

"That makes no sense."

"Tell me."

"She really said that?"

"Pretty much."

"Joey, don't get pissed, but do you think maybe you're more scared than you thought and you misunderstood something she said? Maybe you twisted it in your brain to give yourself an out?"

"No chance. I begged her to let me stay."

"Damn, buddy. That sucks. I wonder if it's hormonal or something. Maybe she'll settle down."

"I don't know, Mel. She seemed pretty intent."

"I don't know what to say."

"Let's just shoot some pool and drink some beer. Maybe I'll forget about her."

"I'll rack." She got up, but turned to Joey. "What are you gonna tell Brenda tomorrow?"

"Who knows? Maybe I'll fucking tell her I quit."

"I'm serious."

"So am I. You know what a pain in the ass she's gonna be? She'll be all self-righteous and shit. I'm sure I'll hear 'I told you so' about a million times."

"It is gonna suck."

"Yeah. Well, she'll have to find out on her own. I'm sure as shit not telling her."

"You know she's going to ask about the appointment."

"I'm sure Liz has already called her. Hell, they probably already know I'm single."

"Maybe." Mel racked the balls and handed Joey a cue stick. "Maybe she'll have the decency to keep her mouth shut."

"Yeah and maybe pigs will fly."

They shot a couple of games of pool and drank some more pitchers. Finally, at ten o'clock, Mel set her cue stick on the table.

"We need to get out of here."

"Maybe I'll just stay here and do shots and blow off work tomorrow."

"And maybe you won't. Get up. I'll follow you home."

"I'm not drunk enough."

"Not a good attitude. I know you're hurting. But drinking isn't gonna make it better. Time should, though. Let's go."

Joey drove carefully the few blocks to her house, grateful to have Mel on her tail. She waved good-bye as Mel drove off and let herself into her house. It felt terribly empty and she felt unbearably alone. She stripped to her boxers and undershirt and climbed into bed.

Memories of the past few weeks played through her head. Things she and Samantha had said, things they'd done. It all culminated in the sheer joy she'd felt when she'd found out they were having a boy. She'd never felt such excitement.

And Samantha had taken that away from her. She'd taken her current happiness, as well as her imagined future joys and crushed them. Joey wiped away a tear just before she passed out.

❖

"Hey, loverboi!" Brenda called as she approached Joey and Mel the next day.

Joey and Mel exchanged glances, before Joey turned to Brenda.

"I assume you mean me?"

"Who else?"

"Who else, indeed?" Mel said under her breath.

"What do you need?"

"Your girlfriend needs you."

Joey's heart skipped a beat. Maybe Mel was right and the previous night had just been a hormonal mood swing. She fought to keep her excitement from showing.

"How so?" she asked.

"One of the little rugrats threw a toy through the wall. I need you to go patch it for her."

Joey felt nauseous. She shouldn't have allowed herself to imagine, even for a minute.

"Can't someone else go? We're busy."

"Too busy for your lady? Bullshit. Come on, I'm doing you a favor. It won't happen again. Get your ass over there."

Joey looked at Mel, who shrugged. Joey didn't want to go, but was still determined not to give Brenda the satisfaction of knowing she and Samantha had split. She grabbed some spackling and tools and drove to the day-care center.

"Oh, wow. I didn't know she'd send you," Samantha said when Joey arrived.

"She thinks she's doing me a favor. And I'm not going to be the one to tell her you dumped me."

"Joey, about that…"

Joey stood, head cocked, and waited.

"I really am sorry."

"You don't know the meaning of the word. Now where's the hole?"

"I suppose it will take a while before you can forgive me."

"You didn't just take you away from me, you know," Joey whispered harshly. "You took him, too. So no, I don't plan to forgive you any time soon."

"I wish it didn't need to be this way."

"It doesn't. This is a choice. Your choice. It sure as hell isn't mine. Now, do you mind? Let me do this and get out of here."

Samantha led her down the hall to the playroom. Joey looked everywhere she could to keep from admiring the swaying hips under the yellow cotton dress. She clenched the bucket of spackle tightly, feeling the handle biting her skin.

"That's a lot of spackle," Samantha said when she pointed out the small, fist-sized hole.

"Better too much than not enough. I certainly don't want to have to come back."

"Would you really rather I tell Brenda and Liz?" Samantha asked.

"I don't know. I wish they didn't have to find out at all."

"It's a small town."

"I'm aware."

"Well, I'm certainly not going to go out of my way to say anything to them."

"Whatever. They'll find out. It doesn't really matter who tells them. Either way, Brenda's gonna be all kinds of smug, and I'm going to want to rip her face off."

Joey went to work filling the hole. Samantha lingered.

"Don't you have something you can do?" Joey asked. "Like tell me where the paint is so I can touch this up?"

"It's out in the shed."

"Fine." She finished with the spackle and retrieved the paint. She was relieved to find Samantha gone when she returned. She knew that painting over the wet spackle might not have been the best job she could do, but she just wanted to get it done. She quickly painted and put the paint away, not bothering to clean her brushes. She'd do that later. She just needed to get away.

She pulled up to the jobsite less than an hour later.

"That didn't take long," Brenda said. "What's the matter? Did you get performance anxiety? Or maybe being around all those kids freaked you out. You'd better get used to that."

"You sent me to do something. I did it. Now I'm back."

"You're losing your touch, Scarpetti. Married life must be getting to you."

Mel stepped over and took Joey's arm.

"Come on. I need your help over here."

Joey allowed herself to be led away, resenting Samantha more with each passing moment.

❖

"So are we surfing today?" Mel asked as they loaded their vehicles at the end of the day.

"I don't feel like it."

"What do you want to do?"

"Go shoot some pool."

"It's a little early."

"It's happy hour. And when did you get so fucking pious?"

"I'm not pious, Joey. I just don't want you to keep drowning your sorrows. You've got to go on."

"I will when I'm ready. Are you coming with me?"

"I guess."

They parked next to each other and entered the lively tavern. Mel went to the bar to get the pitcher while Joey put quarters on a pool table so they'd play the winners. When Mel returned, they grabbed a booth by the pool table and poured their beer. Joey chugged hers and reached for the pitcher before Mel had even sipped hers. She just stared at Joey.

"Damn! You're worse than an old lady," Joey said. "We used to get shitty all the time. What's with you?"

"It used to be for fun."

"Who says it isn't now?"

"Whatever."

"Well, well, look who's off leash this afternoon." Brenda slid into the booth next to Mel. "Does the little woman know you're here?"

Mel looked from Joey to Brenda and back. She slid as far away from Brenda as she could and downed the rest of her beer.

Joey took a deep breath but didn't say anything.

"What the fuck? No smartass remark?" Brenda laughed.

"Why don't you back off a little?" Mel said.

"Why? What's her problem?"

Joey drained another glass that Brenda had refilled from the pitcher.

"What the hell's your problem, Scarpetti? You look like a fucking lost puppy."

Joey tried her best not to allow herself to be baited, but her whole body was a mass of tension and she so desperately wanted to unwind on Brenda.

"Seriously, what's up? You and the missus having trouble?"

"Damn it, Brenda! There is no fucking missus, so would you just shut the fuck up!"

"Hey, I was only messing around. I know you're not married or anything. I'm just giving you grief."

"I'm not sure you understood what she said," Mel said quietly.

Brenda looked at Mel, confusion etched on her face. She looked back at Joey.

"What? What didn't I understand?"

Joey got up and stormed off to the bar, where she ordered another pitcher.

"You wanna tell me what the fuck's going on?"

Joey turned to look at Brenda.

"You won, okay? Does that make you fucking happy? You won. Samantha dumped my ass."

"Oh, man. I don't know what to say."

"Bullshit. Go ahead. Gloat. Tell me you told me so. Get it all out of your system."

"No. I'm sorry, Joey. I really am. I mean, yeah, I never thought it was a good idea, but you seemed so happy. Like your life finally had meaning. I hate to see you like this now."

"What? Are you fucking kidding me? Is this a joke? Because it's not funny. I'm not laughing."

Brenda signaled for two shots. She handed one to Joey.

"Salud, my friend. May the pain lessen soon."

Joey drank the shot, but had nothing left to say. She stood, hunched over the bar, lost in her misery.

Mel walked up and tapped her shoulder.

"Hey, Joey, we're up. You ready to own the table for a while?"

Joey walked back to the table and took a drink of beer. Her world grew fuzzy, taking the edge off the pain for at least a little while.

CHAPTER TWENTY

Mel finally convinced Joey drowning her sorrows wasn't the answer. Instead, they spent their afternoons on their boards catching waves. Joey even admitted it was a better means of escaping. The week passed quickly and Friday after work, Mel walked up to Joey.

"Hey, why don't we get out of town for a couple of days?"

"Where will we go?"

"Santa Brigida."

"Seriously? What's there?"

"Have you forgotten our last trip there?"

Joey wasn't in the mood for another orgy. "What else is there?"

"They're having a beach volleyball tournament this weekend."

"I don't know."

"Buff, scantily clad women bouncing around in the sand. What's not to know?"

"I appreciate what you're trying to do, Mel."

"Don't fool yourself. This is as much for me as it is for you. I need to get out of here, too. And we could both use a little action."

"Whatever happened to Tiffany? Somehow I thought you two would get it together."

"She's too young."

"Is there such a thing?"

"Funny. No, I mean, she's just starting college, Joey. That was like a lifetime ago for us. She's into things that mean the world to her, but aren't that big of a deal to me."

Joey nodded.

"Want me to see if she wants to go with us?" Mel asked. "It might spice things up a bit."

"I think I'd rather find some new blood. I think that would be best."

"Suit yourself. I'll be at your place in a couple of hours."

"Are we bringing our boards?"

"Not in the Z28, my friend. We'll rent some there."

"We'll look like tourists."

"Then maybe we won't surf. Whatever. We can decide that when we get there."

Joey showered, dressed, then stuffed some extra clothes and toiletries into an overnight bag. The idea of a change of scenery was growing on her. She had just finished packing when Mel pulled up.

She hurried out to join her. They turned the music up and rocked out to eighties music. The drive was uneventful and much nicer than their previous road trip.

"Has it really only been a month since we were here last?" Joey asked as they pulled into Flannel's parking lot.

"Just over."

"Damn. It seems like forever ago."

"A lot has happened since then."

"No fucking kidding."

There was a nice Friday night crowd in the bar. Women were dancing to a live band, while others shot pool or just lined the room enjoying the scenery or stalking their prey.

Joey and Mel made their way to the bar and ordered a couple of beers. As they turned away from the bar, they found themselves face-to-face with two women they recognized from their previous trip.

"Hey, you two," the one named Amanda sidled up to Joey.

"Well, hello, stranger," Joey said. "How've you been?"

"I've missed you." Amanda ran her finger along Joey's stomach and up her chest.

Joey didn't like the feeling in the pit of her stomach telling her to walk away. She knew Amanda would be a fine diversion, yet thoughts of Samantha floated through her mind. Samantha cooking dinner. Samantha asleep next to her. Samantha lying naked on the couch.

"Buddy?" Mel was looking at her.

"Yeah? What's up?"

"You with us?"

"Of course."

"You were seriously lost in space. Come on, we're going to sit with these women."

"Right behind you."

Joey slid into the booth, leaving plenty of room between herself and Amanda, who quickly slid next to her.

"What's the matter, Joey? Afraid I'll bite? I'd think you'd be hoping I would."

Joey drained her beer and slid out of the booth to get another. She was grateful for the crowd at the bar, giving herself time to analyze whatever the hell she was feeling. She was lost in her thoughts when she felt a hand on her arm. She turned to see Mel.

"What the fuck, man?"

"What?"

"You act like Amanda's got cooties or something. Have you forgotten our last trip? I, for one, am looking for a repeat, but you're acting like you're fucking frigid."

Joey pulled her arm away and just stared at Mel. She wished she had an answer, but as much as she wanted a repeat performance as well, she couldn't handle the idea of cheating on Samantha.

"Buddy, come on. Talk to me. Your woman just dumped your ass for a fucking ghost. You should be looking for any piece of ass that'll get your mind off her."

Joey thought about what Mel had said and tried to bring back some of the anger she'd felt when Samantha had first told her to take a hike. She drew on the memory of the moment Samantha told her she had moved too fast and how she'd been feeling when she felt like that little baby boy had been ripped from her life. She didn't owe that bitch anything.

"You're right. I don't know what my problem is. Let's have some fun."

She ordered each of them a shot of tequila, which they quickly downed while the bartender poured a pitcher of beer for them. They got back to the table with Joey feeling much more like her old self.

She slid next to Amanda, pressing her into the wall. She traced her finger along the opening of her blouse and over the top of her soft mounds.

"Now, where were we?"

"That's the Joey I remember." Amanda closed her hand over Joey's and guided it under her bra.

Joey's fingers scissored around her nipple and tugged on it while bending her head to suck on Amanda's neck. She smelled of coconut and sunshine. Joey burrowed against her.

"Easy there," Amanda moved her away. "Save something for later."

Joey's body was on fire with need, and she didn't want to wait.

"Is there somewhere we can go?" she whispered hoarsely. "Somewhere for some quick release? Maybe a preview of what's to come?"

"No, there's not." Amanda laughed. "You'll need to be patient."

The band slowed the tempo down and Amanda asked Sara to join her on the floor. Joey and Mel stood to let them out then watched as they moved against each other to the rhythm pulsating through the bar.

"I'm so glad you're feeling better," Mel said.

"Me, too. I'd forgotten how fucking hot these two were."

"No doubt."

They watched as Amanda put her hands on Sara's ass and pulled her to her, grinding her own hips into Sara's. The women kissed, mouths open, tongues visibly moving over each other.

"Holy fuck!" Joey said as her crotch clenched at the sight.

"I want some of that," Mel said.

"I want all of that."

"That's the spirit."

They were speechless as Sara reached her hand into Amanda's blouse and fished out a breast. Holding it in plain view of all around, she lowered her mouth to it.

The rest of the dancers were barely moving as they, too, watched the show. Amanda unbuttoned her shirt so Sara could more easily get to her breast. She moved her hand to Sara's skirt, hiking it up and exposing her to the observers. She ran her fingers along her slit, finally slipping them inside while pressing her palm against Sara's clit.

"Damn, they're not saving anything for us," Joey said.

"I've a feeling there's plenty more where this is coming from."

Amanda withdrew her hand and fixed Sara's skirt before offering her fingers for Sara to suck clean. She glanced over at Joey and winked as the song ended and she tucked her breast away and buttoned her blouse.

Joey was already wet and hard when Sara walked up and kissed her, slipping her juice-coated tongue into Joey's mouth.

"I taste good, don't I?"

"Yeah, you do."

"Share," Amanda said, pulling Joey's mouth to hers. Joey crushed her lips with her own and ran her tongue all around her mouth.

"You sure there's nowhere we can go?" Joey was breathing heavily and craving Amanda's body.

"The night is still young, stud muffin." She took Joey's hand and walked back to the table.

Joey looked around to see where Mel was and saw her bent over the pool table. Sara was lying on the table with her legs wrapped around Mel, who was pressing her pelvis into Sara.

"Someone's not going to be happy their game's interrupted," Joey murmured.

"Are you kidding? What self-respecting butch is going to complain about a spread femme on display?"

"I had forgotten how little y'all care for who sees what."

"Life's too short to worry about others. If it feels good, do it."

"Works for me." She leaned Amanda back and kissed her, cupping her ample breast in the process. She played her thumb over the nipple that was poking through her blouse.

"Suck my tit, please."

Joey looked around self-consciously, then thought what the hell. She unfastened a couple of buttons and pulled Amanda's bra down, exposing a firm, pale breast crowned with a taut pink nipple. She gently cupped the breast and lowered her mouth to suck the nipple.

Amanda placed a hand on either side of Joey's head and arched into her, urging her to take more in her mouth, to suck harder.

Joey took a long draw on her and sucked a large portion of the breast in her mouth. She gently closed her teeth on it and frantically ran her tongue all over.

"Oh fuck, you feel good." Amanda said. She took her breast in her hand, and with her other hand, she guided Joey's hand between her legs.

Joey ran her fingers along the moist crotch of Amanda's lightweight slacks. She pressed them against Amanda's swollen lips, slowly at first, but faster as the need took over. She moved her hand to the elastic waist band and slipped under, searching for, needing to be inside the source of her wetness.

Amanda grabbed Joey's wrist.

"Not so fast."

"Oh, fuck." Joey's breathing was labored, her arousal making her dizzy. "Why not?"

"Not here."

"But…"

"I know. I allow for a lot. But I want you to wait for it."

"Oh, shit, baby. I need you so fucking bad."

Amanda laughed as she helped Joey to a sitting position and put herself back together.

Joey sat back hard against the back of the booth and grabbed her beer. She emptied her glass, sitting it down just as Mel and Sara came back.

"You feeling okay?" Mel asked Joey. "You look a little haggard."

Joey exhaled and poured another beer.

"Just a little frustrated."

Mel looked at Amanda who winked.

"I wouldn't let your friend get what she wanted."

"You both seem pretty good at that," Mel said.

"It's not like you won't get it eventually," Sara joined in. "We just like to make sure you want it."

"Oh, I want it," Joey said. "I don't think anyone can question that."

"Then you don't mind waiting for it," Amanda said.

"It's all good." Joey grinned. "I just need to get my heart rate back to normal and try to make my crotch stop throbbing."

"Oh, sweetie," Amanda cooed and slid her hand between Joey's legs. "There's no reason to stop throbbing."

Joey closed her eyes and tried, to no avail, to make her clit stop swelling.

"Sometimes there is." It was Joey's turn to move Amanda's hand.

"You're really about to blow, aren't you?" Sara laughed.

Joey glared at her.

"Let's dance, Joey. We'll work off some of that energy."

Joey figured there was no harm in dancing with Sara to a fast song, so she followed her to the floor.

She was finally cooling off, dancing and eyeballing the rest of the dancers. She turned her focus back to Sara, who was swaying her hips suggestively as she squeezed her breasts together. She ran her hands over them, which resulted in her nipples popping under her shirt.

Joey stared briefly then tried to look away but couldn't as Sara smoothed her hands down her body and toyed with the hem on her skirt. As she moved her hips in time to the music, she slid her skirt up millimeters at a time until finally the edge of it barely covered her. Joey strained to see the hot pussy she knew was under there, but Sara was skilled at keeping it just out of view.

Joey was a frustrated, wet mess yet again and struggled to maintain her composure. Her gaze met Sara's, and she sensed a dare. She wondered briefly what Sara would do if she dropped to her knees and buried her face between her legs. She knew she wouldn't go that far but couldn't control herself when Sara danced closer.

"I want you to touch me, Joey," she whispered in her ear. "I need your fingers on my clit."

Joey pulled her close with one hand while her other snaked between her legs, her fingers gliding over Sara's slick, hard clit. She rubbed circles on it while Sara closed her mouth over Joey's. Joey returned the kiss, her tongue darting into Sara's mouth as her fingers ran along her opening.

Sara pulled away and laughed, spinning around to the music. Joey stared after her, wondering how she'd survive the night.

The song ended, and Joey and Sara returned to the table.

"Doesn't Sara have the softest pussy?" Amanda pressed her breasts against Joey.

"It's very nice. But I seem to recall yours was very soft and wet, as well."

"Do you know how wet you get me?"

"Why don't you let me find out?"

"I will. I can't wait to feel you fucking me again."

"You're killing me," Joey moaned.

"Poor baby. Would you like me to put my hand in your shorts? Do you want me to take your clit between my thumb and finger and stroke you off?"

"Damn, you're a tease."

Amanda unbuttoned Joey's shorts. Joey moved away.

"You're not gonna do me in public."

"Why not? You wanted to fuck me right here."

"That's different."

"How?" Amanda softly kissed Joey's neck, barely touching it with her lips. "I want to touch you."

Joey looked over at Mel, who was lip locked with Sara. Joey's clit was standing up, throbbing, begging to be stroked. But she wasn't comfortable having Amanda's hand down her shorts in the bar. She glanced around and realized no one was paying any attention to what was happening at their table. Women were making out and caressing each other all over the bar. She unzipped her shorts.

"Good boi," Amanda cooed as she slipped her hand down Joey's shorts and under the waistband of her boxers. Joey held her breath as Amanda's hand moved past her mons, stopping with her fingertips just shy of Joey's clit.

Joey looked at her and swallowed hard.

"What are you doing?"

Amanda laughed.

"I can feel your heat from here."

"If you're not going to touch me, then take your hand out and let me zip my shorts."

"You're so impatient tonight. Has it been a while?" She moved her hand lower, running her finger along Joey's outer lips.

"I thought you were gonna stroke my clit," Joey said through clenched teeth.

"What are you two doing over there?" Sara asked.

Joey yanked Amanda's hand out of her shorts and zipped them, embarrassed that Mel had seen them.

"I was trying to help Joey out."

"You were teasing me more."

"I was getting there."

"You should have let her take care of you," Mel said.

"I can wait. We were just having fun." She poured the last of the pitcher into Mel's glass then made her way to the bar. She felt breasts pressed into her back and heard Amanda whisper in her ear.

"Let's go out to my car."

"Are you serious? Do you know how long it's been since I've done it in a car?"

"Come on." Amanda took her hand and dragged her through the bar and out into the cool night air.

Joey allowed herself to be pulled along, excited at the prospect of finally having at Amanda.

Amanda stopped and fumbled in her pocket for her keys.

"This is your car?" Joey asked, staring at the brand new Dodge Charger.

"I've heard all the comments that this car's too butch for me, so spare me."

"No. That's not what I was thinking. I just realized I'm too old to fuck in the backseat of a car."

"Then we'll fuck in the front seat."

"No, really. You can keep teasing me. I'll make it. I promise."

She took Amanda's hand and tried to pull her away from the car. Amanda pulled her back to her. She laced her fingers behind Joey's neck before running them through her hair.

"Come on, Joey. I'm saying I want you. I need you now. Are you really not going to help me out?"

Joey needed to get back inside. As much as she wanted to rip Amanda's clothes off her, she couldn't allow herself to climb into Samantha's car to do it. She wished she could come up with a graceful way to get out of it.

"It seems to me that since you keep me waiting, I can keep you waiting."

"But there's nobody out here. No one will see us."

"But I also won't be able to get at you as completely as I need to. And, baby, when we do this, I don't want either of us holding back."

"You're really going to make me wait, aren't you?"

"Yes, ma'am, I am."

"Well, damn, Joey. I may not have given you enough credit." She pulled Joey to her and kissed her, pressing her tongue into her mouth and sucking on Joey's.

Joey's resolve wavered as she felt the magic Amanda worked with her tongue. But visions of Samantha kept dancing through her head, and she realized she wasn't ready to do Amanda. She didn't want her. She didn't want anyone but Samantha.

She pulled away.

"Let's get back inside."

"Okay, we'll save it for later."

Joey followed Amanda into the bar, wondering how she'd manage to get out of fucking her. No matter how hot she was, or how much they'd been teasing each other, she knew she couldn't go through with it.

She considered how much it would hurt her reputation, but even that couldn't make her want Amanda. All she wanted was to be alone. She wasn't sure how that was going to happen.

CHAPTER TWENTY-ONE

The mood was ruined for Joey. She didn't want Amanda. She wanted Samantha. The realization made her sick to her stomach. Samantha had no right to hold her hormones hostage. She was irritated as hell when she got back to the booth.

"That didn't take long," Sara said.

"Nothing happened." Amanda sat in the corner with her arms crossed.

"What the fuck?" Mel asked.

"What? I'm not in the mood. Fuckin' give me a break."

"Not in the mood? Bullshit," Mel said.

"Move," Amanda said.

Joey scooted out of the booth to let Amanda out. She slid back in as Amanda moved to sit on the other side of Mel. She pressed her breasts against Mel and ran her hand along her thigh.

"I bet this one can keep up," she cooed.

"You know I can." Mel leaned back and closed her eyes, clearly enjoying the attention.

Joey fumed quietly. She willed herself to want Amanda, to feel the wet throbbing she'd felt just moments before. But all she could think about was the ultrasound, seeing what she thought was her unborn son. Then the joy and exhilaration that Samantha had ripped from her. The pain in her heart was fresh.

She left the threesome at the table and cut through the crowd on her way to the bar. She ordered a double shot of tequila, hoping it would cloud her judgment, but all it did was make her more melancholy.

She sauntered back to the table where Amanda and Sara were all over Mel. Realizing her presence wasn't needed, she left the bar hoping to find some peace in solitude.

Joey wandered along the beach as the cold water swirled around her ankles. The wind slapped her face, and she hoped the cool, foggy air would help her clear her mind. She kept replaying the afternoon Samantha dumped her. She remembered the thrill and excitement and anticipation she'd been feeling as she drove to Samantha's house. How she'd hoped they'd make love to celebrate their healthy baby. She hadn't seen the end coming. She'd been totally blindsided.

She brushed away one unwelcome tear, then another. She finally gave up and let them flow unabated. She sobbed openly and loudly on the deserted beach, finally allowing herself to fully grieve the loss of her family.

Emotionally exhausted, sad and angry, she climbed on a group of rocks and sat to watch the water break around her. She told herself she'd sit for a moment and then head back to the bar.

"Do you have any idea how long we've been looking for you?"

Joey eased her eyes open and cast a blurry gaze at Mel's face. "Huh?"

"We've been looking all over for you. You just disappeared on us."

Joey sat up from the rock she'd been leaning against and tried to shake the cobwebs from her head.

"You seemed to be getting along just fine without me."

"So you decided to run away?"

"I just went for a walk."

"A walk? Joey, you're miles from the bar."

"Seriously?"

"Seriously. At least a mile. We hung out waiting for you after last call, but when you didn't show up, we started looking for you."

"I'm sorry. I didn't mean to fall asleep. Where are the girls?"

"They were helping me look by searching in the other direction. When I found you I called them and told them to go home."

"I'm sorry I beaver dammed you."

Mel laughed.

"I can't believe you used that phrase."

"What? I think it's a great one."

"You're twisted." She sat on the rock next to Joey.

"You want to talk about it?"

"Not really."

"You were primed. Amanda was primed. What happened?"

"I said I don't want to talk about it."

"Fine. Come on. Let's get out of here."

"Well, without the company of Sara and Amanda, where do you suppose we'll be able to stay tonight?"

"I called a cab. Jett said she'd leave the front door open for us."

"Oh, yeah."

They climbed off the rocks and walked toward a gas station where Mel had told the cab to meet them.

"You could have been killed tonight," Mel said.

"How do you figure?"

"You could have fallen off those rocks and drowned."

"I can swim."

"Half asleep?"

"You worry too much."

Mel stared at Joey in the backseat of the cab.

"I may as well worry. Thanks to you I've got nothing better to do tonight."

"Man, I really am sorry. I thought you'd get them both."

"So, what happened?" Mel asked again.

"Didn't we cover this back at the beach?"

"I never got an answer. You were as hot for Amanda as I was. Why the sudden lack of desire?"

Joey turned to look out the window. She shrugged.

"No reason. I just wasn't in the mood."

"That's crap and you know it. Tell me what happened, damn it."

"Fine. If you must know, it was her car," Joey said quietly.

"What was wrong with her car?"

"It was a Charger."

"So?"

"So all I could think about was Samantha, okay? Are you happy? Feel free to laugh and judge and have a great fucking time at my expense."

"Dude, are you serious?"

Joey turned to Mel, who looked genuinely concerned.

"Yes. I'm serious. I couldn't do anything with Amanda because I felt un-fucking-faithful to the woman who dumped my ass."

"Shit. That's rough."

"Tell me."

"How are we going to get you over her, Jo? You've got to be able to move on."

"I tried, man. You know I tried. I was all set to have my way with Amanda. But I couldn't. I don't know when I'll be ready, but it can't be soon enough."

"I hate to see you in so much pain. It's like college all over again."

"It's worse this time. At least then I was young and stupid and could just drown my sorrows. And I could hit on any girl I wanted. I can't do that now. I feel like I'm trying to play responsible adult now."

"Responsible adults don't wander the beach in the middle of the night."

"This one does."

"I'm sorry, Joey. I know you never wanted to grow up and when you finally tried, you got shit on."

"It sucks, for sure."

The cab pulled up in front of a mission-styled house.

"We're here," he said.

Joey and Mel got out. Mel tossed a wad of cash at the cabbie then threw her arm around Joey as they walked up the drive.

"I had no idea you weren't ready to move on. I guess I just assumed you could bounce back, too. Like the old days. I should have realized this was different. I'm sorry I pushed you."

"What? I thought I could do it. Sorry I let you down."

"You didn't, my friend. Not at all. We just know now that scoring will have to wait."

"Well, it sucked that your scoring tonight depended on mine."

"Yeah. We'll make sure that never happens again."

They let themselves in the house and stripped to their underwear in the entry hall before making their way to the air mattresses their hostess had blown up for them.

"Hey, Jo, I really am sorry you're hurting."

"Thanks, Mel. It's not fun. I need to figure out how to make it go away."

"I'm guessing only time will do that."

"Shit."

"Yeah. Good night."

Joey stared at the ceiling, thoughts of Samantha racing through her mind. She had no idea what time she finally fell asleep. It must have been late because Saturday morning came very early.

"Get up, you two lazy bums." A fireplug of a woman with jet-black hair stood staring down at them.

"Holy shit. What time is it?" Mel asked.

"It's late. Get up. You two need food and coffee so we can head to the tournament."

"What time does the tournament start?" Joey managed.

"It starts at nine. It's seven thirty. Get your lazy asses up."

"Oh shit." Joey rolled over and put her pillow over her head.

"Oh no, you don't." The brunette grabbed the pillow and tossed it on the couch. "Get up. What time did you two get here last night?"

"I have no idea," Mel said. "It was after last call when we went looking for Romeo over there. I don't know how much later I finally found her."

"What? Never mind. Tell me over pancakes and coffee. Come on, guys."

Joey and Mel finally got up and followed their hostess to the kitchen.

"Hey, Jett, thanks for letting us crash here," Mel finally said over a cup of coffee.

"You're welcome. But why the hell are you two in your skivvies?"

"We figured our clothes would be covered in sand. We didn't want to track it through your house," Joey explained.

"What the hell? What were you two doing on the beach last night?"

"I went for a walk." Joey knew it sounded lame.

"And then she fell asleep, and I had to find her."

"You passed out on the sand?" Jett asked.

"No. I dozed off on some rocks."

"Damn, that's scary. How fucked up were you?"

"I wasn't."

"Shit."

She put plates in front of them with three huge pancakes and refilled their coffee.

"So where are your clothes?"

"The ones from last night? They're in your entryway."

"No. The rest of them."

"In the car. In Flannel's parking lot."

"Only you two. Jesus Christ. I would love to join you sometime when you come to town, but I'm afraid I'd get in all sorts of trouble."

"Speaking of trouble, where's the missus?" Mel asked.

"She's already at the beach. She's saving us seats, but we can't dilly-dally. Go throw your clothes on. We'll go get your car. Shit. We're going to be late."

"We can get the car after the tournament," Mel said.

"Are you sure?"

"Yeah. We'll just throw our clothes on and go. Do you have a couple of spare toothbrushes?"

Jett hurried them off to different bathrooms to speed up the process, and soon they were piled into her Mercedes SUV and heading to the beach. They parked at a lot three blocks from their destination and hurried to find Heather surrounded by people in the bleachers. They climbed up and sat with her.

"Thanks for saving us seats," Joey said.

"No problem. You look like hell, by the way. Good night?"

"It could have been," Mel piped in, grabbing Heather for a hug.

"What happened? Don't tell me the dynamic duo struck out."

"Long story," Joey said, hoping Heather would let it die.

"I heard you're serious with someone anyway," Heather said.

"You heard wrong."

"I did?"

Joey watched as Heather and Mel exchanged glances.

"I was with someone and now I'm not."

"Got it. Touchy subject?"

"The touchiest," Mel said.

"I'm sorry. Well, let's just relax and watch the women."

Chapter Twenty-two

Joey was relaxing, enjoying the skills and physiques of the women on the court. The morning was passing pleasantly until a man sitting behind them came back from his fifth or sixth trip to the beer stand.

"They're not bad for a bunch of rug munchers," he said.

Joey tensed and looked at Mel who simply rolled her eyes.

She cringed when she felt his hand on her shoulder.

"I didn't mean no offense," he said.

She pulled away and ignored him.

"Shit, there's nothin' but muff divers around here, are there?"

"Give it a rest, buddy," Jett said.

"Hey, sister," the man called to the woman about to serve. "How about you try cock just once? I got one for you."

The woman didn't react; rather, she scored on a perfect serve.

"Don't make us call security," Jett said quietly.

"Fuck me. I know where I'm not wanted." The man walked down the steps on unsteady legs and disappeared into the crowd at the end of the court.

"What a scumbag," Heather said.

"No doubt."

She and Jett went down to the concession stands and picked up hot dogs and beer for their group.

"You sure you can handle a little hair of the dog?" Jett joked.

"I'm telling you. I wasn't messed up last night."

"No? So what was with the long walk on the beach in the middle of the night?"

"I just needed some time to clear my head. I was bummin' hard-core."

"You really got burned, huh? Hey, I'm sorry about that."

"Thanks. It just reinforced that I'm not relationship material. I'll keep my relationships to a six-hour maximum from now on." She wished she believed what she was saying.

"There's the Joey I know and love."

Joey forced a smile as they made their way back to the bleachers.

The early afternoon sun felt good on her face, and Joey found herself occasionally dozing off during the tourney. It was nice to spend time not trying to outrun her demons. She was enjoying friends, sports, and the great outdoors and was thankful for every minute.

"Your body was made to please a man!" Joey heard someone yell, and her eyes flew open.

"Where the hell is that jerk now?"

"It sounds like he's across the court," Jett said.

"He was quiet for so long. I'd hoped he'd been escorted out."

She saw the man stand in the center of the stands across the way. He unzipped his pants.

"I've got something for you right here, sister. Come and find out what you've been missing!"

Everything seemed to slow down. Joey watched as security ran up the stairs, and around a blond woman who tried to step out of their way. She saw the guards grab the man by his arms and struggle to get him to the steps. She watched as the man fought against them and finally broke free, knocking the woman off balance. She fell backward down the stairs and lay motionless on the ground.

"Samantha!" Joey yelled, quickly climbing over people to get down to the sand. She cut across the game in progress, and now the security guards were after her as well.

She knelt next to the still body on the ground.

"Samantha? Can you hear me?" She looked around. "Where are the paramedics?"

As if on cue, the standby paramedics were there, checking her vitals. Two security guards grabbed her by her arms.

"I'm not going to fight you," she said. "I'm sorry. This is my ex. She's pregnant."

The guards loosened their grips on her.

"I wasn't thinking. I shouldn't have cut across the court," Joey continued.

"It's cool. I can see why you'd be upset," one of the paramedics said as the guards released her.

"How far along is she?" the other asked her.

"A little over five months."

They rolled her onto a backboard and carried her across the sand to a waiting ambulance.

"Where are you taking her?"

"Cottage Hospital. Do you know where that is?"

"Can I ride with?"

"Sure. Come on."

And, for the second time in twenty-four hours, she left without telling Mel or anyone where she was going.

They wheeled Samantha into a room in the Emergency Department. Joey hurried to keep up. Samantha hadn't made a sound, and Joey's distress was growing with every passing minute.

Joey sat next to her and held her hand, talking to her quietly as they waited for the doctor.

"You'll be okay, baby. I know I shouldn't call you that. I'm sorry. It's just that it comes so naturally when I'm with you."

She realized she was babbling, but didn't care. She kept up a steady flow of one-sided conversation until a short, balding man walked in.

"I'm Dr. Lamton. I'll be examining your…friend."

Joey stood.

"Do I have to leave?"

"No need."

He lifted her eyelids and shined a light in each eye. He massaged her scalp and nodded sagely.

"She's got quite a goose egg. What did she hit her head on?"

"I don't know. I thought she just hit the sand. Though I suppose she might have bumped it on the metal bleachers."

"That makes sense. I think she has a concussion. We need to get her to wake up."

"They used smelling salts in the ambulance, but that didn't help."

"I've got something a little stronger."

He broke a capsule under her nose, and they watched as Samantha shook her head and quickly opened her eyes.

She looked around, clearly confused, and was even more so when her gaze landed on Joey.

"What? Where?"

"Shh. You just relax," the doctor said. He motioned for Joey to pour a glass of water.

"Let's get you sitting up so we can get you to drink some of this."

Joey and the doctor helped Samantha sit up just as Brenda and Liz scurried into the room.

"What are you doing here?" Brenda asked.

"I rode along in the ambulance. I was worried about her."

"Thanks for that. We'll take it from here."

"What happened?" Samantha said quietly.

Both Brenda and Joey started to speak at once. Brenda glanced at Joey, who backed away from the bed, realizing she really didn't have any right to be there. She remembered the baby and stepped forward, shouldering past Brenda.

"How's the baby?" she asked the doctor.

Samantha's hands went to her belly as her eyes grew wide.

Dr. Lamton moved her hands aside and listened with a stethoscope. He was still and serious. Joey was aware she wasn't the only one holding her breath.

"The baby sounds fine," the doctor announced.

There was a collective exhaling of breath.

"You need to rest now. Don't go to sleep, but just relax, please," Dr. Lamton told Samantha.

"You can head out now, if you want," Brenda said to Joey, apparently worried about her level of comfort.

Joey glanced back at Samantha, then back to Brenda. She nodded.

"You're right. I'll text Mel to come get me. I'll see you guys around."

"Wait a minute," Samantha said. She looked at Brenda and Liz. "Can I please have a moment alone with Joey?"

Joey's stomach was flip-flopping as she watched them leave the room. She turned back to Samantha.

"Look, maybe I didn't have the right to ride along in the ambulance with you," she began.

"Don't be ridiculous. I'm glad you were there for me. I'm surprised you'd do that for me after the way I treated you."

Joey shrugged. "I was mostly concerned about little DJ."

"DJ?"

"Yeah. That's what I call him. Kind of like Dee Junior, I guess." Samantha smiled.

"DJ. I like that."

"Whatever. I need to go. I'm glad you're okay. You gave us all a good scare."

"Well, thank you, Joey."

"You're welcome."

Joey felt a mixture of joy and pain as she walked out to the waiting room, where she found Mel, Jett, and Heather waiting along with Brenda and Liz.

"How'd you know to come here?" Joey asked.

"You were a lot easier to find today than you were last night," Mel said.

"Good."

"How you doin?" Mel asked.

"I'm okay. I've been better. Let's get out of here."

"Let's catch some waves," Jett suggested.

❖

"So how'd things go with Samantha?" Mel asked when she and Joey had paddled out of earshot of Jett and Heather.

"I don't know. She thanked me for being there, and I got all, you know, excited. And then she didn't ask me to stay so I got all bummed."

"I'm sorry, man. You've still got it bad for her. I don't know that I fully grasped that until I saw you shoot out of those stands after she fell."

"Yeah. I've got it bad."

Joey was saved by a nice swell that she paddled from then stood as the wave developed. She surfed it to shore and enjoyed the sheer exhilaration of the ride. She paddled back out to Mel.

"That felt good."

"I'm glad. There's nothing like a few good waves to clear your mind."

They spent the rest of the afternoon communing with the ocean and trying to help Heather improve her surfing skills which were sorely lacking. After numerous wipeouts, she declared she was through with surfing, at which point Mel and Joey decided to give her lessons.

She was finally able to catch three waves in a row. Rather than tempt fate, she straddled her board and just bobbed in the sea.

"Aren't you guys cold yet?" she finally asked.

"There's a bit of a chill in the air," Mel agreed.

"And we haven't seen a decent wave in an hour. Let's go back to the house," Jett said.

"What do you say, Joey?" Mel asked quietly. "You ready to call it a day?"

Joey didn't want to. She liked being in the water. She liked catching waves and focusing on something other than her broken heart. Or how good Samantha looked, even unconscious. The last thing she wanted was to have more time to think.

"Yeah," she said. "We should probably head back to the house."

They all took hot showers and dressed in sweats as the fog rolled in heavy that evening. It was cool and damp on the patio where Joey and Jett were barbecuing.

"So, tell me about this lady," Jett said.

"What about her?"

"How long were you together? How long have you been apart? Why aren't you over her?"

"I don't know. I'm not some chick who writes everything down on her calendar. We were together a while. Not long. We've been apart a week or two. Why aren't I over her? Are you fucking kidding me? Jett, this woman is pregnant. Do you get that? She's pregnant. She's going to have a baby. A diaper wearing, screaming baby. And I still wanted to spend my life with her. She's not some fly by night girl

I picked up one night. This is the real deal. I fell in love. Falling out of love doesn't just happen overnight. Or so I've learned."

"You know you could have been arrested today. That wasn't very bright."

"I don't tend to act very smart where she's concerned. Obviously. Or I would have kept my heart much more guarded."

"You'll find someone else someday."

"Not likely. The being with someone part was hella cool. But the pain of losing her sucks. I don't think I'll chance that again."

"She was your first girlfriend in a very long time, Joey. It had to happen sooner or later. You know your first usually isn't your last."

"Well, she's both. I gave the relationship thing another try. I'm over it."

CHAPTER TWENTY-THREE

Joey got to work the next day to find Brenda in a fouler mood than usual. She pulled Joey to the side.

"Congratulations, my friend. If your goal over the weekend was to fuck with Samantha's head, you succeeded."

"What's that supposed to mean? Jesus, Brenda. I care about her. I see someone I care about get knocked to the ground and not get up, I'm going to react. How the hell is that a mindfuck?"

"Save the crap. You saw a shot at being the knight in shining armor and you couldn't resist."

"You're giving me way more credit than I deserve. I don't think that quickly, thank you very much. I reacted to seeing her get hurt."

Brenda's expression softened. "Well, you've managed to make her miserable in the process. Not that she's been too happy lately. I didn't want to mention that to you."

"I don't want her to be miserable."

"Bullshit. After what she did to you?"

"Still. She made her choice. She shouldn't be sad about that." Although secretly, Joey was thrilled to hear that Samantha might have been hurting, too.

"Well, you really did a number on her over the weekend."

"Are you going to tell me what happened? Or just give me shit for something I didn't do?"

"She was crying on Liz's shoulder all night last night. Missing Dee. Missing you. Wanting to be able to lean on you. Not wanting to be unfaithful to Dee. Jesus, Scarpetti. The woman's a wreck."

Joey felt her heart being pulled in a million directions. She was filled with hurt that Samantha was upset. She was filled with hope that Samantha might still want her. And she was filled with suspicion.

"Why exactly are you telling me this, Brenda?"

"Beats the hell out of me. I guess I figured you have the right to know."

"Sounds like she's working through a lot. Maybe I'll come out in a better place when she's done. Maybe I won't. Thanks for letting me know, anyway."

After work, Joey stopped by the corner market on her way home to pick up a deli sandwich and some beer.

"Fancy meeting you here." Her heart thudded as she turned to face Samantha.

"It's a small town," Joey said.

"Is that dinner?" Samantha asked.

"It is."

"How about you come over and I'll make some spaghetti? I've got frozen sauce so it won't take long to make."

Joey was torn. The thought of time with Samantha sounded at once wonderful and painful. She should just be happy that Samantha had asked and let it go. Feed her ego, but decline the invitation to escape unscathed.

"I don't know if that's such a good idea."

"I'd like to make dinner for you, Joey."

Joey's mind flashed back to all the dinners they'd had together. She wanted desperately to accept.

"No, thanks."

"But I'd like to do something to thank you for helping me out over the weekend."

"You said thank you at the hospital. That was enough."

"What if I just want to spend time with you?"

Joey's heart skipped a beat. She must have misheard. She needed to get out of there before she made a fool of herself.

"I'd better get going," she said.

"But, Joey…"

"I'll see you around."

❖

Samantha surrounded Joey. Her lips captured Joey's, and her hair softly caressed her cheeks. Her mouth was a powerful sucking machine as she kissed down Joey's neck to her chest. Joey tried to cry out as Samantha took one of her nipples in her mouth. She pulled on it with such force, it was almost painful. But the pleasure was exquisite.

Joey eagerly spread her legs as Samantha's hand slipped between them, demanding entry that Joey was happy to grant. She felt her long, strong fingers playing over her clit before sliding deep inside. It felt like her whole hand was inside her, and Joey writhed on her wrist as Samantha kissed her mouth again.

Joey awoke with a start, filled with a need so strong it hurt. She checked the clock. It was one-fifteen in the morning. She got up and grabbed a beer, hoping to cool off. She flipped on the television and saw two buxom redheads licking each other's cunts.

"Damn Mel and her fucking porn." She muttered but didn't turn the channel. She watched as one woman expertly ran her tongue around the other's clit. She enjoyed the sight of the other's pussy spread out as the one examined her before burying her tongue inside again.

"Shit!" Joey said, turning off the television and chugging the rest of her beer. Her body was still buzzing from the dream and now the porn. Her clit was like a rock, and she was sorely uncomfortable.

She lay back on her bed.

"Fuck you, Samantha," she said. "Fuck you for teasing me today. For asking me over for dinner. You're fucking with my head."

She lay on her back and gripped her fitted sheet with her hands. It wasn't helping. She looked down and saw her hard tits poking at her wife beater. She ran her hand over them, sucking in air as her fingers grazed the sensitive tips.

"Shit!" she said again as she lifted the shirt up and pinched and tugged on one nipple then the other. It was sending shock waves to her core. She knew it wouldn't take much to get her there.

She ran her hand down her belly and under her boxers, where she found her clit swollen and slick.

"Oh fuck yeah." She stroked it slowly, tantalizingly slowly. In her mind's eye, it was Samantha catering to her needs. "You like that, don't you? You like how fucking hard and wet you get me."

Her hips moved on their own, gyrating to the rhythm of her fingers rubbing herself.

"Oh baby, you're going to get me off. You want that, don't you, baby?"

She closed her eyes as the storm inside settled in one spot deep in her center, then broke loose, shooting currents to every inch of her body as she gave herself over to a powerful orgasm.

"Oh, Samantha!" she cried out as she rode the waves of the climax.

When her breathing had returned to normal, she rolled over to one side and pulled a pillow close.

"Oh, Samantha," she said quietly as she drifted back to sleep.

CHAPTER TWENTY-FOUR

Joey was sitting on her tailgate, eating lunch with Mel when her phone buzzed.

"Who the hell's texting you?" Mel asked.

Joey looked down and saw it was a text from Samantha. Her heart skipped a beat. Then she was filled with resentment. She didn't want to be Samantha's emotional yo-yo. She read the text.

Please come over for dinner tonight. I need to talk to you.

"Shit!" Joey spat.

"What?"

"She wants me to go over for dinner. I can't do it, Mel. It's still too painful."

"Have you told her that?"

"Of course not."

"Why not go over tonight and tell her that? Explain to her that it's too soon to try to be friends. She may not want to hear it, but she'll have to appreciate the honesty."

"That makes sense. Maybe I'll do just that. Then if she keeps doing this it's because she's mean and I'll have every right to be pissed."

"Way to look at it maturely."

"What?"

"Nothing. I think it's good that you're going. Now text her."

Joey showed up at Samantha's house after an afternoon of surfing and a quick shower. She felt weird not having flowers or wine or anything, but then reminded herself it wasn't a date. She felt even stranger knocking on the door. She slid her hands in her pockets while she waited for Samantha to answer.

After what seemed an eternity, Samantha opened the door and stood wearing a calf-length white skirt and a red blouse.

She pulled Joey to her in a hug.

Joey slipped out of it as gracefully as she could.

"Look, Samantha…"

"No, don't."

"Don't what?"

"I need to talk to you. Let's go out back."

She stopped in the kitchen and picked up a glass of wine for Joey and a bottle of water for herself.

"Samantha, before you start I have to say something."

"I wish you'd hear me out first."

"No. You need to hear me. I can't be friends with you. Wait, that didn't sound right. It's too soon. I mean, I'm not ready. Damn it! It hurts to be here, Samantha. I can't just put us behind me and move on as your buddy. I'm not ready to do that. Can you understand that?"

Samantha reached across the picnic table and took Joey's hand.

"I totally understand that, Joey. And please believe me when I say I'm not trying to be cruel."

Joey pulled her hand back and stood.

"Then you'll understand why I'm leaving."

"Not yet. Please. I heard you out now you hear me out."

Joey didn't move as she processed her options. She needed to get away from Samantha, but she didn't want to be an asshole. She sat back down.

"Okay. But know that every second I spend here is painful."

"What if it didn't have to be?"

"That would be nice. But it's not the case."

"Joey, I realized the other day that I've missed having you in my life."

"I've realized that every day since you dumped me."

"Touché. Let me try to say what I need to say here. Seeing you there gave me that jolt of happiness that's been missing from my world. The rush of love and desire that we shared was all there as soon as I saw you."

"If this is supposed to make me feel better—"

"Even when I didn't know what was going on, you were there for me. Just like you always were when we were together. Joey, what I did was cold and mean. I miss Dee. I can't deny that. But you're alive and here now, and you're willing to step up and take care of me and be there for me. Dee can't do any of those things. It's time for me to let her go and allow myself to love again."

"What are you saying?" Joey didn't dare hope that her dreams might be coming true.

"I'm saying I'm sorry I called things off and I'd really like it if we could try again. If you can forgive me."

Joey sat stone still waiting for the other shoe to fall.

"Joey?"

"I'm just waiting for the punch line."

"There is no punch line. I've never been more serious about anything in my life. I was a fool. I love you, Joey. I want you back."

Joey absorbed the words she was hearing with decreasing trepidation.

"You have to know what that means to me," she said. "But you also have to understand I'm leery. I can't go through that kind of pain again."

"You won't."

"I wish I could believe you."

"How can I convince you?"

"I don't know."

"But you do still love me. And you'd like to be with me. If those things are true, then please say we can try again."

"I guess I'd be crazy not to at least try."

"Do you mean that?"

"I think I do."

Samantha beamed as Joey walked over to sit next to her. She wrapped her arm around her and pulled her close.

"See? This is how it should be," Joey said.

"It is. I can't believe I was stupid enough to ever let you go. Thank you for giving us another shot."

Joey kissed Samantha's forehead, softly, tenderly, breathing in the scent she'd been missing as she did so.

"You smell amazing," she whispered.

"It feels so right to be back in your arms."

Joey tilted Samantha's face upward and lowered her mouth to taste her lips. The kiss was brief, but conveyed so very much. She was overcome with warmth and comfort even as her heart raced and her skin tingled.

Samantha pulled Joey to her again, opening her mouth to welcome Joey's tongue. Joey's heart skipped when their tongues met. All the love she'd been fighting bubbled to the surface and overwhelmed her with sensations, not the least of which was arousal.

She broke the kiss and stood on shaky legs.

"Are you leaving?" Samantha asked.

"No way." Joey extended her hand. "I was thinking we should head inside."

Samantha's eyes lit up. "That's a great idea."

She put her hand in Joey's and stood. Joey led her through the house to the master bedroom.

"I've missed this room," Joey said.

"It's missed you."

Joey pulled Samantha into her arms. "I've missed you."

"I've missed us."

"So true." She kissed Samantha again, her tongue moving slowly around her mouth, tasting every inch of her.

She unbuttoned Samantha's blouse, sliding her hand under it to cup a full breast. She stopped.

"Be careful," Samantha said.

"I know. I almost forgot." She laughed and dragged her hand longingly over the breast. She moved her hand lower as they kissed again, caressing her back and finally kneading her firm ass.

Samantha stepped out of her skirt and panties and lay back on the bed.

Joey quickly undressed and lay beside Samantha, pulling her close for another kiss. As their mouths met, Joey was filled with a strange sensation. Mixed in with the passion she was feeling was a sense of being home. She felt contentment unlike she'd ever felt before as she continued to kiss Samantha.

She kissed down her cheek and nibbled on her earlobe. She sucked down her neck and chest, lifting her head to gaze wistfully at Samantha's off limits breasts.

Joey moved between her legs and kissed one thigh, then the other. She sucked and nibbled, leaving love bites in the privacy of Samantha's inner thighs. She finally kissed up to where Samantha's legs met and lovingly ran her tongue over the length of her, savoring her flavor. The heady, musky taste again brought to Joey the sense of being home.

She was where she belonged. She took Samantha's clit deep in her mouth, rolling her tongue around it. She slid her fingers inside Samantha and moaned at the tight heat that engulfed her. Her own passion flared as she plunged her fingers farther inside.

Samantha moved against her, arching to take her deeper. Joey's head grew light at the sensations flowing through her. Loving Samantha was as necessary to her as breathing. She heard Samantha's breaths coming in gasps and licked harder until she felt her whole body tense as she cried out when the orgasm hit.

Joey continued making love to her until she'd had too many orgasms to count, each one further igniting the fire scorching her insides. She felt engulfed in flames as she moved up Samantha's body to kiss her. The kiss was slow and tender and left Joey dizzy with need.

She rolled onto her back as Samantha lowered her mouth to her breasts. She sucked greedily on one nipple while she tugged and twisted the other. The electricity passed through Joey's body, causing her clit to swell to the bursting point.

Samantha slipped her hand between Joey's legs, finding her wet and ready.

"God, I need you," Joey said.

She watched Samantha smile with a nipple in her mouth as she felt her fingers slide over her clit.

Joey gasped, feeling the energy gathering in her center. She closed her eyes as the energy shot out through her body, releasing the tension as the climax erupted. She rode the waves until they subsided and she could finally think clearly.

She lay breathless as Samantha curled up next to her. Joey wrapped her arm around Samantha and pulled her close.

"That was amazing, baby," Samantha said.

"It was beyond amazing."

Joey reached over and ran her hand over the bump that was Samantha's belly.

"How's DJ doin'?"

Samantha smiled and laced her fingers through Joey's. "I think that's really sweet that you call him that."

"Have you thought of a name for him?"

"I think I'll call him DeeJay."

"No lie?"

"If that's okay with you." Samantha said.

"I started it, didn't I?"

"You did, but I didn't know if you were facetious."

"Not at all. I think it's a great tribute. And maybe it'll alleviate some of your guilt."

"Babe, I'm past the guilt. I mean that. I have every right to move on. I'm lucky I found you, and I'd be foolish to walk away over someone who's not even alive anymore."

"Well, I'm glad you came to that conclusion."

"You know I love you."

Joey's stomach clenched. It was a natural reaction. The fist melted and she was covered in comfortable warmth.

"I love you, too."

"You don't have to say that. I'd rather you wait until you're sure."

"I'm totally sure. It's been pure hell not being with you. You're all I think about. I've missed you like crazy. I've never been more certain about anything than this."

Samantha kissed her again.

"I'm so grateful to have you back," she said.

"We're too good not to be together."

"You sure you're ready to be a mom? I mean, really?"

"I'm sure I care too much about you not to give it a shot."

"Should we get up and get dinner going?" Samantha asked.

Joey rolled over on top of her. "How about a little more dessert first?"

She kissed her hard on the lips, happy with the knowledge that she'd be kissing Samantha for the rest of her life.

About the Author

MJ Williamz grew up on California's Central Coast but now calls Portland, Oregon, home. It's been since she moved to Portland that she really got into her writing. She got her first short story published in 2004 and has never looked back. She now has over thirty short stories published, and *Escapades* is her fifth published novel.

Books Available From Bold Strokes Books

Kiss The Girl by Melissa Brayden. Sleeping with the enemy has never been so complicated. Brooklyn Campbell and Jessica Lennox face off in love and advertising in fast-paced New York City. (978-1-62639-071-3)

Taking Fire: A First Responders Novel by Radclyffe. Hunted by extremists and under siege by nature's most virulent weapons, Navy medic Max de Milles and Red Cross worker Rachel Winslow join forces to survive and discover something far more lasting. (978-1-62639-072-0)

First Tango in Paris by Shelley Thrasher. When French law student Eva Laroche meets American call girl Brigitte Green in 1970s Paris, they have no idea how their pasts and futures will intersect. (978-1-62639-073-7)

The War Within by Yolanda Wallace. Army nurse Meredith Moser went to Vietnam in 1967 looking to help those in need; she didn't expect to meet the love of her life along the way. (978-1-62639-074-4)

Escapades by MJ Williamz. Two women, afraid to love again, must overcome their fears to find the happiness that awaits them. (978-1-62639-182-6)

Desire at Dawn by Fiona Zedde. For Kylie, love had always come armed with sharp teeth and claws. But with the human, Olivia, she bares her vampire heart for the very first time, sharing passion, lust, and a tenderness she'd never dared dream of before. (978-1-62639-064-5)

Visions by Larkin Rose. Sometimes the mysteries of love reveal themselves when you least expect it. Other times they hide behind a black satin mask. Can Paige unveil her masked stranger this time? (978-1-62639-065-2)

All In by Nell Stark. Internet poker champion Annie Navarro loses everything when the Feds shut down online gambling, and she turns to experienced casino host Vesper Blake for advice—but can Nova convince Vesper to take a gamble on romance? (978-1-62639-066-9)

Vermilion Justice by Sheri Lewis Wohl. What's a vampire to do when Dracula is no longer just a character in a novel? (978-1-62639-067-6)

Switchblade by Carsen Taite. Lines were meant to be crossed. Third in the Luca Bennett Bounty Hunter Series. (978-1-62639-058-4)

Nightingale by Andrea Bramhall. Culture, faith, and duty conspire to tear two young lovers apart, yet fate seems to have different plans for them both. (978-1-62639-059-1)

No Boundaries by Donna K. Ford. A chance meeting and a nightmare from the past threaten more than Andi Massey's solitude as she and Gwen Palmer struggle to understand the complexity of love without boundaries. (978-1-62639-060-7)

Timeless by Rachel Spangler. When Stevie Geller returns to her hometown, will she do things differently the second time around or will she be in such a hurry to leave her past that she misses out on a better future? (978-1-62639-050-8)

Second to None by L.T. Marie. Can a physical therapist and a custom motorcycle designer conquer their pasts and build a future with one another? (978-1-62639-051-5)

Seneca Falls by Jesse Thoma. Together, two women discover love truly can conquer all evil. (978-1-62639-052-2)

A Kingdom Lost by Barbara Ann Wright. Without knowing each other's fates, Princess Katya and her consort Starbride seek to reclaim their kingdom from the magic-wielding madman who seized the throne and is murdering their people. (978-1-62639-053-9)

Season of the Wolf by Robin Summers. Two women running from their pasts are thrust together by an unimaginable evil. Can they overcome the horrors that haunt them in time to save each other? (978-1-62639-043-0)

The Heat of Angels by Lisa Girolami. Fires burn in more than one place in Los Angeles. (978-1-62639-042-3)

Desperate Measures by P. J. Trebelhorn. Homicide detective Kay Griffith and contractor Brenda Jansen meet amidst turmoil neither of them is aware of until murder suspect Tommy Rayne makes his move to exact revenge on Kay. (978-1-62639-044-7)

The Magic Hunt by L.L. Raand. With her Pack being hunted by human extremists and beset by enemies masquerading as friends, can Sylvan protect them and her mate, or will she succumb to the feral rage that threatens to turn her rogue, destroying them all? A Midnight Hunters novel. (978-1-62639-045-4)

Wingspan by Karis Walsh. Wildlife biologist Bailey Chase is content to live at the wild bird sanctuary she has created on Washington's Olympic Peninsula until she is lured beyond the safety of isolation by architect Kendall Pearson. (978-1-60282-983-1)

Night Bound by Winter Pennington. Kass struggles to keep her head, her heart, and her relationships in order. She's still having a difficult time accepting being an Alpha female—but her wolf is certain of what she wants and she's intent on securing her power. (978-1-60282-984-8)

Windigo Thrall by Cate Culpepper. Six women trapped in a mountain cabin by a blizzard, stalked by an ancient cannibal demon bent on stealing their sanity—and their lives. (978-1-60282-950-3)

The Blush Factor by Gun Brooke. Ice-cold business tycoon Eleanor Ashcroft only cares about the three Ps—Power, Profit, and Prosperity—until young Addison Garr makes her doubt both that and the state of her frostbitten heart. (978-1-60282-985-5)

Slash and Burn by Valerie Bronwen. The murder of a roundly despised author at an LGBT writers' conference in New Orleans turns Winter Lovelace's relaxing weekend hobnobbing with her peers into a nightmare of suspense—especially when her ex turns up. (978-1-60282-986-2)

The Quickening: A Sisters of Spirits novel by Yvonne Heidt. Ghosts, visions, and demons are all in a day's work for Tiffany. But when Kat asks for help on a serial killer case, life takes on another dimension altogether. (978-1-60282-975-6)

Smoke and Fire by Julie Cannon. Oil and water, passion and desire, a combustible combination. Can two women fight the fire that draws them together and threatens to keep them apart? (978-1-60282-977-0)

Love and Devotion by Jove Belle. KC Hall trips her way through life, stumbling into an affair with a married bombshell twice her age. Thankfully, her best friend, Emma Reynolds, is there to show her the true meaning of Love and Devotion. (978-1-60282-965-7)

The Shoal of Time by J.M. Redmann. It sounded too easy. Micky Knight is reluctant to take the case because the easy ones often turn into the hard ones, and the hard ones turn into the dangerous ones. In this one, easy turns hard without warning. (978-1-60282-967-1)

In Between by Jane Hoppen. At the age of fourteen, Sophie Schmidt discovers that she was born an intersexual baby and sets off on a journey to find her place in a world that denies her true existence. (978-1-60282-968-8)

Under Her Spell by Maggie Morton. The magic of love brought Terra and Athene together, but now a magical quest stands between them—a quest for Athene's hand in marriage. Will their passion keep them together, or will stronger magic tear them apart? (978-1-60282-973-2)

Rush by Carsen Taite. Murder, secrets, and romance combine to create the ultimate rush. (978-1-60282-966-4)

Secret Lies by Amy Dunne. While fleeing from her abuser, Nicola Jackson bumps into Jenny O'Connor, and their unlikely friendship quickly develops into a blossoming romance—but when it comes down to a matter of life or death, are they both willing to face their fears? (978-1-60282-970-1)

Homestead by Radclyffe. R. Clayton Sutter figures getting NorthAm Fuel's newest refinery operational on a rolling tract of land in upstate New York should take a month or two, but then, she hadn't counted on local resistance in the form of vandalism, petitions, and one furious farmer named Tess Rogers. (978-1-60282-956-5)

Battle of Forces: Sera Toujours by Ali Vali. Kendal and Piper return to New Orleans to start the rest of eternity together, but the return of an old enemy makes their peaceful reunion short-lived, especially when they join forces with the new queen of the vampires. (978-1-60282-957-2)

How Sweet It Is by Melissa Brayden. Some things are better than chocolate. Molly O'Brien enjoys her quiet life running the bakeshop in a small town. When the beautiful Jordan Tuscana returns home, Molly can't deny the attraction—or the stirrings of something more. (978-1-60282-958-9)